STARLIGHT OVER HOLLYHOCK FARM

GEORGINA TROY

Boldwood

First published in Great Britain in 2025 by Boldwood Books Ltd.

Copyright © Georgina Troy, 2025

Cover Design by Lizzie Gardiner

Cover Images: Lizzie Gardiner, Adobe Stock and Shutterstock

The moral right of Georgina Troy to be identified as the author of this work has been asserted in accordance with the Copyright, Designs and Patents Act 1988.

Every effort has been made to obtain the necessary permissions with reference to copyright material, both illustrative and quoted. We apologise for any omissions in this respect and will be pleased to make the appropriate acknowledgements in any future edition.

A CIP catalogue record for this book is available from the British Library.

Paperback ISBN 978-1-78513-788-4

Large Print ISBN 978-1-78513-789-1

Hardback ISBN 978-1-78513-787-7

Trade Paperback ISBN 978-1-80656-081-3

Ebook ISBN 978-1-78513-790-7

Kindle ISBN 978-1-78513-791-4

Audio CD ISBN 978-1-78513-782-2

MP3 CD ISBN 978-1-78513-783-9

Digital audio download ISBN 978-1-78513-785-3

This book is printed on certified sustainable paper. Boldwood Books is dedicated to putting sustainability at the heart of our business. For more information please visit https://www.boldwoodbooks.com/about-us/sustainability/

Boldwood Books Ltd, 23 Bowerdean Street, London, SW6 3TN

www.boldwoodbooks.com

To my mother Tess Jackson and godmother Maggie Reynolds for all the laughter.

1

CALLUM

You are invited to attend Keith Preston's (TOP SECRET)
surprise party at
7.30 p.m. on Saturday 8 August
At Beauvoir Manor, Trinity
Please RSVP to Callum Preston

Callum drove up the dusty drive towards Hollyhock Farm, slowing to look to his left at the vans and groups of people milling about in one of the fields. A buzz of excitement coursed through him. He had been on many modelling shoots, but never a proper film set and was looking forward to meeting the star of *Sam Thorne Investigates*, Riley Sharp.

Callum thought of the actor he had seen in a couple of action films and tried to imagine him as Sam Thorne, the detective who: 'once he gets his claws into criminals, there's no escape'. The tagline was a bit cheesy as far as Callum was concerned, but there had been a lot of interest about this new TV character in the papers and about this new detective series set on the island.

He drove into the yard and smiled to see the brightly coloured hollyhocks that grew in front of the granite farmhouse each summer. He parked and got out of his car and saw Lettie Torel, his best friend Zac's older sister, who had the previous year taken over the running of the family farm when her father retired.

She walked over to join him carrying her baby, Isla, on her hip and a large shopping bag in her other hand.

'Here, let me take that from you,' Callum said, reaching out to lift the bag from Lettie. He puffed out his cheeks. 'It's heavier than it looks.'

She sighed. 'I was wondering how long it would take me to carry it up to where they're filming.'

He peered into the bag and saw tins. Knowing how much Lettie's mum enjoyed her baking, he asked, 'Has Lindy been feeding her delicious cakes to the cast and crew while they've been filming here?'

'How did you guess?' She rolled her eyes. 'Mum spends the morning baking and insists we take several up to them every afternoon. Anyone would think the TV company didn't supply enough food for their cast and crew already.' She laughed. 'Anyway, it's lovely to see you here,' she said, giving him a kiss on the cheek.

'Then I hope there's enough for me,' he said. 'Your mum's cakes are the best I've ever tasted.' Callum looked at the pretty little girl in Lettie's arms and smiled. 'Isla gets more adorable each time I see her.'

Lettie beamed at him. 'I agree, but then I am biased.'

He tipped his head to his left. 'So, how's it going having a film crew on the farm?'

She shrugged. 'Not bad at all, if I'm honest. They're very

respectful of the place and take care not to bother the animals. And obviously Mum is enjoying having them here.'

Callum was pleased. He knew how welcome the added income would be for Lettie and Brodie but was aware how much she valued her animals. 'That's good.'

'It's been fun actually.' She waved for him to accompany her. 'Let me take you to where they're filming now.'

He walked with her, taking care not to make any noise when he saw they were filming a scene.

'I'm glad they chose to film the farmhouse,' he said, thinking about how beautiful it looked.

'Me, too. It wasn't in the original plan to record there, but when they saw the colourful hollyhocks, I think they felt it would be silly not to make the most of such a pretty location. We'd better wait here until they finish this scene,' Lettie whispered.

They watched for a couple of minutes and Callum couldn't help thinking how different this was to any of the shoots he'd taken part in for his modelling. With those, the emphasis was on the model and the clothes they were promoting being posed to perfection and on the lighting. There were far fewer people around too.

'And cut! Take a half-hour break, everyone,' a woman Callum presumed to be the director said.

'There's Tasha.' Lettie pointed discreetly. 'Let me introduce you to her and Riley Sharp.'

Callum knew from all the promotion for *Sam Thorne Investigates* that the actor had been on the island for a couple of months, filming at various outside locations for the new television series. He wondered whether he should take advantage of meeting the actor and try to book him to be interviewed on his daily radio show.

'I know what you're thinking,' Lettie said, grinning.

'You do?'

She nodded. 'Yes, you should ask him.' She frowned. 'No, you should ask his PA Tasha. She looks after his diary and might be the right person to persuade him.' Lettie leant in slightly closer to Callum and lowered her voice. 'I've heard he can be a bit difficult, although I haven't seen it myself.'

Callum walked with Lettie to the outskirts of the group of people talking seriously together. 'Where shall I take these?' he asked, lifting the bag slightly.

'The food truck is just there. You'll probably find Mum in there too.' She grinned. 'Dad keeps saying that if we can't find Mum when they finish filming here that she'll probably have run off with them.'

Callum smiled. 'I'll take these. I won't be long.'

The door to the food trailer opened and Lindy went to step out. 'Callum, good to see you.' She noticed the bag in his hand. 'Are those my cakes?'

'They are,' he said, carrying the bag inside for her and leaving it where she indicated. 'I hope you'll keep me a slice of one of them.'

'Always,' she said, kissing him on the cheek. 'Are you staying to watch the filming for a bit?'

He nodded. 'Yes. Lettie is outside with Isla.'

'I might see you in a little while.'

As he went to join Lettie again, Callum spotted Riley chatting to a woman who was pointing to something on the tablet she was holding. He stopped walking, unable to take his eyes off her. She seemed to sense she was being watched and looked over at him.

His stomach did a flip as the woman with long, shiny auburn hair looked over at him, her green eyes locked with his, causing

Callum's breath to catch momentarily in his throat. She was beautiful.

Riley said something and the woman immediately focused her attention back on him.

'That's Tasha,' Lettie said, coming over to stand by Callum. 'She's pretty, isn't she? Highly efficient too, from what I've heard. Although, I suspect she needs to keep everything running smoothly for someone as busy as Riley.'

'You know her then?'

Lettie shrugged. 'Sort of. We've chatted a few times and I recently helped her find somewhere to rent while she and Riley are here filming.'

'I see.'

'In fact,' Lettie added, 'it's the cottage in the same grounds as Beauvoir Manor where I suggested you book your family to stay for your grandfather's secret birthday celebrations.'

Callum stared at his friend. 'Really?'

She laughed. 'Don't look so shocked. The cottage, well, it's more of a big house really, but it's further along the drive and I doubt you'll even come across them while you're staying in the manor house.'

He hid his disappointment. 'I suppose they like to be private, don't they?'

She nodded. 'It was one of Riley's stipulations.'

Callum thought of the impending party he had arranged for his grandfather's eightieth birthday and all the family and friends who would be attending. Most of his family would be staying in the manor house with him.

'Don't look so concerned,' Lettie said. 'The cottage really is a little way away.'

He wasn't convinced. 'It might be but you know my family can be pretty lively when they all get together.'

She raised an eyebrow. 'That's true.'

Callum sighed. 'Maybe I should get to know them a bit before my family and I go and stay at the manor? At least then we wouldn't be complete strangers.'

'Good idea.' She raised a finger as Lettie often did when an idea occurred to her.

'What?'

'You could always invite them to the party.'

Callum wasn't sure that was such a good idea. 'I hardly think Riley Sharp would want to come to my grandfather's party.' He thought of his grandfather who was known as one of the characters on the island who seemed to get along with most people and was always the life and soul of any get-together.

'Why not?'

Callum frowned. 'I doubt it'll be his kind of fun.'

'Maybe not, but if you invite them then at least they'll know there's an event happening and what it's celebrating. And,' she said, giving him a cheeky wink, 'it won't be so easy for them to make a fuss.'

He gave her suggestion some thought. 'I'll see how it goes,' he said non-committally.

Lettie nudged him. 'Look, they're coming this way. Come with me and I'll introduce you.'

2

TASHA

'If you've finished, I'd like to make the most of this break from filming,' Riley said, frowning. His chiselled features softened into a bright smile. Tasha looked to see who this show of charm was for and saw Lettie and a gorgeous man coming their way.

Her breath caught in her throat and her pulse raced. Who was this man? He was gorgeous enough to be an actor, but she didn't recognise him from anywhere, so doubted he must be.

'Hi, I hope we're not interrupting anything?' Lettie asked.

'Of course you're not,' Riley said, ruffling Isla's wavy hair, making her giggle.

'Oh good. I wanted to introduce you to a family friend. This is Callum Preston. He's a radio DJ with his own show.'

Tasha noticed Callum briefly give Lettie a concerned sideways glance but he didn't contradict her.

'Callum, this is Riley Sharp. He's the lead in *Sam Thorne Investigates* and this is his brilliant PA Tasha Dodds.'

'Good to meet you, Callum,' Riley said, looking him up and down before shaking Callum's hand.

Tasha wasn't surprised to see Riley doing it and was sure this signature move of his was designed to make men he saw as competition feel uncomfortable. It often worked, she had noticed, but she enjoyed seeing that Callum didn't seem at all fazed.

'It's a pleasure to meet you, Riley.' Callum looked from Riley to Tasha, and yet again she felt as if she had been thumped in the chest.

'Nice to meet you, Tasha.' He smiled at her. 'How are you liking being on the island?'

'I haven't seen too much of it,' Riley said, always having to be the one to reply. Tasha wasn't surprised he always assumed people were addressing him; after all, he was the celebrity, but she had met other famous people who were much more polite and humble than Riley could ever be.

'How about you, Tasha?' Lettie asked. 'Although I suppose you've probably been busy with work while you've been here.'

'I have.' She wished her voice hadn't come out so high-pitched. She saw Riley give her a confused look and knew she needed to calm down. She was a professional and used to working with charismatic people.

'There he is,' Tasha heard Lindy Torel's voice. She loved the farmer's wife and especially enjoyed her delicious baking. She knew Riley had a soft spot for her too.

Riley turned on his heels and opened his arms wide. 'My favourite lady. What delights have you brought to tempt me today?'

Lettie grimaced, making Tasha want to laugh, but Lindy seemed amused at his efforts to charm her.

'Well, there's the usual Victoria sponge, a carrot cake...' She raised a hand to the side of her mouth and lowered her voice. 'I know you're not keen on that flavour, but the director specifically requested it.'

'And the dark chocolate cake?' he asked.

'I've a piece kept by for you in the food trailer, if you want to come and eat it while you have a free minute or two.'

'You don't have to ask me twice,' he said, immediately walking away with her without bothering to say goodbye.

Tasha smiled politely. 'He loves your mum's cakes,' she said for something to say to fill the awkward silence.

'She's over the moon that he does,' Lettie said. Isla wriggled, wanting to get down, and Lettie lowered her to the ground. 'I'm going to need to take her for a walk so she doesn't start whingeing. Isla doesn't have much patience for staying still, I'm afraid.'

'I'm sure most of us didn't at her age,' Callum said.

Tasha noticed Lettie give Callum a slight nod. 'Callum has something he wants to ask you though, so I'll leave you two to talk business.'

Intrigued, Tasha waited for him to speak.

He stared at her for a moment, and she wasn't sure whether she should say something. Then Callum said, 'Sorry, I don't mean to ambush you. I thought that as you keep Riley's diary maybe you were the person to ask whether you thought he might consider coming on my show for an interview and if he would, when he was free to do it.'

'I see,' she said, trying to work out how difficult it might be to persuade Riley to do as Callum asked. 'It's difficult to say without speaking to him first and checking his availability, but I can let you know either way sometime tomorrow, if that suits you.'

He seemed surprised for a moment. 'That would be perfect. Thanks, Tasha.'

'Do you have a preferred contact number, or should I phone the radio station direct?'

Callum shook his head. 'No, I'll give you my number.'

'Hey, Callum.'

Tasha and Callum looked over to the tall, sandy-haired man striding towards them, who Tasha now knew to be Lettie's partner, Brodie, who was also the local vet. He slapped Callum on the back.

'How's things with you?'

'Good, thanks.'

'Hi, Tasha,' Brodie said. 'How's everything going? Only two weeks of filming left, isn't it?'

She nodded, sad at the prospect of leaving the pretty island. 'I wasn't pleased at first to have an extra couple of weeks added to the schedule, but the weather has been amazing and I'm hoping the added time here gives me the opportunity to see a bit more of the place.'

'I hope you do get to see more of it. There's a lot to see despite the island only being nine miles by five in size.'

'If you do have any free time,' Callum said quietly, 'I'd be happy to show you a few of my favourite places.'

'There you go,' Brodie said. 'I know Lettie would offer, as would I, but there's so much going on at the veterinary practice and of course here. And there's Isla.'

Touched by their willingness to make her visit as enjoyable as possible, Tasha raised her free hand. 'I completely understand.'

She smiled at Callum, wanting to accept his offer but unsure whether it was a good idea if the effect he had on her after such a brief meeting was anything to go by. It wasn't as if she would be staying here much longer, let alone her promise to herself not to get involved with anyone unless there was a real chance of the pair of them having a future together. She had been caught out like that with her last serious relationship, with Toby, and that break-up took her far longer to get over than she had expected.

It was part of the reason she had left the bank where they had both worked for five years and gone into a completely different line of work.

'No need to make up your mind yet,' Callum said, seeming to sense her reticence. 'But you have my number now if you do want to take me up on the offer.'

It was kind of him to let her off the hook so easily. 'Thanks, I'll do that.'

3

CALLUM

Callum hoped he hid his embarrassment well enough for Tasha and Brodie not to notice. Why had he been so quick to offer to take her out? Fool. He was acting like an awkward schoolboy for some reason and that wasn't like him at all.

'Well, I'd better be going. If Riley does want to do the interview, just let me know.' She nodded. 'See you soon, Brodie. Please say my goodbyes to Lettie and Lindy.'

'Will do, mate.'

As he made his way back to his car, Callum couldn't help thinking how quickly life could change. Or his emotions at least. He had been happily single for the past couple of years ever since his engagement had ended abruptly when Zena decided spending the rest of her life in Jersey wasn't something she intended doing. He had thought it an excuse at the time, but she had gone travelling with a girlfriend and the last he heard of her she was living in Australia somewhere.

Callum saw Zac and Lettie's father, Gareth, taking Spud – the family's dog – into the house and waved. He thought about Zac, Lettie's brother and his best friend since primary school, and how most of his teens had been spent on this beautiful farm and how close Gareth and Lindy had come to selling up only the year before. He looked around him at the beautiful granite house, the colourful flowers and the two larger barns and smaller outbuildings, one of which Gareth had let Zac, Callum and two other friends who made up their band use for practice several nights a week after school.

He was relieved they had found a solution as to who would take over the farm after Gareth's health scare and had been as surprised as the rest of Zac's family when Lettie gave up her life in London working in fashion to return to the island and run the farm.

He got into his car and drove slowly back down the drive, not wishing to cause any dust or noise as he went in case they had begun filming again. Apart from travelling with Zac just after they had both gained their degrees at university, going away on annual holidays and the odd photo shoot for his modelling, Callum had only lived away from Jersey for a brief two-year period and had since been content to stay on the island. Unlike Zac who spent most of his time touring as a sound engineer.

Callum drove back to his two-bedroomed flat. The mortgage had been painfully high at first, but ever since he had worked on a popular radio show and gained a large number of followers on social media, he had been able to earn more. He understood why Lettie didn't mind returning to live on the island after spending several years away working in fashion in the capital, and Callum was grateful that now he earned better money life had become much easier. Yes, he decided, his life might not be perfect, but it was good, and the last thing he needed was to let his attraction for Tasha Dodds get the better of him, because her life wasn't over here and he had no wish to move away.

* * *

He had showered, changed into his tracksuit bottoms and an old T-shirt and was sitting on his small balcony drinking a cool lager when his phone rang. He looked at the screen and, not recognising the number and not wishing to interrupt the peace and quiet, was about to ignore the call when he remembered he had given Tasha his number.

He accepted the call. 'Hello?'

'Callum? This is Tasha Dodds, Riley Sharp's PA.'

Callum smiled at Tasha's expectation that he wouldn't know who she was unless she mentioned Riley. 'Hi, Tasha. Can I assume this call is to give me good news?' he asked before taking a drink from the bottle.

'It is. Riley took a little persuading because he's not one for interviews, but I convinced him that the show needs all the promotion he can give it and, for once, he agreed with me.'

'That's great news. Did he have a day and time in mind to visit the studio?'

He listened as she told him when Riley could make it. 'That's great. Thanks for making this happen, Tasha, and I'll see you then.'

He rang off and punched the air. Getting Riley Sharp to agree to come on his show was a massive coup.

Knowing he would be seeing Tasha again soon was an added bonus.

4

TASHA

Tasha stood to the side and watched Riley Sharp charm the blushing receptionist as she stepped from behind the desk and went to shake his hand.

'It's a pleasure to meet you, Mr Sh... Sh... Sharp.'

'Please,' he said, taking her hand and lowering his head to kiss the back of it, keeping eye contact at all times. 'Call me Riley,' he said in his sultriest voice, causing the receptionist to sigh and look for a moment as if she might faint.

Poor girl, Tasha thought, understanding only too well the effect her boss had on people when they met him in the flesh for the first time. His piercing blue eyes, six-foot-plus frame, toned physique as well as his perfectly symmetrical face and dark, almost black, perfectly styled hair were breathtaking. Initially. Knowing Riley as she now had for the past three years since starting work as his personal assistant, she thought he had probably spent most of his teenage years perfecting this first impression. She was relieved that his deep voice and beauty no longer made her feel weak at the knees.

He still had the ability to magnify her stress levels though.

He was a master of that, she mused, frustrated that so many of her more recent working days and evenings were spent doing damage control after he had upset yet another actor, director or member of the crew he was working with. She caught his sideways glance in her direction as he lowered the receptionist's hand and turned slightly towards Tasha. She tensed, aware that if the radio host didn't appear soon Riley would almost certainly leave without going through with the interview.

She took a steadying breath and willed the man to appear, closing her eyes in relief when the door opened and a flustered man burst into the reception from a door at the back of the room.

'I'm so sorry to keep you waiting.' He took Riley's hand in both of his and shook it enthusiastically. 'Thanks for welcoming our guests, JoJo,' he said, giving the receptionist a grateful smile. Then turning his attention back to Tasha and Riley, he stepped to one side and held out an arm. 'Let me show you through to the studio.'

She followed the men upstairs and took a seat next to Riley, hoping this idea of hers had been as good as Riley's manager presumed. It wasn't common knowledge outside of the cast and crew, but Riley's cheerful, friendly personality was as fake as his posh English accent. The past two months filming on the island's picturesque beaches and secret valleys had been exhausting, with one tantrum or argument after another.

Most of the crew were no longer speaking with Riley unless their lines called for them to, and three assistants had been fired after offending him in some imagined way. His previous two shows and last year's film might have been a roaring success, but she wondered how long it might be until people began to talk outside filming circles about his rude manner.

Thankfully, today he seemed to be on his best behaviour,

and Tasha was enormously relieved. He was here to help raise interest for the TV cop series, aware that he now needed to do something to rectify all the damage he had done by his disruptions on the film set.

She glanced down at her tablet, which showed the running order of the questions she had agreed with the radio host prior to Riley consenting to take part in the interview. So far so good. She listened to host Callum's lovely voice as he ran through what he intended doing.

'I've got a shout-out to make and will then introduce you,' he explained to Riley, shooting a glance at Tasha. 'Then we'll get straight into it if that's OK with you?'

'Sounds fine.' Riley gave his brightest smile that he saved for people he wanted to charm. Tasha knew that look, though, and could tell he wasn't happy the host hadn't seemed more enthusiastic to see him again. 'We're happy as long as you are.'

Tasha also knew that was untrue and by the brief movement of surprise in Callum's eyebrows she sensed he did too.

'Great, let's do this.' Callum gave them a nod and focused his attention onto the sound panel. 'Welcome to another sunny afternoon at BBC Island Radio. I'm your host Callum Preston and today, as most of you know, we have a very special guest who's been filming on the island for the past couple of months. He's a star of television and film.' He lowered his voice and moved slightly closer to the microphone as if he was sharing a secret with his audience. 'Mr Riley Sharp has kindly agreed to come into the studio. Yes, that Riley Sharp – and we couldn't be more excited to welcome him here.' He sat back and looked at Riley. 'Welcome, Riley. Thank you again for agreeing to come and speak to us.'

'It's my pleasure, Callum,' Riley said, seeming, Tasha was

relieved to note, happier now he had been given the sort of attention he had grown to expect.

She thought back three years to first meeting Riley when he had seemed far less arrogant and still surprised and grateful to have been in the top-ranking psychological thriller series on television that year. It was only a few months after that when he was offered a supporting role in a massive film and had been nominated for a BAFTA and a Golden Globe. After that, there was no stopping his ego. How the mighty can rise only for their behaviour to be reported on. He had developed a reputation, at least in the acting world, for being difficult to junior cast members and crew. It had completely changed that meteoric trajectory when more and more directors refused to work with him. It served him right, as far as Tasha was concerned.

Riley brought the microphone closer to him. 'Hello, listeners in Jersey. Thanks for inviting me here today, Callum. I am delighted to be on your show and share some behind-the-scenes news about our brand-new series *Sam Thorne Investigates* with your wonderful listeners. I hope they all look forward to watching.'

Tasha reminded herself that despite Riley's behaviour she liked her job, most of the time. She would have loved to find work with a more likeable actor. Unfortunately, Tasha knew that those celebrities tended to keep their assistants for years, so she hadn't heard of any vacancies that suited her.

Maybe if working as Riley's PA hadn't been her first role in show business after leaving banking wanting a more varied life-style, she might have had more confidence to stand up to him or leave sooner, but she loved her job, or at least the part of it that didn't include Riley's tantrums. She couldn't forget her gratitude to Riley for giving her the chance to work for him, and she was certain that not many other people in his position would have taken on someone with no experience in show business like he had done.

Then there was the niggling doubt that even though she had proved she could cope with Riley's demands, other more established actors would still choose an employee with much more experience than her if she did apply for another job.

'This is the detective series you're currently filming here in Jersey,' Callum said, bringing her back to the moment. 'Can you tell us how everything is going?'

Tasha wondered how the public would react if they knew. She braced herself for the nonsense Riley was about to spout.

'Extremely well,' Riley answered proudly. 'The production team are delighted with the scenes they've already captured and looking forward to wrapping up the final ones in the next two weeks.'

Liar, Tasha thought, biting her lower lip to calm her irritation as well as keep herself from blurting out the truth. Despite Riley's and his manager Dale's assurances to the director, Riley's behaviour on set had been the cause of delays. How could someone she believed to be over-rated as an actor fake being so likeable?

She listened anxiously as Callum asked the questions and Riley answered them. He was charm personified and as much as it irked her to know people were unaware of his true personality, she was grateful he was doing something to rectify the damage he had seemed intent on doing for the past two months.

She suspected the film Riley was initially cast in and should have been working on next, but which had been recast the previous week, probably had a lot to do with him agreeing to do this interview. It might also be why he was suddenly taking the TV series a lot more seriously. If other offers for work weren't forthcoming soon, Riley would be mortified. He needed a second series to be commissioned as soon as possible, as did Tasha, if she wanted to have her salary paid.

Catching movement from the corner of her eye, Tasha turned to see a younger man in the next room giving Callum the thumbs up before seeming to take a call. Tasha had accompanied Riley to enough radio stations to know that the person in the next room was usually a sound assistant. Maybe not though. She focused her attention back to the interview and Riley's next answer. So far, so good.

Dale would be as relieved as her that this was going better than either of them had dared hope it would.

5

CALLUM

Callum arrived home to his flat after his show ended. It had been a long day, and he opened a bottle of lager and went to sit outside on his small balcony to make the most of what was left of the day. The show had gone better than he expected and he was relieved. Getting Riley Sharp on the show had been a huge coup, which he hoped hadn't gone unnoticed by his bosses at the studio, especially as his contract was up for renewal in the next couple of months.

'You in?' his sister Erin bellowed from inside the flat.

Hearing her voice, Callum wondered what excuse she would make for her arrival, suspecting she had either heard him chatting to Riley Sharp on his show, or that someone at her hair salon might have mentioned it. There was no way Erin would admit it was because she wanted to know more about the actor.

'If the front door is unlocked then you can assume I am,' he teased. 'Grab yourself a drink and come out here to join me.'

He closed his eyes and thought back to seeing Riley and Tasha again at the studio. He felt more tired than he usually did after a show. Then again, this one had been more important than most, with such a prominent actor coming in to be interviewed, but both of them had seemed happy enough with how things had gone.

'Well?' Erin sat on the chair next to him and took a sip of the white wine she had poured for herself. 'How did you manage to land someone as massive as Riley Sharp on your show?'

'Lettie invited me over to watch the filming for a bit at Hollyhock Farm and introduced me to him and his assistant. I then asked her whether she thought he might agree to come on.'

'I couldn't believe it when one of my clients sent me a text telling me you were talking to him, so I immediately tuned in. How do you think it went?'

'Well, I think...' Callum thought a bit more about the reaction of his audience. 'I think the listeners will be happy,' he said, unable to miss the look of amazement on his sister's face.

'I'm glad.' She slapped his arm. 'Well done you. Anyway, that's enough about Riley Sharp.'

'I thought you were a fan of his,' he asked, surprised.

She shrugged. 'Right now I've got more pressing things to worry about.'

'Like what?'

She glared at him. 'I know you're mixing with celebs now, but have you forgotten Grandpa's party?'

Of course he hadn't and he was aware his sister knew that only too well. 'What, because I've given it so little thought, you mean?' She could be really irritating sometimes, he decided. 'I've only had all the invitations printed and sent them out; arranged, thanks to Lettie's contacts, where Grandpa and most of the family, including you, I might add, will be staying for one glorious week; and booked the band to play for the evening at the manor.'

'All right, don't make an issue out of it,' she grumbled, getting up to leave. 'I only asked. I do have other places I can be instead of here listening to you showing off.'

'I'm sure you do.' Callum reached out to take his sister's forearm, pulling her back down onto her seat. 'Sorry, I'm tired. I didn't sleep much last night, preparing for the interview today.'

'Why didn't you prepare earlier in the evening?'

He narrowed his eyes at her, irritated. 'Because as soon as I finished for the day, Dad called and I had him on the phone fretting for almost two hours about party preparations.' He drank some of his beer. 'Regardless of that, I shouldn't take it out on you.'

'No, you shouldn't.' Her voice softened. 'Then again, I shouldn't have been so snarky.'

Callum thought how things often played out this way with his only sibling. One goading the other, then a little bickering and finally quickly moving past it and forgetting they had ever squabbled. He wondered if it was their subconscious way of releasing irritation after a difficult time.

'It's fine.' Wanting to change the subject, he said, 'I think you're going to love the manor house. It's beautiful and the grounds are spectacular with perfectly mowed lawns, colourful borders and huge trees. I'm so glad we're all going to stay there together, apart from Mum and Barry, even though most of us have our own homes here, but it'll be extra fun being in the same place for a week.' He thought about their dad's fiancée Betsy, and their stepdad, Barry.

'Yes, and we both know that since Dad and Betsy can't be in the same house as Mum and Barry for too long without one of them falling out with the other, that works out well. I think they'll be fine for the party because they both love Grandad, but not for twenty-four hours, let alone a week.'

Callum agreed, but now wished he hadn't been so quick to offer his flat to his mother and stepfather. He was shattered after weeks with little time off and still needed to freshen the place up and change the bedding to get the flat ready for their arrival. It had been the sensible thing to do though, and his mum had been happy to accept his offer.

'I can't believe you found this manor house for us,' Erin said. 'I looked it up online but could only find a couple of old photos.'

'That's because the owners are very private and only occasionally rent out the place, and then only do it through an exclusive rental company.'

'How did you find it then?'

'Through Lettie Torel. She knows the owner of the agency and put me in touch with her.'

'Wow, talk about having friends in all the right places,' Erin said.

He smiled at his sister. 'Apparently the owners are going away for a few weeks and offered it to us for a slightly lower rate than they usually charge because the previous booking cancelled too late for them to find anyone else. It's got a cottage in the grounds too.' He didn't add that Riley was already staying there and would be for at least the next two weeks with his PA, because he doubted Erin could refrain from finding a way to introduce herself to him.

'I'm looking forward to seeing it,' she said. 'And I can't wait to stay there. What's it called again?'

'Beauvoir Manor.'

She beamed at him. 'It even sounds impressive. It's probably good that we're holding the party at a private place away from other people in case our lot get noisy.'

'Which they're bound to do,' he said, hoping the cottage

where Tasha and Riley would be staying was far enough away for the sound of his family having fun not to carry that far.

He supposed he would find out soon enough when they moved in. Callum groaned inwardly and hoped he wasn't going to have to spend the next week apologising and trying to make up for any issues with Tasha or Riley.

6

TASHA

Tasha grimaced as she heard Riley swear at the woman playing his love interest in the series. Yet again he was directing focus away from his own laziness learning his lines to the debut actress's brief hesitation before replying to what he'd just said. No one would have noticed, Tasha seethed, certain even Riley wouldn't have done if he hadn't needed someone to blame for how badly today's filming was going. Again.

It hadn't taken him long to forget how much he needed this series to work, or how desperately he needed to do all he could to save what little respect he had left in the business.

'That's enough, Riley,' the director snapped. He turned to the pink-faced actress. 'We'll go one more time. And Ruby, if you could speak your line as soon as Riley has finished speaking, that should do it.'

'Yes,' Riley sneered. 'The conversation is supposed to be punchy, not drawn out.'

One of these days someone was going to stand up to Riley, Tasha thought, hoping she wouldn't have too long to wait for that to happen.

'Right, let's do this, then we can call it a day.' The director gave Ruby a sympathetic smile.

Unable to stand another moment of Riley's bullying, Tasha walked off set back to the dressing room to tidy up, ready for them to make a hasty exit. This was her first time on the island and she loved it. Well, she'd loved what she had managed to see of the place, being at Riley's beck and call twenty-four-seven. She might not like the idea of leaving her job but she wasn't sure how long she could stand working for him.

It wasn't only her that felt this way about him. The tension among the rest of the cast and most of the crew was palpable and increasing by the day, and the delay in completing filming was costing the production more each day. Tasha sensed an undeniable undercurrent whenever she was on set and had a horrible feeling something bad was about to happen.

Then again, she wasn't ready to admit that her parents' reservations about her leaving her role as a PA to the chairman of the bank to take the position working for Riley had been valid. Her argument with them the night she had broken the news of her resignation and why she was leaving the bank had caused the strain between them and, as much as it saddened her, she hated to admit she might have been a little too hasty to drop everything to chase a dream.

No, she decided. That wasn't true. It might be an ordeal working for Riley sometimes but she loved travelling with him, being on film and TV sets and watching the creative process. She even enjoyed helping him learn his lines, though he could be lazy and often wanted to put off doing them until the last minute.

Anyway, where would she go if she did leave him? She had lost touch with most of her friends over the past three years, not having time to meet up with them much, until one by one they had stopped inviting her to parties to celebrate engagements, weddings, or even christenings when one of them had had a baby.

Tasha knew some of her friendship group thought she had changed because they'd ghosted her, or due to sarcastic comments in chat groups. She had noticed a few months ago that no one seemed to leave messages in their group chat any longer and suspected a new one had been set up that hadn't included her. The realisation hurt, but she couldn't blame them. She had been absent from their lives for too long now.

Surely though, just because she was away a lot and in a different place to them relationship-wise, that didn't mean they didn't matter to her. She had been thinking more often about contacting one or two of them and arranging a visit back to Sussex to catch up with them again. But when?

Each time she broached the subject with Riley, and Tasha started to try and work out dates, something had come up, or his filming schedule had changed, until in the end she had realised that to arrange something only to have to pull out at the last minute would be far worse than not doing anything. She hoped that when she did have time for a decent visit home she could make it up to them.

She lost track of time folding Riley's expensive clothes, which he had dropped onto the floor, and tidying away others from the wardrobe department. Standing with her hands on her hips, Tasha stared at the mess of cups, half-drunk glasses of water, bottles of vitamins and glass flasks half filled with green shakes he insisted on being brought in to him each morning, only to take a couple of sips and declare it disgusting before demanding a different one. How did his dressing room always end up being so messy?

The man was becoming a nightmare. Correction, she mused,

he was already that. He was becoming impossible and as much as she liked what she did for a living she decided that as soon as an opening became available working for someone, no, anyone else, she would apply for it.

The door burst open, crashing against the wall behind her and only just missing Tasha's elbow.

Riley marched in, his face puce with temper. 'Grab my things.'

'What's wrong?' She hurriedly zipped up the nearest bag, deciding there wasn't time to discard all the detritus from his day. Tasha was used to his rages but whatever had just happened it was clear Riley was only just managing to contain himself before really losing his temper.

'I've just overheard one of the runners chatting to the caterer and moaning how it's my fault we need to stay here for an extra two weeks.' He leant closer to her. 'My fault,' he screamed in her face. 'As if.' He stomped out of his dressing room and down the corridor in the direction of the exit.

If only Riley wasn't so delusional when it came to himself, she mused. The man was always highly critical of others, demanding perfection from them, and for some reason always assumed that was what he gave, which he rarely did now.

Assuming Riley was making his way to the car that had brought them to and from the studio yesterday, she swept the rest of his belongings into the largest bag and, tucking her own bag under her shoulder, grabbed both the other bags and followed him.

At least they had a beautiful house to return to and relax overnight.

No one spoke to her as she left, which was a relief. She was becoming more embarrassed every day, and it wasn't as if she was the one treating everyone badly. She shouldered the door open and squinted as she stepped back into the bright sunshine, relieved when two strong hands took the larger bags from her.

'We're parked just over here,' Bill, their driver, explained. He lowered his voice as they walked. 'Himself is already in the car. Sulking, he is. Gawd knows what's happened to upset him this time.'

'People are moaning about having to film for another two weeks.' She wondered whether the change in schedule affected Bill's life in any way. 'I'm sorry if it puts you in a difficult position with your next job.' A thought occurred to her. 'You're not going to be replaced by another driver, are you?' Bill never seemed fazed by Riley's rudeness but she wasn't so sure other drivers would take too kindly to his snappiness.

Bill sighed. They reached the car, and he opened the boot, giving her a cheeky smile. 'I shouldn't be bothered. I can soon find someone to step in for me with the next job. I'm happy to keep looking after the pair of you for another couple of weeks.'

She smiled, relieved.

Tasha got into the car and tuned out Riley's rants. She was yet to hear back from the property manager and hoped the owners would agree to her and Riley extending their stay at the cottage. *Cottage*, she thought with amusement. This was the grandest, largest cottage she had ever seen. She and Riley had driven past the manor house further up the driveway each time they had arrived or left this place and had noticed cleaners appearing to get it ready for new guests.

She decided to change the subject. 'I wonder who's moving into the manor house?'

Riley groaned. 'I wish it was staying vacant. Or that we could have stayed there instead of here.'

'You know it was already booked up when we found this place.'

He mumbled something under his breath, then added, 'As long as they keep to themselves and don't start coming down here and pestering me for autographs and selfies.'

'I'm sure they won't.' She hoped not. She was busy enough looking after him without having to police the cottage gardens against eager fans.

'As always, I booked this place under my name so that you can stay here anonymously,' she said, hoping to reassure him.

'Whatever.'

She closed her eyes as he moaned yet again about the poor young actress who had initially been over the moon to be cast opposite him. Tasha wondered what she thought of him now. She hoped the girl's experience filming her first series wouldn't be ruined by Riley's nastiness and that she knew enough about filming to be aware that Riley's behaviour was not all that typical. He was the worst person Tasha had worked for, but also the most successful, giving her the chance to see countries and stay in suites at the most prominent hotels in the world.

Other assistants she knew who worked for celebrities were often sent to basic nearby accommodation, and most of the time that's what she had done too, but while they were on the island it made sense for her and Riley to both stay at the cottage. He liked having her on call, whenever he needed her to help him go through his lines, order in food, or any other job he could think of to give her. She thought of her studio flat in Clapham, which she'd given up before coming to Jersey. It hadn't ever truly felt like the home she had intended to make it. Probably because she was rarely there for very long with all the travelling to locations she had done with Riley.

She wondered if she might feel like she had roots somewhere if she was in a relationship with someone, but again how would that be possible when working for Riley took up so much of her time? The only man she had dated since working for Riley had soon become jealous of her lack of free time, even though she and Riley had never been more than boss and employee to each other.

Regardless of the benefits she had gleaned during the past three years, she was becoming more aware that by working with Riley, she was often found guilty by association among the cast and crew of shows he worked in, and the sooner she found somewhere else to work the better as far as she was concerned.

Not that she had much free time to apply for anything else right now.

Tasha decided that as soon as she had changed their flights home, she would look for other accommodation for herself on the island.

There was a lull in Riley's moaning, and Bill took the chance to change the subject.

'How did the radio interview go yesterday, Mr Sharp? I forgot to ask.'

'It could have been worse, I suppose.'

'I thought it went very well,' Tasha said, thinking how good Callum was at his job.

'Maybe.'

He really was in a bad mood, Tasha thought miserably. She hoped he snapped out of it soon, otherwise the evening ahead was going to drag.

'Hey,' Riley said, frowning. 'Did you pick up my phone yesterday?'

'Your phone?' She tried to recall when she might have last seen it. Riley was always leaving it somewhere.

'Yes. I've been racking my brains to think when I had it last, and I think it was at the studio.'

Tasha closed her eyes. 'Are you sure?'

'I said so, didn't I?'

Not quite, she thought, but kept her response to herself. Aware that his next comment would be for her to retrieve it for him, she took her phone from her pocket and found Callum's number. He didn't answer her call so she sent him a text. 'I'll get it back as soon as I can.'

7

CALLUM

Callum felt his mobile vibrate in his jeans pocket and after taking it out looked at the caller ID. He didn't recognise the number and never liked answering calls from strangers, so ended it and pushed the phone back in his pocket. Seconds later it vibrated again. Not wishing to miss a call from one of his family, Callum sighed and withdrew his phone. This time there was a text.

> Sorry to message you like this, but this is Tasha, Riley Sharp's assistant, and I need to ask you something if that's OK. I'd be grateful if you would call this number as the matter is urgent.

He thought of the patient woman who had accompanied Riley Sharp to the studio. She didn't say much, but Callum hadn't missed how she seemed to take in everything around her and it was clear to him that she kept everything in Riley's diary in perfect order. The auburn-haired, green-eyed woman had a quiet strength about her and if she was asking him, a relative stranger, for help then how could he not immediately do as she asked?

Intrigued, Callum returned her call.

'Callum?' she asked before he had barely registered the phone ringing.

'Yes. Hi, Tasha,' he said, his stomach flipping over when he heard her voice. 'I'm just returning your call,' he said, trying not to sound as delighted as he felt to have an excuse to speak to her.

'Hi, Callum, thanks so much for getting back to me so quickly.'

He listened as she explained about Callum's lost phone. 'And if he did leave it at the studio, I was hoping I could arrange to pick it up from you as soon as possible, if that's all right?'

He tried to recall whether he remembered seeing the phone in the studio after the pair of them had left. 'Let me call my assistant and see what I can do. Then I can bring it to you, if that's easier.'

'Are you sure that won't be putting you out too much?'

If it meant seeing her again then he was only too happy to do it, not that he had any intention of letting Tasha know that. 'I really don't mind. I know how much I hate it when I mislay my phone.'

'That's so kind of you. Let me send you the address where we're staying.'

'There's no need. You're at Beauvoir Cottage, aren't you?'

There was a few seconds' silence. 'Er, how did you know that?'

It dawned on him how important privacy was to most celebrities and that he probably shouldn't have let her know he already knew their address, so he decided to be open with her. 'Lettie mentioned it to me.'

'She did?'

Tasha didn't sound pleased.

'Only because she knows I'll be staying at the manor house next door.'

'Really?'

He wasn't sure if that was a happy response, but at least she didn't sound as angry now. 'That's right. I'll be there with most of my family to celebrate my grandfather's eightieth. It's a surprise party.'

'That sounds lovely.'

'I hope it works out well. As far as he's concerned he's being taken somewhere for a birthday meal. He has no idea where, so is ready for some sort of surprise, but not all his family and friends being together on the island to celebrate his big day.'

'What an incredible way to celebrate his birthday.'

'My father is packing a bag for him and of course he'll be able to return home for anything else he needs, but we thought a week together in a beautiful manor house would be something special and memorable.'

'I think it sounds idyllic.'

'I hope it turns out that way. I must admit I'm looking forward to it, but we have quite a bit of preparation still to do and we have to hope that the weather stays good.'

'I suppose you will want to make the most of the gardens. I've only driven past the ones in front of the manor house but everything looks like something from Chelsea Flower Show.'

'That's good to know. I haven't been there yet, only seen the photos the agent showed me when I went to sign the contract for our stay. No, the weather is important because we have quite a few of Grandad's friends flying over and we can get those days when fog settles on the island and all flights are delayed or cancelled. I'm hoping everyone can get here to celebrate with him.'

'I'll cross everything that happens then.'

'Thank you,' he said, thinking how kind she seemed. 'I'll have a look for the phone and if I find it I'll bring it to the cottage if that suits you?'

'That would be perfect. Thanks, Callum.'

'It's no problem at all,' he said honestly.

She ended the call and Callum hoped he did find the lost phone.

The following evening, Callum placed Riley's phone on the coffee table in front of him, meaning to email Tasha and ask whether he could pop it round in an hour or so, but before doing that he decided to quickly reply to another email so he could tick off one more item on his list of jobs to do in preparation for the party. He had just pasted in all the information when there was a bellow from his front door.

'You in?' Erin called as she let herself in.

'Kitchen.' He frowned, trying to remember what he had been about to add to the email to the taxi firm he had booked to collect several of the guests from the airport upon their arrival.

'What you doing?' She stopped on the other side of the small table by the window briefly before picking up a clean glass from the draining board and pouring herself some water. 'It's hot and sticky outside. I can't stand this weather, drives me nuts and makes my hair go all kinky.'

Typing the same word twice, Callum looked over at her. 'Did you want something or are you just here to bother me?'

She leant against the worktop and took a sip of the water. 'Someone's grumpy today.'

He glared at her. 'I'll be even grumpier if you don't leave me in peace to deal with this.'

'Grandad's party?'

He sighed. 'Yes.'

'Everything not sorted yet then?'

He gave her a look of disdain. 'What do you think?'

'Ah.'

He reread the email and, satisfied it gave all the information the person had requested, sent it off. 'I'm trying to cover all bases. This was about the taxis I've booked for guests.'

She looked around the room. 'I think you're very brave offering your place to Mum and Barry.'

'Why, don't you think it looks OK?'

She shrugged one shoulder. 'Not at all – it looks amazing compared to my messy flat.'

He wished Erin wouldn't make him panic unnecessarily. 'What then?'

'Well, we both know Mum is bound to make changes to where you store things, or tidy wardrobes and stuff like that. She always has to declutter and move things to how she feels they look best.'

Erin was right, but he had too much on his mind to care much about that now. 'Then I'll just have to move it all back again to how I like it after she's left, won't I?'

'I guess. And you don't mind giving up your place for them?'

'Not if it keeps everyone happy, no.'

Erin spotted the phone and picked it up, turning it over in her hand. 'Who does this belong to? It's not your usual one.'

'It's Riley Sharp's,' he replied without thinking.

'What?'

'He left it at the studio and I need to return it to him.'

Callum sighed, trying to decide whether to mention Tasha and Riley's situation to his sister.

She gasped and stepped over to the table. 'What is it? I can tell there's something you're keeping from me.'

Stifling a groan and knowing from experience that it was far easier to give in straight away and tell his sister something than to put up with her going on about it, he relented and explained about Riley and Tasha's staying in the cottage and his concerns about disturbing them.

Her mouth dropped open for a couple of seconds, before drawing back into a wide delighted smile. 'This is amazing news.'

'I can see I shouldn't have told you.'

Erin squealed in excitement. 'Rubbish, you didn't have much choice. We both know I would have got it out of you somehow.' She laughed. 'I'm only teasing you. This is exciting though.' She took another sip of her water. 'I can't believe I'm going to meet Riley Sharp in the flesh.'

'Hold on. No, you're not.' Callum glared at her. 'He's very protective of his privacy, Erin. You're not to bother him. Promise me.'

Shaking her head, Erin laughed. 'You really do worry about everything, don't you?'

'I do not,' he lied. 'Only the important things.'

His laptop pinged.

'Maybe that's him emailing you,' she joked.

He looked down and saw Tasha had replied. 'His PA actually.'

He smiled at his sister's aghast expression. 'Close your mouth, Erin, you look as if you're doing an impression of a goldfish.'

He typed a quick response before he closed his laptop, picked up the phone and stood.

'You're going to take it to him? Now?'

'Yes.'

'Can I come with you? Pleeeeease.'

'No.'

'I promise I won't gawp at him.'

He knew his sister well enough not to trust her to keep calm. 'There's not a chance I'm taking you with me, so if you don't mind leaving now, I'll be on my way.'

'You can be incredibly selfish sometimes, Callum. Do you know that?'

He gently pushed her out of the flat and locked the door behind them. 'We can't always have what we want, Erin,' he said, thinking about how much he wished Tasha wasn't on the island for only another two weeks. He would have loved the chance to spend time with her and get to know her better, but life often didn't work that way, he thought, trying to resign himself to the fact that she would soon be leaving Jersey and he might never have the opportunity to see her again.

8

TASHA

Tasha read Callum's email with relief.

'Callum's located your phone,' she called out, hearing Riley mutter something as he slammed the fridge door closed in the kitchen along the hall. 'He's bringing it here now.'

She was relieved he had been successful but when Riley stepped into the dining room, which she was using as her office, instead of looking pleased he seemed sulky.

Unsure why he should react in that way, she asked, 'I thought you'd be pleased. It's not like you to be without your phone. I thought you'd have missed it.'

He didn't react immediately, then looked at her in silence for a moment.

Tasha tried to work out why he was behaving this way. Then it dawned on her. 'Are you avoiding Brooke?'

He raised an eyebrow. 'Maybe.'

Riley had been dating model Brooke Farrow on and off for almost a year, as far as she could recall. More off than on, Tasha mused, recalling the seemingly endless rows the pair had had as their inflated egos clashed time and again.

'You've broken up?'

He groaned. 'To be honest, I'm not sure. I feel like we are but Brooke seemed to have a different opinion. I'm not sure how much longer I can deal with her drama.'

Tasha watched him leave the room, trying to work out how anyone could be as oblivious to their own behaviour as Riley managed to be.

Remembering Callum was on his way, she quickly went to her room and freshened up. It was one thing trying to act cool but she intended doing that with brushed hair and fresh breath.

She heard a car and hurried down the stairs to greet him, wondering whether he had been to the cottage before.

'Hi there,' she said, giving him a wave as he parked the car. 'It's good of you to come so quickly.'

He got out and walked towards her, holding out Riley's phone. 'It's no problem at all. I was at a loose end and I imagine Riley's eager to get this back. I know I'd hate to be without my phone for long.'

'I suppose he is,' she said, aware that if she had heard Callum's car from her bedroom then Riley must have done from his down the hall. She took the phone from him. 'Thank you. Um, if you've got time maybe I could show you around? Or we could sit outside and have a drink before you go on to whatever you need to do next?'

He smiled. 'I'm happy to do both of those things.' He looked around. 'It's beautiful here, although why they call something this grand a cottage beats me.'

Tasha laughed. 'I agree. When I told Riley we were coming to stay in a cottage he wasn't impressed.' She didn't add that he wasn't that cheerful after seeing the place either, preferring something far more modern and minimalist.

It made sense for her to at least show Callum the place

before she told Riley she had his phone. She took a discreet look at Callum's handsome face and thought how his kindness shone through. Then she considered how deceptive people's looks could be. There was Riley's friendly on-screen character and boy-next-door looks that tugged at his many fans' hearts, and if there was one thing she had learnt above all others since working for him it was not to take people at face value ever again and to watch what they did more than listen to what they said when referring to themselves and others.

'I presume this is Victorian,' he said as he studied the frontage of the building with its pillared front porch and crenellated balcony above, on which stood a large planter containing scarlet hanging geraniums interspersed with purply-blue lavender. He turned to her.

'This is beautiful.'

She nodded. 'I thought the same thing when I first came here. Shall we go inside and have a look around? There's a housekeeper but it's her day off today so we're seeing to ourselves.' More that she was looking after Riley's needs for food and drink most of the time.

Tasha led the way inside. 'I love how symmetrical the building is and I adore the pale blue shutters on either side of each window against the stark white of the rest of the house.'

'I agree. It's beautiful.' He turned and indicated the view behind her. 'And how about this for a view when you wake up in the morning.'

She turned and stared, entranced at the colourful array of flowers filling each of the borders. 'They must employ several gardeners to keep everything this pristine.'

'I suppose they must.' Callum stretched out an arm indicating Tasha lead the way. 'I'm excited to look around this place.'

Tasha walked through the cool hallway with its perfectly

polished parquet flooring that flowed into each of the down-stairs rooms. After showing him the black and white kitchen with its white marbled worktops and tiles, she led him up the thickly carpeted stairway to the first floor where three bedrooms including hers were immaculately made up, their windows slightly open to let in any breeze. When they'd arrived she'd decided she didn't mind which bedroom she took because each was as perfect as the next.

'The primary is at the end of the corridor, but that's Riley's. I'm not sure whether he's in there learning more lines.' She knocked lightly and when there was no answer, she opened the door to the cream and pale blue room, cringing at the strewn clothes and open wardrobes.

'I think we should miss this one.'

'I'd feel odd going into his room anyway.'

'I would have loved to show it to you because it's probably the most incredibly beautiful bedroom I've ever seen.' She thought of all the apartments, hotels and homes she had accompanied him to and shrugged. 'Riley's taste is very different to this place.'

'How so?'

Tasha smiled up at Callum, wishing she could answer honestly, but as much as he seemed friendly enough she didn't really know him and didn't want to say anything disloyal about Riley that could be relayed back negatively to him. She needed this job too much, at least right now, to dare risk that happening. She saw Callum's eyebrows lower in a thoughtful frown and realised he was wondering why she was taking so long replying to a simply question.

'Just that he favours minimalist modern.' She shrugged, forgetting herself for a moment. 'Then again, we're only staying here for a short time.'

Tasha stood, embarrassed to have almost spoken freely about her boss's antics to Callum. Turning, she began leading him back downstairs. Where was Riley? The least he could have done was come and thank Callum for locating and bringing back his phone. Instead, he had gone off somewhere and not even bothered to say thank you. How typical of him to assume that was what someone would do for him in their free time and it not be worthy of a show of gratitude.

9

CALLUM

Callum wasn't sure why their easy chatter had tailed off. She seemed concerned about something and he decided to broach the subject in case it had been anything he had said to cause her change of mood.

'Everything all right?' He saw her turn to him from the corner of his eye.

'Yes, thanks. Why?'

He shook his head, not wanting to make things even more awkward. 'You seemed a little quiet, that's all.'

She gave a short laugh and he could almost feel her annoyance.

'Is something the matter?'

She shook her head and gave an apologetic smile. 'No, Callum, you've been amazing putting yourself out like you have.'

Unsure whether to voice his thoughts, Callum decided that if this was Tasha letting him know she needed to vent then he really had no option but to do it.

'Is it Riley? Is he difficult to work for?'

She seemed surprised at his question and didn't react immediately.

He was beginning to wish he had kept his thoughts to himself when she said, 'He can be a little bit difficult at times.'

He looked at her more closely, trying to work out whether Riley was in some way abusive to her. If she did have a problem with him, Callum wanted her to know he was there to support her.

'I know we don't know each other all that well, but you have my number now and I want you to know you can always call or message me if you ever need any help.'

He saw her frown. 'Help?'

Damn, had he overstepped the boundaries of what she felt acceptable? He hoped not. 'Er, or if you need assistance with something. Anything.'

He was rambling now and feeling more awkward by the moment.

He felt her hand rest on his forearm and looked down at it.

Tasha moved back. 'Sorry, Callum, I know what you mean. And I am grateful for the offer. Thank you. I can deal with Riley though. He can be rude and impossible with his demands at times, but he doesn't dare push things too far with me, if that's what you're worried about.'

'That's good,' Callum said, relieved to hear it.

She sighed. 'He acts like a spoilt brat quite a lot of the time, which is why we're having to reshoot several of his scenes. He's gone through so many assistants since his career took off that I hope he's slowly beginning to realise word is getting around in the film and TV business and soon there won't be anyone willing to work for him.' She shrugged. 'Plus, I threatened to leave only last week and even Riley worked out that I wasn't joking.'

The thought of Tasha going anywhere saddened him and Callum wondered if maybe he was getting to like this woman a little more than he should. After all, he barely knew her and their time together was designed to solve a work issue for her, nothing personal. Anyway, he reminded himself, she wasn't from the island and was only working here for another couple of weeks so he needed to gather himself and stop being silly.

His phone rang. 'Sorry,' he said, taking it from his back pocket. 'It's my father.' He smiled, ending the call. 'I imagine it'll be him worrying, yet again about preparations for the party. I'd better go and call him back.'

'Thanks again for today, Callum.'

'My pleasure.'

He gave her a wave before walking out to his car.

* * *

Two hours later Callum sat in his small living room rereading the same line in the thriller he was resting on his lap. He placed his book on the chair cushion beside him and wondered about Tasha having to deal with Riley, especially as he was a difficult employer to work for. Callum thought how hard it must be for Tasha to be staying under the same roof as the man and unable to get that respite he had always savoured by being able to go home after a day's work.

Callum picked up his mug of cooling coffee, relieved to have finally sorted out the bulk of his to-do list for the party. He wondered what it would be like seeing more of Tasha, then reminded himself that with the cottage being down a drive longer than the lane his home was situated on, and Tasha accompanying Riley to set each day, it was probably unlikely that he would see much, if anything, of her at all.

It was probably just as well, Callum decided, as he took the empty mug to the kitchen and washed it. He checked his phone, wondering if it was early enough to visit his father and Betsy before they left to go and eat at wherever place they had chosen for their meal that night. He decided to do it and take his swimming shorts and a towel with him, so that if they were out he could make the most of the hot weather and go for a swim in St Brelade's Bay.

10

TASHA

Tasha knew she still had to mention Callum's family party. The last thing she or the Prestons needed was Riley being his usual entitled self and marching up there to complain, or worse getting someone else to do it, like the police, but Riley was busy arguing loudly with Brooke on the phone in the living room. They had been at it for the past hour and Tasha's head was pounding, both from the hot weather on set and yet more drama from Riley. Tasha waited in the kitchen, as they screamed at each other. She closed her eyes and rubbed her temples lightly with her fingertips.

Eventually she heard their tone change and once again they were blowing kisses to each other down the phone. She wished they would make up their minds one way or another and either work at their relationship or end it once and for all.

Riley walked through to the kitchen. 'What's the matter with you?' he asked.

She took a calming breath. 'I have something I need to talk to you about.'

He groaned. 'What now?'

She explained about the Prestons hiring the manor and moving in for the next week.

He rested his hands on his hips, scowling. 'Why don't we have the big house? I thought we were here because it was the bit the owners rented out. Why do we only have the cottage?'

'Because there are only two of us,' she said, watching him prepare to respond. 'And they're a large private party. The place was booked out but became unexpectedly vacant, so I'm sure the owners were happy for the Prestons to hire the place.'

He began studying his phone again, clearly bored with the conversation. 'Pay them to swap, or move, then. Whatever it takes.' When she didn't respond he looked up at her. 'What's the problem?'

Tasha was too busy trying to control her rising temper to be able to answer him.

'Tasha, why are you staring at me like that? Go on. You know how I feel about not being treated in the manner I expect.'

She reminded herself that she needed this job, although it was getting more difficult by the day not to give in to her need to tell Riley exactly what she thought of him and his disregard for anyone else's feelings. She couldn't lose her temper right now and she had no intention of trying to persuade anyone to change anything about the property arrangements.

'There is nothing wrong with this place Riley; we both know that. We don't even take up all the bedrooms in the cottage and we're out at work most of the day. So, on this occasion I'm not doing anything about trying to change things.'

'You're not?'

She wasn't sure whether he was testing her loyalty and decided that even if he was she didn't care. 'No, not this time. This is a stunning place. We even have the woods over there and these beautiful grounds and the huge pond. There's no realistic reason to change anything.'

He glared at her, furiously leaning towards her, his nose inches from her. 'You won't do it?' he asked quietly. 'You're choosing to disregard my instructions?'

Refusing to be intimidated and closer to telling him to shove his job where the sun didn't shine than she had ever been before, Tasha took one step back. 'That's right.' His eyes widened. 'Callum very kindly brought your phone back to you, not that you bothered to even thank him. We don't need that huge manor house. His family, on the other hand, are staying there, with friends travelling to the island for the party. They're looking forward to a big family celebration and I will not ask him to change anything to appease your whim.'

She turned to leave the room. Stopping at the kitchen door as a thought occurred to her. She turned back to him. 'I can give him your number though if you'd like to tell him we wish to swap properties with him.'

Not bothering to wait for a response, she went into her temporary office in the dining room and closed the door. Once inside Tasha held on to the top of the table, trying to gather herself. She didn't know whether she was trembling because of her fear of upsetting Riley, or because she was so angry with him for being so uncaring about anyone else.

Hearing him stomp outside, Tasha decided she needed a cup of tea to calm herself down. She returned to the kitchen and switched on the kettle before taking a mug from the cupboard.

Tasha had barely had time to close the fridge after returning the milk to the shelf when the kitchen door opened and Riley stood at the doorway, arms crossed and a scowl on his handsome face. He relied far too much on his looks to charm people, she thought, as he stared at her, seemingly either trying to disarm her or work out whether to give her a lecture.

She had no intention of letting him think he'd intimidated her as he continually did to others. 'Well, have you decided what you'd like to do?' she asked.

He glared at her. 'The way I see it you haven't left me much choice,' he grumbled. 'We both know there's not enough accommodation here to sleep too many people, so I suppose I'll have to put up with the Prestons keeping the manor house.'

She was taken aback that he had given in so easily but had no intention of letting him know it. Tasha picked up her mug and went to leave the kitchen. 'If that's all, I'll go and answer some of the emails we received today.'

Finally, Riley turned his back on her.

'If that's the way you feel about it, then I'll leave things how they stand.' He walked out of the room and all Tasha could to was stare at his retreating back, astounded that for once she had stood up to him and got her own way. It was a strange feeling but one she decided she liked.

11

CALLUM

He couldn't believe today was the day the family all arrived from their homes in England, Spain and France. He had already welcomed his mother and Barry and settled them into his cottage and was now on his way to Beauvoir Manor to meet Erin and prepare for the rest of them to arrive. His car was packed with gifts for his grandfather and the large poster they had of him to display on the stand Erin was taking, together with his bag with enough clothes to last the week everyone would be staying there.

He wished they were all staying for longer but it had been exhausting enough arranging everyone to come for this one week. They all loved his grandad, Keith, and Callum hated to think how impossible it might have been if his relations hadn't all wanted so desperately to make this birthday celebration a huge success.

He carried the last of the things into the hallway, deciding to let the others choose which rooms they wanted to sleep in. Whatever it took to keep everyone happy so that his grandfather had the best birthday, that's what he intended to do.

Hearing a car pull up outside, Callum rushed outside to find his friends Brodie and Joe getting out of Brodie's ancient Land Rover, and he hurried over to greet them.

'Don't look so worried,' Brodie said, opening the back door of the vehicle. 'Lettie's mum, Lindy, has packed home-made cakes and scones, and your sister will be bringing the cake with her.'

He stepped back to let Callum look into the vehicle. 'It's packed in there,' Callum said, delighted to see so many cool boxes and bags of food. 'I'll message her too, of course, but please tell Lindy how grateful I am that she's doing so much of the baking.'

'We all love Keith,' Brodie said. 'And Lindy said she was thrilled to have her offer to help out accepted by your family.'

'Joe's a legend in his own lifetime,' Callum said, thinking of a recent sea rescue Joe had carried out with other firefighters. 'It's hot out here so I think we should take all this food into the house as soon as possible. We don't want it to start spoiling.'

'Good point.' Brodie lifted out the first three bags. 'I don't want to have to be the one to admit to Lettie and Lindy how we messed up all their hard work with all this baking.'

Callum picked up the two nearest cool bags. 'Neither do I.' He followed Brodie into the hallway then led the way through to the vast kitchen.

'This place is incredible,' Joe said, giving a whistle of approval. 'Your grandad will love all this. Will he be staying here tonight with the rest of you?'

Callum left what he was carrying on the kitchen table. 'No. He's at home tonight to give us a chance to finalise everything. He knows we've planned something, but he thinks it's a meal at one of the restaurants in town. The rest of the family will come here tonight and help me set up the orangery where we'll be holding the party, and it needs to be ready for when Dad brings him here with Betsy tomorrow evening.'

'Does Keith know he's staying somewhere other than his own place?' Joe asked.

Callum shook his head. 'No, but Dad and Betsy will pack up a few things for him and discreetly bring them. Knowing Grandad, he'll want to be partying until the very end.'

Joe laughed. 'And knowing Keith, he'll probably be the last one standing.'

Callum didn't doubt it. His grandfather might almost be eighty but he had the stamina of someone half his age when it came to socialising.

'Orangery?' Brodie laughed. 'This place is even bigger than I thought.'

'Is someone going to come and help me carry this lot inside?' Erin bellowed from somewhere in the hallway.

Callum exchanged amused glances with Joe. 'I suppose we'd better go and help her.'

It only took a few minutes to unload Erin's car and another twenty to unpack everything and store it safely away in the fridge and walk-in pantry.

Callum stood admiring the filled room before closing the door. 'You guys are amazing. Thanks so much for doing all this. I just wouldn't have had the time to do it by myself.'

'Or done it as well as we have,' Erin teased, slapping him on the back of his shoulder. 'Seriously though, big brother, I think you've done well finding this place and arranging all this for Grandad. He's going to be bowled over.'

'Can I get you all a drink to say thank you before the others arrive?' he offered.

'Not for me,' Erin said. 'I'm going to park the car out of the way and bring in my stuff. I want to bags a room before the rest of them descend on us and hang up my dress for tomorrow night.'

Brodie shook his head. 'I need to get back to Lettie and the baby. I promised to help feed the animals tonight.'

Joe shrugged. 'And I have to go with him because he brought me here.'

'I'll show you both out.' Callum walked with them to the front door and just as both his friends stepped outside they saw a shiny black car with tinted windows slowly passing the house along the driveway.

Callum watched in silence as it passed, wishing he could see whether Tasha was inside but presumed she must be.

'Who's that, do you think?' Joe asked.

'That will be Riley Sharp and his assistant Tasha. They're staying in the cottage down the drive while he's here filming.' Both his friends immediately turned to stare at him but before they could speak, Erin shrieked.

The three of them turned to her to see what was wrong. 'Sorry, I'm just excited to be staying this close to my crush.'

Callum withheld a groan. 'But he's here because he wants privacy, so you're not to venture down there. Understood?'

She gave him an angelic, wide-eyed look. 'Totally.'

Callum wished he believed her but right now he had to hope his sister behaved herself and was too busy with Grandad's birthday celebrations to go and bother the annoying actor.

'However, there is something I've just thought of.'

Erin had that self-satisfied look on her face that he knew meant she had come up with an idea she really liked.

Callum sighed. 'Go on, what is it?'

'I think it's all very well us having to keep away from them physically, but our family can get rather overexcited when they're all together, and not a little noisy.'

'And you're worried the noise will carry to Riley's cottage, I suppose. I've been worried about that too.'

'Exactly.' He went to respond but Erin raised her hand, holding it in front of his face briefly before lowering it. 'I do have a solution though.'

'Which is?'

'Isn't it obvious?'

He frowned and gave her question some thought. 'You think we should invite Riley and Tasha to Grandad's party, don't you?' he asked, dreading her agreeing.

'It does make good sense,' Joe said.

'You see?' Erin gave Callum a pointed look. 'I'm not the only one to think this is a good idea. That way if they do come, they'll not mind the noise because they'll probably be making some of it.'

'And if they don't want to come to the party?'

She shrugged. 'Then how can they complain about a party they were invited to attend, if it's their choice not to bother going?'

Callum was pretty sure that Riley would complain if he felt like it whether he had been invited or not but wasn't in the mood to argue with his sister.

'Fine, then I might pop down there later and invite the pair of them.'

He saw the mischievous twinkle in his sister's eyes.

'What now?'

'Nothing,' she said, grinning, clearly amused.

'What, Erin?'

'I suspect you were hoping for a reason to go down there all along.' When he didn't respond, she added, 'You know? To visit Tasha?'

'Erin?'

'Yes?'

'Go and find something useful to do and stop bugging me, will you?'

He watched his sister laugh and saunter away, aware that he was only irritated because she had been right. He was only too happy to chat to Tasha again.

12

TASHA

'Who the hell was that lot?' Riley grumbled as Bill drove the car smoothly down the long driveway.

'That will be Callum and his family and friends. Remember? The family party I told you about yesterday.'

'Well, I hope they know better than to come and bother me asking for autographs.'

Arrogant fool, Tasha thought. Most people would be wondering how to get along with their temporary neighbours, but not Riley.

The driver slowed to a stop in front of the cottage and Tasha waited to see if Riley had anything else he felt he needed to whinge about before they went inside. Unsurprised when he didn't, she followed him out of the car after the driver had opened the door.

'The property manager messaged a little while ago to say they've restocked the fridge and pantry for us while we were out,' Tasha said, reading the email she must have missed earlier. 'She hopes we find everything to our liking.'

'Did you tell her that I can only drink that one particular brand of bottled water?'

Tasha wasn't sure why he was asking this, especially as he had been drinking the water since their arrival weeks before. 'She knows all your requirements.'

Seemingly satisfied, Riley walked into the building and she followed, struggling not to show her irritation with him.

He ambled into the living room and slumped heavily on the pale blue and gold brocade sofa, a bored look on his face.

Not wishing to spend any more time with him than necessary, Tasha went back to the car to help Bill fetch their bags. 'It's fine, I can take these,' she said. 'You get on to your next job and we'll see you at 7 a.m. tomorrow.'

'Fine. I'll bring his croissants from the bakery. Are you sure you don't want me to bring you something in the morning?'

She shook her head. 'No, thanks. I'll eat before we go.'

'I'll be off then.' Bill gave her a wave. 'You're filming at Green Island tomorrow, I believe.'

She picked up her handbag and two larger bags containing Riley's clothes and other bits he liked to have with him for filming, like the copy of his script, snacks, his special shampoo and conditioner he insisted the hairdresser on set used and his own make-up sponges and sable brushes.

'Thanks, Tasha.' He raised an eyebrow. 'Himself seems in one of his less friendly moods today. You'd think he'd be happy to spend time in a place like this, wouldn't you?'

'You would think so.'

She went inside, took Callum's things to his room, unpacked and left the bags behind a chair ready to repack in the morning with whatever he chose to take for that day.

The one place Riley refused to allow anyone apart from her

to enter was the primary bedroom suite with its unmade bed and cups and plates with detritus from whatever food or drink he hadn't finished the night before. She put them all together on the chest of drawers nearest the door, then walked down the short hallway leading first to a dressing room where she was greeted with clothes on the floor beneath empty hangers and the en-suite bathroom to the right with damp towels strewn all over the floor. She took several minutes to tidy up and replace towels from the airing cupboard along the hall midway between his room and hers.

Satisfied that Riley's room was as tidy as she could make it, she went to her room and having chosen what to wear the following day, changed into a pair of shorts and a thin summery top. She sat on her bed wishing she didn't have any work to do and could simply slip under the sheets and fall asleep. This was the most comfortable bed she had ever slept in and she knew she would miss it when she did leave. She fell back against her downy pillows and closed her eyes.

The most difficult part about staying here longer was going to be putting up with Riley's moods and persuading him to get out of bed in the mornings.

Deciding to get up before she did actually fall asleep, Tasha made her way through to Riley's bedroom to fetch the dirty crockery and take it down to the kitchen.

Spotting the stunning view from his bedroom window, she walked over to one of them and gazed out at the pond and wood beyond.

She opened the window slightly to let in a little more air and looked up the driveway in the direction of the manor house, noticing that she could only just see a couple of upstairs windows. She wondered how the party preparations were coming along and whether all the guests had arrived yet, when she noticed movement out of the corner of her eye.

It was a pretty, blonde-haired woman of about her age wandering cheerfully across the lawn. She didn't look as if she was heading anywhere in particular, or in any hurry, and Tasha was concerned about Riley's reaction to seeing a stranger so close to the cottage when she had assured him she had chosen this place for the privacy.

Tasha groaned, aware she needed to go outside and speak to the woman and discreetly find out who she was and what she was doing down here. If she was one of Callum's guests hopefully she wouldn't mind being asked to stay closer to the main house or bypass this property on her walk. Tasha heard the girl singing something but didn't recognise the tune. She hoped she wasn't about to upset her by asking her to move.

Tasha grabbed the crockery and hurried downstairs and out of the front door, her thoughts racing as she tried to think how best to address the issue with the woman. Stepping outside, Tasha had only gone a little way when she heard laughter. Had someone joined the woman? She went to find out and as she walked around the end of the house, she saw Riley with his hands on his hips and head thrown back.

Unsure what to do for a moment, Tasha decided to leave them to it. Riley seemed perfectly happy and she was grateful not to have to endure an awkward conversation with someone who was most likely related to Callum, especially after all Callum had done to return Riley's phone.

'Hey, Tasha,' Riley shouted, waving her over to join them. 'Come here for a second.'

Groaning inwardly, Tasha did as he asked. She smiled politely and held out her hand towards the woman when she reached them. 'Hi, I'm Tasha, Riley's assistant.'

The girl beamed back at her. 'I see. I'm Erin. Erin Preston. I gather you've met my brother Callum.'

Tasha's stomach did a little flip at the mention of his name. 'That's right.' Tasha smiled. 'He was very kind finding Riley's phone recently. We're grateful to him, aren't we, Riley?'

She didn't look at him when she asked the question, knowing him well enough to be certain he had his most charming smile on his face and would act exactly as he was expected to.

'We are. In fact, I was hoping to see him again sometime to thank him personally.'

There was a slight silence before Erin spoke. 'If you're doing nothing now, I'm sure Callum wouldn't mind you popping by the manor house to say hi. If you're not too busy, that is?'

Tasha wasn't sure. 'Won't he be getting everything ready for the party tomorrow though?'

Erin shrugged. 'He's got all of us helping him do that. No, I'm certain it'll be fine.'

Tasha didn't like to point out that if Erin was here chatting to them then she wasn't being much help with the party preparations. She waited for Riley to decide what he wanted to do.

'Great idea,' he said. 'I was hoping for a tour of the house and grounds, wasn't I, Tasha?'

It was the first she had heard of it, Tasha thought, but didn't argue and instead forced another smile, wishing she had Riley's talent for charming people.

'Great,' Erin said. 'Let's go.'

'Shouldn't we wait while you check he's OK with us bothering him?' Tasha asked, not wanting to be one of the reasons Callum's preparations were interrupted.

'No, my brother will go mad if I don't invite you both.' Erin cocked her head. 'Come on, I promise we won't be long. Anyway, if we're to be neighbours for the next week I think we should get to know each other a bit, don't you?'

'Of course we should,' Riley agreed, linking arms with Erin and making her giggle in delight.

Tasha followed the pair of them, hoping Callum's relations wouldn't mind them intruding. She suspected the next week was going to be a very long one.

13

CALLUM

He heard his sister's laughter before he saw her.

'Where the hell have you been?' he bellowed from the orangery where he stood at the top of a ladder tying string to hold up one side of a specially ordered banner for his grandad's surprise birthday party. 'We could have done with your help hours ago.'

'Where's your manners?' Erin said.

Callum looked over his shoulder at her, surprised to see Erin wasn't alone but walking into the room arm in arm with Riley Sharp. Tasha followed and was looking directly at Callum.

Callum's ladder wobbled, causing him to drop the string and quickly grab hold of the top of the ladder to steady himself.

'Hey, steady on,' his stepfather Barry said, grabbing the sides of the ladder. 'Don't want any accidents now, do we?'

'I bumped into these two when I was out walking,' Erin explained, looking very pleased with herself.

Callum swapped surprised glances with his mother who stood on the top of another ladder to fix the other side of the banner. He doubted they had come across each other by accident, especially as Riley and Tasha always seemed to keep to themselves. He had a sneaking suspicion his sister had planned for this very thing to happen.

'I see.' He smiled at the new arrivals. 'Hi there.'

'Hi. We didn't mean to interrupt anything,' Tasha said.

'It's fine. I'll just finish tying this side, then will fetch you all a drink if you'd like one.'

'Don't worry,' Tasha said at the same time Riley said he'd love one.

Barry held up another piece of string for Callum to thread through a lower hole in the banner. He focused on what he was doing, trying not to be too cross with Erin for going to the cottage grounds when he had explicitly told her to leave Riley and Tasha in peace.

'Everything straight, Mum? Barry?'

Barry gave him a thumbs up and Callum realised the look on his mother's face he had taken for surprise was in fact delight. Surely she wasn't pleased to see Erin with the film star? Callum stepped down to the floor as Barry helped Callum's mother off her ladder.

'It's time we had a break anyway,' Callum said, deciding that even though he would rather continue finalising decorations in the orangery it was a bonus to have Tasha here and be able to spend a little time with her.

'It's looking splendid,' Tasha said. 'And if you do need any help, please just ask.'

'I'm Michelle, Callum and Erin's mum,' he heard his mother saying, turning to see her take Barry's arm and pulling him into the small group. 'This is my husband Barry. He's the children's stepfather.' She lowered her voice. 'Their actual father is Keith's son, James. He's my—'

Erin moved to stand next to their mother. 'I think they get the gist of who we are now, Mum.'

Callum saw Tasha gently bite her lower lip as her eyes twinkled in amusement.

'Keith?' Riley asked looking bewildered.

'It's Keith's eightieth,' Barry explained. 'He's the reason we're all staying here and who we're celebrating at the party. He's a good sort and we're all very fond of him.' He turned to Michelle. 'We all get along well, don't we, love?'

'Well enough,' she said, barely hiding her sarcasm and reassuring Callum he had made the right decision inviting his mother and Barry to stay in his flat while they were on the island. He hadn't initially expected his mother to want to travel over for his grandfather's party, but she had insisted she should be there, having known him for thirty years.

Callum suspected her being at the celebrations had a bit more to do with wanting to see how his father and fiancée Betsy really got along. He had a feeling that although his mother had tired of her marriage, she had been with James for so long it must still be difficult for her to see him with someone else, especially someone with whom he seemed extremely happy.

'You get us all some drinks, Callum,' Michelle said. 'I'll show this charming young man through to the living room so we can make ourselves comfortable and get to know each other a bit before the party.'

What? Callum went to explain that Riley and Tasha weren't guests but not wanting to embarrass anyone, thought better of it.

Tasha gave him a knowing smile. 'Come on, I'll help you get those drinks.'

As soon as they were in the kitchen out of earshot of the others, Callum looked at Tasha and shook his head. 'I'm sorry.

Mum has a habit of taking over things even when she's not organising it.'

Tasha laughed. 'It's fine. I think like most people she was a bit taken aback to see Riley standing there.'

'I suppose so. Riley didn't seem to be bothered to have been dragged away, thankfully.'

Tasha raised her eyebrows. 'He will have been delighted, I can assure you.' She glanced at the doorway and lowered her voice. 'He's been in a foul mood for the past few days, so I'm only too happy to see him cheerful.'

'What's bothering him?'

Her face reddened slightly. 'He felt he should be staying in the manor house and your family at the cottage.' She frowned. 'Maybe now he's met you all, and especially Erin, he might not mind quite so much.'

Callum couldn't help finding it funny that his sister's actions had helped them all without her meaning to. 'I imagine he can be tricky to deal with and that you have to do what's best at the time where he's concerned.'

She arched an eyebrow. 'You could say that. And yes, sometimes I need to make snap decisions and work things out afterwards.'

'Sounds fun,' he said sarcastically.

She laughed. 'It can be.'

'I suppose we should make some drinks.'

They carried through a tray of cool soft drinks to the others and as soon as the pair of them reached the seating area and set the tray down, Erin took Callum to one side and lowered her voice.

'Isn't it exciting?' she said. Callum frowned, unsure what she might be referring to. 'You know, Riley Sharp agreeing to come to Grandad's surprise party.'

He realised this was his sister's way of telling him what she had just done. 'You asked him then?'

'I didn't feel I had much choice really,' she admitted. 'Now that he and Tasha have met everyone and have seen us setting up.'

He thought about what she said. 'I suppose not.'

Callum wasn't all that bowled over by Riley Sharp, but he did like Tasha and agreed it made sense to ask them. Anyway, he mused, having Tasha at the party would make it an even more special occasion as far as he was concerned. He doubted his grandfather had ever heard of Riley but supposed some of his guests might have done and could appreciate having the celebrity at the party.

They joined the others. 'I gather you've both been invited to Grandad's party tomorrow night.'

Tasha seemed uncomfortable with the idea and Callum hoped she wasn't going to turn down Erin's invitation.

'Don't say you haven't got anything to wear,' Riley teased. 'We both know you always come prepared for anything and always have a smart evening dress in your suitcase.'

She seemed to consider then accept the idea. 'He's right, I do. Yes, I'd love to come to the party. I'm intrigued to meet your grandfather.'

Happy to know Tasha would be joining them, Callum relaxed.

'That's great.' He indicated the direction of the orangery. 'You are welcome to stay and finish these drinks before Erin, Mum, Barry and I need to get on and finish the decorations. I've got to go to the airport and collect the rest of the family as they start arriving tonight.'

'Yes,' Erin grumbled. 'And I've been tasked with fetching the others from the harbour when the boat comes in.'

'Well, we don't have anything much to do for the rest of the day, so we can help too, if you like?' Riley said.

Callum saw Tasha frown at Riley's offer. 'That's very kind of you but we'll be fine. Don't you have filming tomorrow?'

Tasha gave him a grateful smile. 'He does and he also has lines to go over this evening.'

'Don't remind me.' Riley arched an eyebrow and grinned at Erin.

'How exciting,' Erin said. 'I've never watched anyone learn lines for filming before.'

Suspecting his sister was edging for an invitation back to their cottage, Callum quickly spoke. 'And there's no chance of you doing it today either. Not with everything I need you to help me with here.'

Riley took Erin's hand and raised it to his lips, kissing the back of it. 'We have a whole week to see each other, and you're welcome to come and help me after the party.'

Callum didn't think he'd seen such delight on his sister's face before and hoped Erin wasn't going to get too carried away with her adoration of the actor.

A feeling of dread surged through him. Erin might be an adult with a thriving hairdressing business, but she also let her heart rule her head and he knew from experience how devastated she could be when her relationships came to an end.

Callum groaned inwardly. By the look of adoration on her face as she stared at Riley Sharp, Callum was going to have to keep a discreet eye on his sister for the rest of the week. It was the last thing he had planned on doing. As much as Erin acted tough, he had helped her through enough break-ups to know that someone as charismatic and confident as Riley Sharp could hurt her deeply, and he had no intention of letting that happen if he could possibly help it.

14

TASHA

Tasha checked her watch the following morning. She had already called Riley several times but he still wasn't downstairs and as much as he didn't bother about keeping their driver Bill waiting, Tasha hated being rude, believing Bill's time was just as valuable as Riley's.

She marched upstairs and into his room.

'Get up now, Riley,' Tasha said, trying her best not to show quite how irritated she was with him. She pulled open the curtains so that the enormous bedroom was immediately swamped with bright sunlight despite it only being 6.45 a.m.

As expected, Riley groaned and pulled his covers over his head, his back to her. 'Stop bothering me.'

'You can't be late, not when you're the reason they're all having to do this extra filming.' She didn't care if he was cross with her for reminding him. She walked to the other side of the room and opened the rest of the curtains on her way. 'Riley, you're already in trouble with Dale and the producers. Do you really want to draw more negative attention to yourself? Anyway you did promise to be on your best behaviour, don't forget.'

He didn't bother to respond.

'Remember Dale telling you this is your very last chance,' she said, hoping the reminder of his manager's recent threat might spur Riley into action. It didn't.

'I've made you coffee; it's on your bedside table. Now, please drink it and get in that shower. Bill will be here to fetch us in just under fifteen minutes.' She was sorely tempted to throw a jug of cold water over him but didn't have the energy to deal with the fallout of his reaction if she did do something that drastic, even if it probably would have the desired effect.

'I'll meet you downstairs in fifteen minutes and if you're not there then, I'll have no option but to give Dale a call.'

Big threat, she mused, aware that Riley couldn't give a damn if she completely lost her temper and threw things at him. Not that she had ever done anything like that, although she had been sorely tempted to many times. Riley would more than likely be amused and tease her about finally finding a backbone and standing up to him. Before firing her. She had no intention of being his amusement for the day.

She needed to get him to the location for filming then he would be someone else's problem, at least while he was working, and she knew from experience that Riley's manager was the only person he ever seemed to listen to. She wondered when the man would deign to return to the island, because it was getting to the point where Dale had little option but to step up and deal with the temperamental actor if he ever expected filming for this series to finish.

She poured herself another cup of tea and added a dash of milk while listening out in case she heard movement from Riley upstairs. She stilled when she heard the bathroom door slam shut in Riley's determination to let her know she had annoyed him. She couldn't care less how angry he might be as long as she managed to get him into the car and get to today's location on time.

Tasha picked up her bag and placed it on the counter to check yet again that she had everything she needed for a day out filming. There was no need for her to take Riley's brand of water because there was always enough of that waiting for him. Her tablet was charged as was her phone. She reached up and touched her sunglasses. Yes, she was ready. She blew on her tea to cool it slightly and tapped her foot, anxiously waiting for her boss to get a move on.

Hearing a car pull up outside, she peered out of the window and, seeing Bill, waved. Ten minutes early, as always. Without bothering to ask him, she poured a cup of black coffee, placed two biscuits on the saucer and carried them out to him.

She heard Riley's bathroom door slam and relaxed slightly.

'Morning, Bill. Here you go.'

'Thanks, Tasha. I could do with this.' He glanced up at some upstairs windows. 'His lordship up and about yet?'

'In the shower as we speak, I'm relieved to report.'

Bill laughed. 'How's his mood?'

She rolled her eyes. 'Not good.'

'Ah, well. Nothing new there then.'

She laughed. 'I'll go and chase him along. See you in a few minutes.'

* * *

If anyone ever tried to tell her how glamorous filming a TV series was Tasha would give them a few home truths. Her family assumed she'd left her old, steady job for a more exciting one but never seemed to care that her working hours were long and the pay lousy. Not that she blamed them at all. It had been her decision to give up working in the investment bank three years before to take a different direction in her career, and she guessed they didn't want to hear about how dull her job could really be.

She watched from a distance as Riley redid a take for the sixth time. They had gone through his lines several times the previous evening after returning from the manor house and she was certain he knew them. Why was he being so useless today?

She sat back in her chair and thought about the party later that evening and whether her dress would be right for it. Amused by her silliness, Tasha reminded herself that she had only brought the one smart dress so, whether she was happy with it or not, she would still have to wear it. There would be no time to go shopping for another one after filming wrapped.

She wondered how Callum was getting on with the preparations and whether all his relations had now arrived on the island and settled into the manor house. She wasn't sure why she was feeling nervous about the evening. It was only going to be a family affair after all and it wasn't as if anything was expected of her or Riley. Riley. She hoped he would be on his best behaviour. The Prestons, or at least those she had met so far, seemed like ordinary decent people and she would hate for Riley to ruin this special party when everyone had gone to such lengths to make it a success.

15

CALLUM

Callum wondered how Tasha's day was going as he helped Betsy set out the cutlery and napkins on the large table along one wall of the orangery while his father and Erin finished making canapés to serve their guests on arrival. He looked forward to his grandfather's arrival and getting the whole surprise element out of the way. The thought of it going wrong was worrying him more the closer that moment got.

'Stop fretting.' Betsy followed her nudge in his ribs with a smile. 'Everything will be perfect. We all know it will even if you don't. And just remember, if anything you've planned does go a bit wrong, your grandfather won't realise it wasn't as you had hoped it to be. I'm sure he'll just be delighted everyone has been thoughtful enough to arrange something this exciting behind his back and for friends and relations to fly over to the island just for him.'

He wanted to believe she was right. 'I suppose that makes sense. I just worry that we'll only have one chance to surprise him.'

She stood in front of him, hands on her hips. 'You've thought of everything, Callum, and Keith will be delighted with the party, however it turns out.' He must have looked alarmed because she rested a hand on his shoulder and grinned, shaking her head. 'It will all be perfect, is what I'm trying and failing to say.'

Erin burst into the room and raised both hands excitedly in the air. 'I've just heard from Mum that she called Grandad to wish him happy birthday and she's fairly certain he has no idea about tonight.'

Callum hoped his mother was right but wanted to find out more. 'How can she be so sure?'

'Apparently when she asked him whether he was doing much to celebrate, he told her he was having a small family meal somewhere but that it was a surprise as to where.'

Calmed slightly, Callum felt his shoulders lower. 'Maybe he really doesn't suspect anything then?'

Betsy picked up the remnants of wrapping from the napkins and scrunched them in her hands. 'It sounds like he doesn't.' She gave him a pointed look. 'I think it's time you stopped worrying and went to get ready. I think everything's nearly done here.'

Erin nodded. 'It does look amazing in here, and Dad and I have finished with the food. All we need to do now is get our party clothes on.'

An hour later, Callum dried his freshly shaved face just as his phone pinged. He suspected it was the prearranged message from Betsy telling him she and his dad had fetched Grandad and were on their way to the manor with him. He put down the towel next to the washbasin and picked up his phone to check.

Keith is with us in the car and excited to meet up with you at the restaurant. See you in about fifteen minutes. Betsy

Nervous all over again that he might have forgotten something, Callum pushed his phone into his trouser pocket and hurried downstairs to where his sister and mother had been greeting the rest of the family and friends. He wished he had managed to finish the party preparations earlier and get upstairs to shower and shave when the rest of his family had done.

He reached the bottom step and his phone pinged again. Taking it out, he saw a message from Tasha and eagerly opened it, hoping she was still coming.

Running late after a Zoom call but will be with you as soon as we can get there. Apologies if we're not in time to greet your grandfather. Tasha

Relieved she was still going to be joining them, Callum sent off a quick reply.

No problem. See you when you get here. C

'There you are,' Erin said, rushing out of the kitchen to him. 'Do we know what's happening yet? Has Dad collected Grandad?'

'Yes, and yes. They should be here in about fifteen minutes, or thereabouts. So we'll need to make sure everyone has a drink in their hands and is waiting in the orangery, not in their rooms, or out in the garden chatting.'

Callum and Erin raced around filling glasses and finding family members dotted around the garden and gathered them in the orangery when their mother shouted for their attention from the doorway.

'I've just seen James's car coming down the drive. Quick, Callum, you'd better go and greet them. Erin and I will go and keep everyone quiet while you bring them inside.'

He waited for the car to stop and went to open his grandfather's door. 'Happy birthday, Grandad.' Callum helped his grandfather out of the car and gave him a hug.

Keith looked at the manor house. 'I'm trying to fathom why we're here? Is this a new restaurant, or hotel?'

Callum shook his head.

James and Betsy joined them. 'All in good time, Keith,' James said. 'Why don't you lead the way, Callum?'

Callum walked with his grandfather, relieved not to be able to hear anyone talking. The last thing he wanted now was for his grandfather to recognise one of the voices and ruin the surprise he was about to receive.

'It's this way.' He led them down the hall and through the sumptuous living room.

'It's a grand place, whatever it is,' Keith said.

Callum relaxed slightly, glad his grandfather was impressed with the place. 'Nearly there.' He stopped in front of the orangery double doors and waited briefly for his father to step forward and take hold of the other door handle. Giving his father a nod, they pulled back the doors to reveal the elegant room filled with beautifully laid tables, each with arrangements of flowers created by his mother and sister.

'Surprise!'

Keith stared around him, trying to take in the scene. Callum watched as he surveyed the guests. His mouth drew back into a wide smile, and Keith turned to look at Callum. 'Did you do all this?'

He shook his head. 'It was a joint effort. Erin, Dad, Betsy, Barry and Mum have all been working hard and everyone is here.' He thought of Tasha and Riley. 'We have two more guests who are staying at the cottage and should be along soon.'

Keith raised his hands. 'This is the best birthday present ever,' he said. 'All my family in the same room.' He noticed a cousin he hadn't seen for years and pointed at him. 'You're here, too.'

Callum watched the guests swarm to greet his grandfather and sighed.

'You've done well, son,' his father said, patting him on the back. 'This is going to be a night to remember.'

'I'll get you a drink, Grandad,' Erin said, giving Callum a delighted grin.

The local band Callum had booked for the event began playing some of Keith's favourite songs from a list James had collated, and Callum decided to start enjoying the evening and making the most of all his hard work.

He felt a hand rest on his arm and looked to his side, delighted to find Tasha. His heart almost stopped.

She looked incredible. She always did, he thought, but he had only ever seen her dressed for work or relaxation before. Tonight though she was as glamorous as any film star he had seen being interviewed on a red carpet. She had put her long hair up in a bun with tendrils curling down on either side of her tanned face. Her eyes looked even bigger now that they were made up and her lips, with the shiny red lipstick on them, made him want to grab her and kiss her.

'You're here,' he said, barely able to draw breath and wishing he had thought of something a little less obvious.

'So am I.' Riley stepped from behind her. 'This looks amazing.'

'Thanks very much. I'm glad you could both make it.'

Before he could do anything else, Callum was aware of the cacophony of voices stilling one by one.

'That's Riley Sharp, isn't it?' one voice said.

'What, that bloke off the telly?'

'Yes, the one who's over here filming for that *Sam Thorne Investigates* series.'

'Ooh, I wonder why he would he be here,' another said and laughed.

'I think I'd better introduce you both to my grandfather, if you don't mind.'

'Lead the way,' Riley said, seeming happy under the glare of everyone's attention.

Callum didn't have a problem getting his grandfather's attention, seeing as all the guests bar a few were staring in his direction at the unexpected guest.

'Who's this young fellow then?' Keith asked. Seeing Tasha, he added, 'My apologies, I didn't see you there.' He reached out to shake her hand. 'I'm Keith, the eighty-year-old.'

Tasha smiled. 'Nice to meet you, Keith. I'm Tasha and this is my boss, Riley.'

'I told you it was him,' one of the voices whispered nearby.

'Tasha and I are staying at the cottage further down the driveway,' Riley explained, shooting a beaming smile to the group of guests gossiping about him at the nearest table and sending them into another flurry of excitement. 'It was kind of Callum and Erin to invite us to your incredible birthday party. I hope you don't mind that we came?'

Keith shook his head and laughed. 'Now why would I do that? It's a pleasure to meet you both.'

'Thank you.' Riley took a glass of champagne Erin held out for him and Tasha. 'Good to see you again, Erin.'

Callum saw his sister's cheeks redden slightly. 'I'm glad you both came.'

'Now,' Keith said, 'there are a few things I've always wanted to know about filming these stunts you do in films. Would you mind me asking you about them?'

Tasha gave Callum a knowing look and he had to stifle a laugh, aware Riley would like nothing more than to talk about himself and his work.

He watched the pair of them walk over to the nearest table and sit down to chat.

'I thought that went well,' Tasha said quietly.

'Yes, it did. I have to admit I'm relieved.'

'He seemed to know who Riley is.'

Callum wasn't sure why Tasha was surprised. 'I think most people know who he is, Tasha.' He indicated the nearest French doors to the terrace. 'Shall we go outside for a little while and chat while Grandad and Riley are talking? Knowing my grandfather, they could be a while and he won't want me interrupting him to tell everyone to help themselves to the food.'

Tasha laughed and pointed to several of Callum's relatives loading food onto their plates from the buffet table. 'I think any announcement is already a bit late.'

'Good. They don't appear to need me in here for now.' He smiled at her. 'Shall we go while we have the chance?'

She nodded. 'I'd like that.'

16

TASHA

She only just managed to hide her delight at Callum's stunned reaction when he saw her arrive at the party. She accompanied him outside, glad he had suggested they do so.

It was a relief to get away from Riley for a while. She wondered what people would think if they knew what a diva that man was to deal with. First his suit hadn't been right for how he wanted to present himself to others that evening.

'They will be expecting a film star,' he snapped. 'And that's what I intend giving them.'

'You're not the star of tonight's show though, Riley,' she had retorted before she managed to stop herself.

He had been shocked but then turned on his heels and went back to his room to change, yet again.

By the time they left for the party he had spent several minutes preening in front of the living room mirror until he was content that the Ralph Lauren chinos and shirt his stylist had recently sent over for him gave him a look he was satisfied with.

If he wasn't her boss, she would have left him earlier and

made her way to the party without him. Tasha supposed that if nothing else this job as his assistant was teaching her patience. Becoming aware that Callum was speaking to her, she turned to him.

'Sorry, I was thinking about something that happened earlier.'

He frowned. 'Everything all right?'

She sighed. 'Yes, thanks. Just the usual Riley stuff.'

'I'm not saying he seems spoilt,' Callum said, his eyes widening, 'but I can imagine he isn't easy to work for.'

'He isn't.' She shook her head. 'Anyway, I've spent far too long waiting for him already today and don't intend wasting any more time at this wonderful party thinking or talking about Riley Sharp.'

'Good idea.' He held out his hand. 'Shall we take a walk in this incredible garden?'

Why not, she thought, taking his hand and enjoying the feeling of her hand in his as they strolled across the lawn past fragrant flower borders and breathing in the sweet scent of roses, lavender and rosemary in the warm evening air as she walked.

'I don't think I've ever been anywhere this perfect. I've certainly never stayed anywhere as idyllic as this place.'

'Not even with your boss?'

She shook her head. 'No, Riley prefers modern places and would much rather stay in the city than the country.'

He laughed. 'Sorry.'

Confused, Tasha looked up at Callum. 'Why do you say that?'

'You didn't want to talk about your boss and I've immediately brought him up.' He stilled and stared at her in silence. For a moment she thought he might kiss her and decided she hoped he would.

Then his eyes moved up from hers and he seemed to peer over her shoulder towards a border of rhododendrons on the other side of the lawn.

'What is it?' Tasha asked, trying to see what had grabbed his attention but failing.

He shook his head and smiled, although she noticed it didn't quite reach his eyes. 'I thought I saw movement in the bushes over there but must have been mistaken.'

'Maybe it was one of the gardeners,' she suggested. 'There must be an entire team of them to keep all this land as pristine as it is.'

He didn't seem sure for a moment, then nodded. 'I can't think why they would be working at night, but I suppose they could be checking something.'

Hearing his sister shriek with delight, Tasha wondered if it might have something to do with Riley. She hoped not. Erin seemed lovely and although Tasha knew she could be wrong about things, she doubted Callum's sister was used to men like Riley. He had mentioned how pretty Erin was and even in the time she had worked for him, Tasha had experienced the devastation when three of his romantic engagements had fallen apart after each fiancée discovered he had been unfaithful to them. She would hate the same thing to happen to Erin.

As they neared the orangery, she couldn't help thinking how much she would have preferred to spend the evening by herself with Callum. Then she reminded herself she was here to help celebrate his grandfather's eightieth birthday party, not to start anything romantic with a man she might never see again once the week was over.

She followed Callum's gaze and saw he was watching his sister dancing with Riley. Erin was in Riley's arms, gazing up at him adoringly. Callum didn't look pleased, and Tasha understood why.

'I'm going to suggest everyone finds a table and starts eating,' Callum said. 'A few people have food but most haven't yet. I remember my mum saying that if you let guests drink for too long they end up drinking more than they mean to and no longer feel hungry. We don't need mountains of food left over.' He raised his eyebrows.

She looked at the long table laden with food to her right. 'I see what you mean.' She noticed his grandfather's table had no spare seats but that there was a table further to the left that only had two people sitting at it. 'Would you like me to go and reserve a few seats at that table?'

Callum looked over and nodded. 'Great idea. Better keep one for Erin and Riley because by the looks of things they've not considered eating yet.'

'Good idea. I won't be long.'

As Tasha went and made herself comfortable at the designated table, she pulled out three of the chairs slightly and waved for Riley's attention. He spotted her almost immediately and stopped dancing, probably wondering what she wanted. Tasha waved him over, pointing to the table. Erin came with him and as they moved through the guests Tasha noticed they were holding hands. Already? He was moving fast. The thought made her mood dip and she hoped she didn't have to spend the next few days working on damage control.

Tasha looked over to Callum who was now standing next to the music trio. As soon as they stopped playing he thanked them and picked up the microphone.

'Hi, everyone,' he said as guests slowly stopped speaking and gave him their attention. 'As you all know, we're here this evening to celebrate my grandad Keith's eightieth birthday.' Tasha watched Keith raise his glass and give Callum a wink. 'I first want to thank you all for keeping the secret from him.'

'I'll never trust any one of you again,' Keith teased.

When everyone stopped laughing and commenting, Callum continued. 'This party has been a joint effort, and I think it worked out better in the end for us that the people who had originally booked this place cancelled.'

Keith seemed surprised. 'You did good, my boy.'

'Thanks, Grandad. I'd like you all to raise a glass to Keith Preston, my wonderful grandfather who has made an impression on each and every one of us at some point over the years.' More cheers and teasing erupted until Callum had to put out his hands, palms down. 'Thanks, everyone. I know you're all eager to get partying, but please do eat all of this food; we'd hate for it to go to waste.' He raised his glass. 'Firstly, though, Grandad, this evening is for you. We love you and hope you have an amazing night. To Keith.'

'To Keith.'

Tasha raised her glass and watched as family and friends toasted the smiling man who she imagined must have looked very like Callum when he was younger. He was certainly popular and she was glad Keith was having such a special evening. What a lucky man to have such a caring family. She thought about her own strained relationship with her family and felt a pang of envy that she would never experience anything similar to the love she was witnessing now.

She watched Callum being patted on the back and thought how different he was to any other man she had ever spent time with and wished she wasn't on the island for such a short time. She sat down at the table as soon as Callum joined his father and grandfather after his speech, and she looked around wondering where Riley and Erin had got to.

Tasha's stomach grumbled, reminding her that it had been at least six hours since she had last eaten anything. Deciding not to wait any longer, she got herself a meal and then picked up her cutlery and began eating the delicious food from her plate.

Tasha ate the tasty fresh lobster and what looked like tiny lobsters but which she now knew to be langoustine, a sweeter more delicate flavoured shellfish. She took a sip of her champagne, listening as Riley and Erin finally settled themselves down in two of the vacant seats at the table. Riley explained to an enraptured Erin how he got his first break in acting.

'It was when I was in a school production of *Charley's Aunt*,' he recalled. 'One of the mothers, a producer for a TV series about children being evacuated during the Second World War, spotted me and gave her card to my mother.'

'That must have been incredibly exciting,' Erin said. 'How old were you?'

'Sixteen, but then I could pass for twelve. Mum always knew I wanted to act and took me along to a couple of auditions and then I got the part.'

'And the rest is history,' Erin said, her hand resting on her chest. 'What a delightful story.'

It was certainly fiction, Tasha thought, aware that he had spent several years after college going to open auditions until he landed his first part in an advert for floor cleaner, before being cast in a television soap before going to Hollywood and being lucky enough to land a supporting role in a film that went stratospheric.

She took another sip of her drink, struggling not to contradict Riley when she noticed Callum looking at her.

'Dance with me,' Callum said, arriving at the table and taking Tasha's hand.

'One sec,' Tasha said, reaching out to pick up her half-empty glass of champagne. She took a sip.

'We need to get you a fresh glass of something,' Callum said. 'You must have been nursing that for a while now.' He reached out a hand to her. 'So, do you want to?'

Confused, Tasha frowned. 'Um, want to what?'

'Dance with me.'

She put the glass back down onto the table and nodded. 'Lead the way then.'

As soon as they reached the dance floor set out in front of where the trio played, Callum took her in his arms. Tasha couldn't help thinking how natural they felt together. It was strange how she barely knew Callum, but he somehow seemed very familiar. Was this feeling what people meant when they said that when you met the one, you would know? She pushed the thought aside, aware she was being fanciful.

'Sorry I got waylaid and didn't eat dinner with you,' he said, smiling down at her.

'It's your family party, of course you should spend time with them,' she said, not wanting Callum to feel guilty. 'Anyway, I'm used to looking out for myself at events. In fact, I'm usually working, now I come to think of it.'

'Well, you're not working tonight.' He scanned the room. 'Talking of work, did you see where Riley or my sister went? They were at your table but they're not there now.'

Tasha presumed Callum was concerned about his sister falling for Riley and completely understood. Erin seemed sensible enough but from her own experience sense seemed to vanish just when you needed it most.

'I'm afraid I didn't.' Not wanting Callum to worry, she said, 'Would you like to go and look for them?'

He shook his head. 'No. Erin is a grown woman and won't take kindly to me interfering, however well it's meant.'

Tasha could understand that. Then again, she mused, it must be nice to have an older brother who looked out for you. Maybe if she had a sibling she might not feel quite so lonely.

17

CALLUM

He had hoped to find time away from his family to dance with Tasha and was enjoying every second. She was a remarkable woman, independent and clever as well as beautiful and kind. She never spoke about any family though, he realised, and wondered whether there was a reason for that or if she just didn't feel she knew him well enough to speak about them. Maybe she didn't have family.

'Having fun?' he asked as one song ended and another began.

'I'm having a wonderful time.' She beamed up at him, causing his stomach to flip over. All he needed was to fall in love with someone who would soon be leaving.

'I'm glad.' He raised her hand and she twirled underneath it, laughing.

Someone tapped him on the shoulder. Seeing it was his father, Callum slowed to a stop. His father was scowling. Concerned, Callum gave his dad a questioning look. 'What's wrong?'

'Sorry for interrupting your fun.' His father directed his comment to Tasha.

'Please don't worry about it.' She glanced up at Callum. 'Is something the matter?'

James waved them over to the side of the room where the music wasn't as loud. After checking no one was close enough to overhear them, he lowered his head. 'There's someone lurking in the garden. I didn't want to alert any of the guests, least of all your grandfather, so thought I should mention it to you. Maybe you can go and have a discreet look outside.'

Callum thought of the movement he believed he'd seen in the rhododendron border. 'Don't worry, I'll go right away.'

'I'll come with you.' Tasha took his hand when he went to argue.

'You go and have fun, Dad.'

'Thanks, son.'

Callum hurried with Tasha, glad she had offered to join him. He hoped there wasn't anything too untoward going on outside but was confident Tasha had experience dealing with overzealous fans turning up on Riley's doorstep at some point since she began working for him.

'Let's hope we can find whoever this is quickly.'

Tasha didn't answer but he noticed she had a look on her face that made him wonder if she might suspect something already.

They stepped out onto the terrace and walked towards the lawn. 'Pretend to be speaking about something and see if we notice any movement. Whoever it is won't want to be spotted, so we'll need to be subtle.'

'I agree.' She went to say something else when he saw her eyes narrow and she put her hand on his upper arm. 'Don't look now but I'm sure there's a person to my right in the border next to the one you thought you spotted someone hiding in earlier. I'll turn slightly and laugh; you have a look past me when I do that.'

She did as planned, and Callum, his head down as if he was speaking to Tasha, looked across the lawn in the direction she had mentioned. Several of the deep pink flowers moved at the same time and as there was no wind he knew it could only have been someone behind them who had caused it.

As he looked back at her, Callum spotted a couple kissing passionately at the corner of the building. Recognising the long fair hair as his sister's, he peered at them to be certain. A bright light caught his eyes, blinding him. Callum squeezed his eyes against the glare.

'What's the matter?' Tasha asked.

'I thought I saw my sister kissing your boss, but then a harsh glare hit me.' He shook his head. Then it dawned on him why the light had been so brief, yet piercing. It must have been a camera flash that he had seen.

'Erin kissing Riley?'

He noted Tasha sounded as shocked as he felt but was suddenly more concerned about who might be watching them.

'I think there's someone with a camera taking photos of them.' Annoyed to have their privacy invaded, he felt his temper rising. 'I'm going over there now.'

'I'll come with you.' She took his hand once again. 'If they're busy watching Riley and Erin, they might not notice that we've spotted them.'

'Let's hope not.'

They broke into a run, reaching the border in a few seconds. As they neared, Callum let go of Tasha's hand and barged into the border, knocking over a middle-aged man, sending his camera and large lens flying over his head and landing behind him on the immaculately manicured lawn.

'Hey, what the hell do you think you're doing?' he shouted, pushing Callum away and getting slowly to his feet.

Callum almost fell but after stumbling regained his balance. He picked up the camera. 'Never mind me,' he said angrily. 'What are you doing here? Isn't it obvious this is private land?'

The photographer snatched his camera from Callum's hand and checked it. 'I was invited, if you must know.'

Shocked, Callum tried to work out who might have done such a thing. None of his family would do anything to risk ruining his grandfather's birthday.

'That's a bare-faced lie.' Tasha brushed away the leaves that had ended up on her dress.

'No, it isn't,' the photographer insisted angrily.

Callum had had enough. 'I invited the guests. And I know for certain you weren't one of them. This is a private gathering. Now if you'll step out of the damn flower bed you can tell me what you're doing here and more importantly who told you to come.'

The man glowered at him without responding.

Enraged, Callum added, 'Now, before I call the police and have you arrested for trespassing on private property.'

Grumbling to himself, the man frowned. 'There's no need to do that.'

'So,' Tasha said. 'Who told you where you'd find Riley Sharp?' She rested her hands on her hips and Callum could see she wasn't a woman to be fobbed off if she wanted to know something.

'Fine.' He brushed dirt from his trousers and slung his camera strap over his right shoulder. 'It was Dale Mackie who gave me the call.'

'You flew from London?'

He shrugged. 'Dale's covering my expenses. At least that's what he promised.'

Callum wanted to know more. 'First of all, who's Dale Mackie?'

'Riley's manager,' Tasha explained.

Callum saw by Tasha's face that she wasn't surprised this manager had arranged something underhand. 'But why would he do this when Riley was hoping for privacy?' It didn't make sense as far as he was concerned. 'Surely his manager is there to protect him from people like him.'

'Hey, there's no need for that.'

Aware he had been rude, Callum frowned. 'I'm sorry, I don't mean to be offensive but you must admit what you've done is annoying at the very least.'

'I've done nothing I wasn't asked to do.'

Tasha turned on him. 'Don't give me that nonsense. You were hiding in a bush for at least the last hour or two. Nobody hides unless they're doing something they know others won't approve of.'

The man shrugged. 'Fair enough.'

She stepped forward and Callum realised she hadn't finished. 'I want those photos wiped. Now.' She folded her arms when the man didn't react. 'And I want to check that they've gone.'

Before the photographer could answer, Riley called out, 'Anything the matter, Tasha?'

She sighed and turned to respond. Callum gazed at his sister to try and gauge how she was doing. She seemed OK, he noticed with relief.

Just then he heard a car slowing down, quickly followed by a voice yelling from the other side of the wide border. 'Quick, let's get out of here.'

The four of them turned to the drive in time to see the photographer slink away through the flower bed and into a blue hire car that seconds later sped up the driveway towards the entrance gates. The driver was laughing and waving at them.

Callum clenched his teeth together, furious to have let the photographer go without having deleted the photographs of Riley and his sister in each other's arms. 'Damn, that's done it.'

'Will one of you kindly explain what's just happened?' Erin asked, looking from Tasha to Callum.

'It seems,' Tasha began, 'that Riley's manager decided to pay for a photographer to come here in secret and take photos of you.'

'Why the hell would he do that?' Riley snapped. He slipped his arm around Erin's shoulders. 'Sorry, Erin, but I have a feeling those photos will be in several newspapers tomorrow.'

'Yes, and no doubt splashed all over the internet,' Tasha grumbled. 'We'll probably be finding them in various magazines over the next few weeks, too, I expect.'

'What?' Erin glanced at Callum.

Callum wasn't certain but he thought he noticed a hint of delight mixed in with the shock on his sister's face.

'You mean photos of us kissing?' Erin asked.

Turning to face her, Riley placed a hand on each of her shoulders. 'I'm so sorry, Erin. Unfortunately, this sort of thing tends to be a part of my life more often than not.' He glanced at Tasha briefly. 'Although I never expected it to happen when we're somewhere like this and far away from public view.'

Riley scowled at Tasha, clearly furious. 'Why didn't you get him to delete the photos when you had the chance?'

'I was about to do so,' she said. 'But you called out to me and he took that opportunity to run off. Now he's gone.' She stepped closer to Riley. 'Anyway, never mind me, it was Dale who arranged all this. If you want to blame anyone then ask him what he thought he was doing setting this up.'

'Dale? But why would he?'

Tasha gave Callum an apologetic smile and he knew their evening together was at an end. 'I'm sorry, Callum, but we're going to have to go back to the cottage.'

'I think you're right,' Riley agreed. 'Sorry, Erin,' he said, giving her a peck on the lips. 'I need to get in touch with my manager and find out what he thinks he's playing at.' He looked at Callum. 'I really am sorry about all this. I never would have given permission for your grandfather's party to be used in this way.'

Callum saw the sincerity on his face and believed him. 'I'm sure you wouldn't.' He hugged Tasha and gave her a peck on the cheek. 'You go off and do whatever you need to and maybe we can catch up sometime tomorrow.'

'I'd like that,' she said, making him feel a bit better. 'I'll be able to give you an update then,' she said to Erin. 'But I'm afraid I can't see that we'll be able to stop those photos being published now. They're probably already being uploaded at various newspaper offices as we speak.' She smiled at Callum. 'I'll pop round when we've finished work for the day.'

He nodded. 'Great.'

Callum put his arm around his sister's shoulders as Tasha and Riley walked across the lawn in the direction of the cottage.

'You OK, sis?' he asked, concerned for her.

She didn't respond immediately, but just when he was getting worried, Erin looked up and beamed at him. 'Can you imagine, I'm going to be in all the papers kissing gorgeous Riley Sharp. Isn't that amazing?'

He wouldn't have put it quite like that, but not wishing to ruin her excitement Callum sighed. 'I've no idea why you find that thought appealing.'

She glowered at him. 'Why shouldn't I?'

Was she serious? Callum decided not to get into an argument with his sister when their grandfather's party was still going strong.

18

TASHA

'And you didn't know anything about Dale's plans?'

'What do you take me for?'

Tasha thought it best not to answer that question. She studied Riley's earnest expression, searching for clues that he was lying. She reminded herself he was an actor and that pretending was what he did best, so she gave up.

'Fine. But I think you should get Dale on the phone and have a word with him.'

He shrugged and shook his head as he poured himself a beer. 'Why? There's no point now, is there? You said yourself that the photos would already be out there.'

Did he really think that, or was it just that Riley didn't care about anyone else's feelings but his own? 'What about Erin?'

'What about her?' He took a sip and seemed genuinely confused.

'How do you think she's going to look to her clients when they see her kissing you in the garden?'

He considered her question for a moment and his cocky attitude petered off slightly. 'I hadn't thought of that.'

Of course he hadn't. How typical. 'And what about Brooke?' she asked, picturing Riley's tall, glamorous girlfriend, a spoilt woman used to getting her own way. Not that Tasha was surprised about how Brooke behaved; she'd grown up as the only child of a wealthy hotelier father and model mother, and was one of the main characters in the top reality TV series currently on television. 'How do you think she'll react when she sees the photos?'

Riley leant against the granite worktop in the kitchen and closed his eyes, groaning. 'She'll go ballistic.'

She will, Tasha thought, not looking forward to the fallout when the pair next saw each other. 'And knowing Brooke, she'll have words to say to poor Erin too.'

He winced. 'She will, won't she?'

'Yes.' When would he ever learn? Tasha wondered. 'You're going to have to get to Brooke first before she tracks Erin down. Somehow smooth the waters or at least warn Erin about her. As far as you know, Erin might not even know you have a girlfriend.'

'Brooke isn't my girlfriend. We broke up.' He gave a triumphant shrug.

Tasha had worked for the man long enough to suspect he wasn't being completely truthful. 'You mean you had another argument after you made up the other day?'

'We did, as a matter of fact.'

Was the man determined to annoy her? 'Well, did you just have an argument or did you actually break up? Because if you didn't finish things with Brooke she probably just thinks you're sulking and has no clue the relationship has ended.'

'You can be really annoying sometimes, Tasha. Has anyone ever told you that?'

How typical of Riley to turn the focus onto her. 'I'd place

money on the fact that you didn't tell Brooke things were over between you. And that's just not fair. I know it might be news to you, Riley, but most men don't go around kissing other women when they already have a girlfriend.'

'Are you sure about that?' he asked, seeming genuinely perplexed by the notion.

Riley's phone rang, saving her from arguing her point any longer. When he didn't bother picking up his phone, Tasha did. She looked at the screen.

'It's Dale. You'd better speak to him.'

He groaned. 'What should I say?'

Tasha clenched her teeth together as she battled to contain her rising temper. 'Ask him what he thought he was doing sending that photographer. Remind him the man was trespassing on private land, at a private party that wasn't yours,' she added, feeling her resolve to remain polite waning. 'Oh, and ask him to do what he can to stop those photos being sold to the newspapers and magazines.'

She handed him the phone. Unable to stand being in the same room and hearing Dale's dulcet tones, Tasha walked to the door. 'I'll go and change quickly, then I'll catch up with some paperwork while you speak to him. Let me know when your call is over and I'll come back inside.'

'Hi, Dale,' she heard Riley say, but closed the door before hearing the manager's voice and went outside to check her emails.

Deciding to find somewhere peaceful to work, Tasha crossed the lawn and walked over to a gazebo partially hidden by some tree branches. She brushed several leaves from the wooden bench and sat. Placing her phone onto the table in the middle, Tasha heard laughter and music coming from the party.

She leant forward onto her elbows, resting her chin in her

cupped hands, and thought of Callum, wishing she was still up there with him. He seemed almost perfect. Decent, kind, thoughtful, and very much a family man. As sad as Tasha was not to have longer on the island, she couldn't help thinking how lucky she was to have met him and spent time with him. Even the little time they had so far spent together.

As much as Riley irritated her sometimes, she knew that it was only his misbehaving on set that had kept them on the island for the extra time and the reason she had been able to spend any time with Callum at all.

Laughter rang out and Tasha wished she could go back to the party, at least for a little while. If she did, she would need to at least ask Riley whether he wanted to go too, and that really wasn't an option, not after the photographer incident. No, she needed to be professional about it and stay at the cottage in case he needed her for anything while he sorted out the issue.

'Tasha!' Riley's voice bellowed from the front door. 'Where are you?'

'Over here.' Thinking it best if she went to him, Tasha picked up her phone and got up to go and see what he wanted. Before she got very far, Riley was marching over to her and despite the dusk light Tasha saw that his expression was thunderous.

Her heart sank. She hoped this wasn't going to be one of those evenings when she had to spend her time calming his temper and helping him see reason about whatever it was that Dale had said to upset him.

'What did he say?' she asked, going back to sit in the gazebo, realising Riley was on his way to join her there.

'That bloody man.' Riley sat and shook his head.

Tasha braced herself to hear more.

Riley scowled. 'He only tried to make out he had done this for my career.'

Tasha attempted to hide her confusion. She shook her head. 'I can't see how he worked that out.'

'That's what I said. Apparently, this is all my fault.'

'What? How did he come to that conclusion?' As much as Riley could be impossible, Tasha couldn't understand how Dale thought he could get away with laying the blame on him for arranging secret photos to be taken when Riley had known nothing about it.

'He was rather rude, I thought.'

Dreading what was coming next, Tasha asked, 'In what way?'

Riley didn't respond immediately but stared at her. 'You'd always be honest with me, wouldn't you, Tasha?'

She often felt she was far too blunt with him but thought that maybe it was her being straight when so many other people around Riley just agreed with anything he said. 'Yes, I try my best.'

He frowned, then exhaled slowly. 'Bloody Dale said he felt my popularity had been waning recently.' Riley narrowed his eyes. 'If it is that's because Dale isn't finding the work for me.' He shrugged. 'He said he believed that a little scandalous story about me in the papers would bring much-needed attention back to me and that's what I needed right now.'

'He did?' She was surprised. Dale mostly agreed with Riley and didn't often argue. Tasha was intrigued to hear more.

'Dale said if the papers get hold of this, which they will because he'll no doubt be the one selling the photos to them, that I can then tell my side of the story. Brooke will probably be offered to sell her side of the story too.' He laughed. 'Which we both know she'll do in a heartbeat. She loves attention, that one.'

Tasha pressed her lips together, desperate not to react. It never ceased to amaze her how oblivious Riley could be about his own behaviour and how he came across to others, yet he was only too quick to criticise other people's reactions to things.

'It seems to me that all you and Dale are focusing on is your career and selling the story. Have either of you considered how this will affect Erin? Despite what you said about you and Brooke breaking up, you haven't made that clear to her; she still feels she has some sort of ownership over you and you're still in contact. What happens when she kicks up a fuss, or worse comes to Jersey and decides to confront Erin? Have you thought about that?' She tried to stop from adding, 'Do you even care how this is going to make her feel?'

'You might be surprised to know, Tasha, that you're wrong. Brooke and I officially broke up.'

'When?'

He gave her a piercing look. 'You're my PA, Tasha, not my nanny. I don't tell you everything. But there is no us when it comes to Brooke and me, not any more. So there's nothing for me, or you,' he added pointedly, 'to tell Erin. Is there?'

She tried to gauge whether he was being truthful with her, or just wanting her to stop going on about it. He kept eye contact with her and she presumed he was being honest. 'Fine. I just hope that is what's happened, for all your sakes.'

He looked in the direction of the party. 'Should I go back to the manor house now?'

She considered his question briefly, then shook her head. 'No. It's a family party. I do think you need to tip Erin off about the photos before she sees them, or someone else shows them to her. It's only fair that you do it tomorrow morning.' She thought of Riley's reluctance to get up in the mornings. 'Early, though, Riley.'

'Yes, I heard you,' he snapped.

She hoped he had.

19

CALLUM

'Callum!' Waking from a deep sleep after finally getting to bed at 4.30 a.m., only three and a half hours before, Callum opened his eyes and winced as his head immediately began pounding. Why hadn't he thought to close the curtains? he thought, irritated with himself.

'Callum, have you seen this?' his father roared before marching into Callum's bedroom and waving a tablet in front of his face.

Grabbing the tablet as it grazed his nose, Callum pushed himself up to sit, and rubbed his eyes. 'What is it?'

James tapped the screen repeatedly with his forefinger. 'Look. That's your sister kissing that full-of-himself actor outside last night. Some sleazy photographer must have made quick work to get that in the newspaper.'

Callum blinked a few times and tried to focus. He realised he was staring at the front page of one of the papers. 'Erin will be ecstatic to see this,' he said, his voice croaky.

James snatched the tablet from his hands. 'What the hell do

you mean? Why on earth do you think she'll be happy with this?'

Callum explained what had happened the night before. 'It's fine, Dad. We told you about this photographer chap, remember?'

His father calmed slightly. 'Maybe, but I didn't expect to see my daughter in a clinch with this Riley chap.' He pointed to the screen again. 'Did you read it?'

'No, you took it from me before I had the chance.'

His father held the tablet in front of him again. 'Well, there,' he said, tapping angrily with his finger again. 'It says that this Riley character has a girlfriend. Brooke someone-or-other who is going to be devastated. And I don't know about you, but I'm not happy to think of your sister's name being raked through the mud by getting herself involved in some sort of love triangle.'

His dad had a point. Callum reached out for the glass of water he must have thought to take up to his room earlier and drank from it. 'I'll get up and go and speak to her. Give me a few minutes to shower and I'll meet you downstairs.'

His father sighed, sounding slightly calmer. 'Fine. I'll put on the coffee. She's not up yet, so won't have seen this.'

Callum threw the covers back and got out of bed. As he dressed after his shower it dawned on him how his sister often said that the first thing she did upon waking was to pick up her phone and look at her social media. He hoped that his dad was right and she wasn't awake yet.

As he entered the corridor, Callum realised how peaceful it was. He heard snoring as he passed his grandfather's bedroom and smiled. It had been a great party and Grandad had celebrated his birthday until the very end. He hoped that this drama with Riley wasn't going to ruin anyone's day.

As he neared the kitchen he heard muffled voices. He

opened the door and walked in to find his father comforting his sister.

He exchanged concerned looks with his father as Erin wiped her eyes with a tissue.

'So you've seen the news then, Erin?'

'Yes,' she sniffed. 'And I've just put the phone down on Riley-sodding-Sharp, who had the nerve to call me to explain, apparently. Although I'm not sure what there is to explain apart from the fact that he has a girlfriend and never mentioned that to me.'

Callum went to commiserate with her when someone used the heavy knocker to announce their arrival at the front door.

'Who the hell is that?' Callum groaned, hurrying out to the hallway to answer the door before the rest of the household was woken from their much-needed sleep.

He pulled the door back and saw Riley. His tanned face was paler than usual and held a concerned expression.

'What do you want?' Callum asked.

He noticed the man had the decency to look shame-faced. 'I've, er, come to speak to Erin, if she'd let me.'

'If you wait here, I'll go and ask her.' Callum waved Riley into the hallway and closed the front door.

'Erin,' he said once he had closed the kitchen door behind him. 'Riley—'

'I know.' She looked up at the ceiling and closed her eyes for a couple of seconds before smoothing down her dress and taking a steadying breath. 'I've got a few things I want to say to that man.' She raised an eyebrow at Dad. 'I might be a while. If I'm gone for too long you might need to send a search party out to look for him.'

He laughed at Erin's remark, wondering why he ever worried about his sister. She was tough and could stand up for herself without any problem. 'I'm not sure whether to wish you good luck, or him,' he said.

She opened the kitchen door. 'Definitely him.' He heard her speaking to Riley for a few seconds then their voices trailing off. 'I think I'd better go and find Tasha,' he told Dad. 'This business is bound to bring up extra work for her and I want to offer her any assistance she might need.'

'Good idea.' His dad smiled. 'I don't know why I worry about your sister when she's probably more capable of standing up for herself than the rest of us.'

Callum laughed. 'I was thinking the same thing,' he admitted as he left through the back door.

He walked down to the cottage hoping Tasha was in and that he wouldn't be disturbing her. Riley had been the star of the party after his grandad, and the guests had seemed delighted to see him having fun with them, being well-mannered and not drinking too much. Callum had begun to think he might have got the guy wrong. Riley had charmed all guests, old and young. Erin had had more fun than he had seen her have in a long time, and it was a shame that so soon after the party things were turning sour for some of them.

He was nearing the door when he heard Tasha calling out to him. 'Over here.'

Callum turned to look for her, spotting a small clearing in the wood and catching glimpses of her yellow sundress in what looked like some sort of gazebo. He hurried to join her.

'You're looking very nice.' Callum stepped onto the wooden structure and sat near her.

'Nice?' She laughed. 'I was hoping for a bit better than that.'

He knew she was teasing but realised he had been a bit flat with his compliment. 'Beautiful and very summery. Better?'

She tilted her head from one side to the other. 'Maybe. It's good to see you.'

'You, too.' He relaxed slightly.

'Riley said he was going up to the house to speak to Erin. Do you know if he's there yet?' She grimaced. 'He did try to call her to tip her off about the articles but said Erin had already seen them and wasn't happy.'

'I'm not surprised. My sister was unaware he had a girlfriend. Erin isn't the sort of person to kiss someone who's in a relationship.'

Tasha frowned. 'I was worried about her finding out before he spoke to her. Silly man. Honestly, I wonder what he's playing at sometimes. He told me he and Brooke had split up.' Tasha shook her head. 'They do so quite often. I gather they had a fight and he assumed they were on a break. She might not see it the same way though.'

'What a mess. At least his girlfriend doesn't live on the island. That would be awkward for Erin.'

'Yes. I think Riley is anxious about clearing this up with her and intends contacting Brooke as soon as he's spoken to Erin.' She stared out to the garden for a moment. 'Riley spoke to his manager Dale again this morning and told him he hoped there was a future for him and Erin.'

He wasn't sure if he'd misheard. 'Sorry, what?'

'I know.' She raised her hands in disbelief. 'I've met Brooke. She's used to getting her own way and can be rather temperamental. I'm not sure how this is going to turn out, but one thing I can be sure of is that she won't let Riley go easily.'

'And where will that leave Erin?'

Tasha shrugged. 'I've no idea and I have to admit that worries me.'

'Same here.' He was beginning to think that his the short

time before Tasha left the island was going to be filled with drama about Riley and the two women he had managed to get himself entangled with.

'I'm going to have to go back to the house and help finish the clearing up,' he said, wanting to take the opportunity to get to know Tasha a little better and make the most of having time alone with her. 'First though I was wondering if you would like to go for a quiet walk. Just the two of us.'

She nodded. 'I would like that very much. All this chaos is exhausting and I fear this is only the beginning of it.'

They walked along a path between lavender borders. 'This scent is wonderful, don't you think?'

She breathed in slowly. 'Glorious. I think we should pick loads and put it in vases in every room in the cottage,' she suggested, laughing. 'We need all the help we can get calming everyone before the tension mounts too much.'

'Great idea, although I doubt the owners of this place, or the gardens, would welcome us pinching so much.'

She nudged him and laughed. 'I was joking.'

'I know you were.' He reached out to see if she would take his hand, delighted when he felt Tasha's cool, soft fingers taking hold of his. 'This is just what I needed this morning.'

'And me.'

They walked on a bit. Intrigued to know more about her, Callum said, 'You've met most of my family but I realised this morning I don't know anything much about you at all.'

He wasn't sure but thought he felt her tense momentarily. 'Like what?'

Unsure what to suggest, Callum thought for a moment. 'I don't know. Um, where you're from? Are you an only child or one of a dozen children? Are your parents still together, or divorced like mine?'

20

TASHA

Tasha's heart dropped. She didn't want to talk about her family with him but sensed he would wonder why that might be if she didn't respond in some way. 'Near Chichester in Sussex. I'm an only child and my parents are still very much together.'

She hated that Callum had asked about her family. His seemed such a large and close family and she was embarrassed to show how disconnected she was with hers. She thought of all the effort his family had put into giving Keith the best birthday possible, while with her family she was considered disloyal if she didn't do as her parents thought she should.

She knew she shouldn't be so concerned about what someone else thought of her family, but this was someone she liked rather more than was probably good for her. If there was one thing she did know about Callum, it was that he was trustworthy and kind. Not the sort of man to throw information back in her face or use it against her, as her ex-boyfriend Toby had been prone to do.

'Sorry, I've got so used to being very private that I now find it a bit difficult to open up to people.'

'That's fine,' he said, giving her hand a gentle squeeze. 'It's none of my business anyway.' He gave her a sweet smile. 'And it's not as if we've known each other very long.'

'That's true, I suppose.' Feeling a little better, she added, 'And I've only met your family because of the party and staying next door.'

'There, you see? All perfectly understandable.'

They walked on a little further, then Callum stopped her by gently pulling her hand. 'I do like you though, Tasha. I know you're returning to England soon but I would like to stay in touch, if you're up for it.'

She liked the idea. Very much. 'Yes, that sounds good. Riley will hopefully be back to film the second series in a few months and if I still haven't given in my notice I should be accompanying him.'

'That's true.' He laughed. 'What do you think the odds are that you'll still be working for him by then?'

She had no idea and said so. 'This situation isn't helping either. Although, to be honest, he has been taken aback by it. Usually Riley is carefree and uncaring who he hurts, but this time I've seen another side of him and he really is concerned for Erin.'

'You sound surprised.'

She shrugged. 'That's because I am.' She thought of Brooke, and as much as she didn't like the woman she couldn't help feeling badly for her. 'Although I'm not sure how bothered he is about Brooke's feelings, so he clearly hasn't changed all that much.'

Callum frowned. 'That is a shame.'

Her phone buzzed. 'Sorry, I have to see what this is about.' Seeing that the email was from production, Tasha opened it and read.

'Problem?'

'I'm not sure.' She stared at him, wondering if she dare ask Callum for his help. She thought of Riley's behaviour and how it could all end badly for Callum's sister. No, she decided, she couldn't ask him. She realised Callum was giving her an amused, knowing smile. 'What?'

'Is there something you want to ask me.' He laughed. 'Or, going by the range of expressions that have passed across your face in the last minute or so, maybe you don't want to ask me.'

She groaned. 'Has anyone ever remarked on how perceptive you can be?'

'Many times. I think it's got something to do with inter-viewing personalities for my shows. I need to read them to know when to push my questions and when to change the subject.'

She raised her eyebrows. 'Well, you've certainly got a knack of picking up when someone is arguing with themselves about whether or not to ask you something.'

He laughed. 'Just tell me what it is.'

She cringed. 'I'm not sure.'

'Go on. What have you got to lose?' He grinned at her. 'I really am happy to help you in any way I can.'

She placed her phone down onto the table in front of them and pointed to the email, explaining as she read. 'You probably know how tight timing is for this extra filming. Well, there's now an issue with one of the supporting actors. It's only a small part and I know there will be people on the island with experience to step in, but the problem is time.'

'I'm sorry, I have no idea what you're asking of me.'

'This is an email from the producer's secretary. She's tipping me off that the actor due to film opposite Riley soon has had some sort of meltdown and can't face finishing the last scene.

He's only done one so far, so they can quickly reshoot that but still need someone to agree to do it.'

'Right,' he said, clearly confused.

She stared at him thoughtfully. 'I'd like to put your name forward to the director to play the part. It's opposite Riley,' she said, wanting to be transparent and not set Callum up for any nasty surprises. 'He tends to have a way of making less experienced actors feel anxious, as you can probably imagine.'

She could see Callum wasn't convinced. 'And you think he won't have that effect on me?'

Tasha raised her eyebrows. 'I've seen you with him, remember. You're always polite but you're no pushover. You also have experience of shoots with your modelling.'

'Exactly – shoots, maybe the odd advert but not having a part in a television series.'

She gave him a pleading look. 'Please at least consider the suggestion for me. It's a tiny part in two scenes and I know you'll be fine with it.'

'I'm glad you do.'

Not wishing to make him panic, she added, 'Look, I still have to put your name forward. I can show the director photos I've found online.'

His mouth slowly drew back in a smile. 'You've been searching for me online?'

Why had she said that? 'For this.' It was a fib and she hoped he didn't realise the email from the producer's secretary was the first time she had known about the part being vacant. 'Oh, go on, Callum. Say you'll do it.'

When he didn't answer, she tried a different tactic. 'Fine, then at least confirm you don't mind me putting your name forward.'

'OK, I'll agree to that.'

She picked up her phone to respond to the email before Callum had a chance to change his mind.

21

CALLUM

He dried the last handful of cutlery, wondering how Tasha had managed to persuade him to let her put his name forward. He had no interest in acting. The few adverts he'd filmed had been bad enough. Slow and boring was what he mostly recalled about doing them. He frowned. Maybe it wouldn't be too bad, he mused. He would be able to see Tasha when they were recording. She was always somewhere nearby Riley when she was working. He might even be surprised and enjoy himself. Feeling calmer about the whole thing, his mind wandered to Erin. He hoped his sister was doing all right and getting on with Riley, seeing as she seemed to like him an awful lot. She would be fine, too, he decided. He put each piece of cutlery neatly away in the kitchen drawer, feeling much better than he had shortly before. His phone buzzed and, seeing it was a message from Lettie, Callum put down the cutlery and read it.

> Why don't you bring Tasha and pop round for a bit. It would be lovely to see you both and you can tell us how the party went. L

Happy to have a reason to visit the farm again, Callum hung up the tea towel before he turned to his father. 'I thought I'd pop by and visit a couple of friends while Grandad is out with his friends for lunch. I have something I need to ask them but shouldn't be too long.'

'Take your time. Your grandfather has several people wanting to meet up with him. I'll see you later.'

He got into his car and was about to drive off when he thought of Lettie's message and decided that if Riley was out somewhere, Tasha would be alone at the cottage and might want to join him for his visit to the farm. He turned left and drove the short way down to the cottage, pressing the hooter twice in quick succession.

Tasha appeared from the garden, a questioning look on her face. 'You've not changed your mind, I hope?'

He shook his head. 'Not at all. I just wondered whether you might like to come with me for an hour or so. If you're not too busy, that is?'

She stared at him thoughtfully for a couple of seconds, then raised a finger in the air. 'Wait there. I'll be two minutes.'

Unable to help himself, Callum smiled. Maybe today was going to be brighter than he had expected. She came running out of the house carrying her phone and sunglasses and got into the car.

'That was quick.' He laughed.

'I wanted to escape before Riley gets back.' She tapped the dashboard. 'Quick, let's get a move on.'

He put the car into gear and slowly drove back up the driveway, having to pull over when he saw a taxi coming from the opposite direction. Callum watched it pass by, frowning. 'I wonder who that was?'

'Sorry?' Tasha looked up from her mobile. 'I didn't see them,

I'm afraid. Too busy checking my emails for the hundredth time this morning.'

He drove on and after checking nothing was coming turned onto the main road. 'You must get a lot of them.'

She groaned. 'They seem never-ending.' Then, smiling at him, added, 'But it's my job to keep on top of all the correspondence, so I shouldn't moan.' She placed her phone onto her lap and looked out of the window, breathing in deeply. 'The air here seems so much fresher than at home.'

'Maybe it's because we're so near the sea.'

'I suppose it could be that.' She opened the window fully and rested her arm on the door. 'You never mentioned where we're going.'

'Didn't I?' He loved that she had readily agreed to join him without knowing where.

'Is it to the farm?'

'It is. I thought I could show it to you when there aren't a pile of people and vans there.'

'Sounds good to me.'

They drove on in silence and Callum loved how comfortable they were with each other. He was beginning to get excited to show her the farm as it usually was.

'Here we are,' he said, slowing down and turning into the driveway. Someone was buying bags of vegetables from the honesty box and Callum had to drive around their badly parked car.

Tasha laughed when the old man shouted at Callum to slow down. 'You were barely moving.'

'I know. And he was the one parked so badly too. Cheeky devil.'

He continued down the driveway smiling as Tasha oohed and ahhed at the animals.

'How come I hadn't realised there were alpacas?'

'Because Lettie will have kept them well out of the way, knowing her.'

'Will I be able to see some Jersey cows this time?'

'Yes. Did you know all the animals at Hollyhock Farm are either rescues or retired?' he said, proud of his friends for giving these animals such an amazing life.

'I love it more like this than I did before.'

He slowed right down. 'You must have seen the farmhouse from a distance,' he said, pointing ahead to get her attention from the animals in the field to their left.

'No, I haven't. We were told to turn off the driveway before we reached the yard so that we kept away from the barns and went straight up to the larger fields at the back for any filming. We'd done some filming in the woods, of course.'

Callum hadn't realised that was the case. Anticipating her reaction, he slowed and turned into the yard and immediately heard Tasha gasp. 'What do you think?'

'Those hollyhocks either side of the front door and along the wall are breathtaking,' she said quietly. 'I don't think I've ever seen such a pretty farmhouse.'

'It is pretty special, isn't it?'

'Yes.' She sighed. 'And your friends own this place, is that right?'

'Lettie's only been running this place for the past year since her father retired. Her parents now spend a lot of their time travelling.'

'It's so pretty. Like one of those pictures I remember from books with nursery rhymes when I was a child. What an incredible place this must be to live. Shall we get out?'

'Yes, let's do that.' He couldn't wait to show her around. Not only would the place be perfect, at least he hoped it would, but

Callum presumed there might be an additional payment involved for filming at the farmhouse and he was sure Lettie would welcome the extra income.

'Oh, look, there's Lettie,' Tasha said as Lettie came out of the farmhouse, her little girl on one hip and her farm dog Spud walking slightly ahead of them.

Lettie waved. 'Hi, guys.' She kissed him on the cheek and then Tasha. 'Welcome to Hollyhock Farm.'

'This place really is so full of character.'

'That's kind of you to say.' She glanced at the hollyhocks. 'This is my favourite time of year when they're out. Gorgeous, aren't they?'

'Absolutely stunning.'

'Thank you.'

'I only agreed to allow filming here if they agreed to keep away from the barns and the animals. Most of them are quite old and I didn't want them to become stressed by too much noise or unnecessary numbers of people.'

'I presume they've been good keeping to the zones marked in the contract.'

'They have,' Lettie said. 'I made it one of my stipulations of them coming here.'

'Why don't you show Tasha around, Callum. Then come inside and I'll make you both something to drink.'

'Thank you, that's really kind of you.' Tasha smiled up at him and he wished he had more opportunities to see her this happy.

'Right,' Lettie said, shifting the baby slightly higher onto her hip. 'I'll leave you both to it and see you in a bit.'

'I'd like to show you other parts of the farm that you won't have seen yet.' Callum took Tasha's hand. 'Let's go and have a look, shall we?'

He led her past the barns and, taking their time, accompanied her to the top field and pointed out the views across more fields and out to the sea.

'Oh, this is breathtaking up here.' Tasha sighed. 'I wouldn't mind living here myself.'

'You're not the only one.' Callum laughed. 'I'll take you down to the wildflower meadow.'

'Sounds good to me.'

He waited for Tasha to take more photos by the stream and then walked back with her to the farmhouse so she could speak to Lettie.

'I think Lettie is happy with the extra bit of money coming in. She has a lot of animals to keep fed.'

'They must pay reasonably well, I imagine,' Tasha said. 'Although I don't know the figures, so I might be wrong about that.'

Lettie must have been watching for them as they approached and came out of the front door just as they entered the yard. 'So, what's the verdict?'

'I think I've now found my favourite place ever,' Tasha said. 'It's certainly picturesque.'

'I'm glad you think so,' Lettie said, smiling. 'Right, let's get that drink. Follow me.'

Any tiredness Callum had felt earlier that day after the party and ensuing drama between Riley and his sister vanished. He had enjoyed spending a bit more time with Tasha. Maybe agreeing to film a couple of scenes wouldn't be all that bad after all. He thought of his sister and recalled a dream she had once had to work on actors' hair on a film set.

'Lettie, would you mind me asking something of you?'

'I'm intrigued. Go on, what is it?'

'Could you keep Erin in mind should there be a hairdressing vacancy on set, do you think?'

Lettie looked surprised. 'I wasn't expecting you to ask that. Of course I will.'

'Thank you.' He shrugged. 'I doubt it'll happen but she'll never forgive me if I come here and don't think to mention it, just in case it does.'

22

TASHA

Tasha found it difficult to concentrate on what Lettie and Callum were saying as she lifted her phone slightly to peek at the screen and check whether she had received a response. She had enough on her plate with Riley's personal dramas right now not to want him to have another tantrum over changes to the filming schedule.

She hoped the director's secretary got back to her soon with her boss's thoughts about considering Callum to take over from the upset actor. She liked the idea of spending more time with Callum and couldn't deny that she was liking him more the longer she was in his company.

She realised her right heel was bouncing up and down as it sometimes did when she was nervous and that Callum was trying to act as if he hadn't noticed. Forcing herself to sit still and at least try to appear calm and less agitated, Tasha willed the production team to hurry up and look at his photos. Perhaps someone else had come up with an alternative suggestion. Her heart dipped at the thought. Surely not. She gritted her teeth.

No, she would focus on everything turning out well, at least until it didn't.

Baby Isla began grizzling so Lettie stood. 'She's hungry, I'm afraid. I'm sorry to cut this short but I'd better prepare her bottle before she really gets in a state. My daughter isn't known for her patience.' She moved Isla up and down in her arms and kissed her on the top of her downy head.

'No problem at all.' Tasha got to her feet, as did Callum. 'Thank you again for allowing us to come and look at your stunningly beautiful farm and gorgeous animals.'

'It's no problem at all. I'm happy you enjoyed it.'

Lettie kissed Callum on his cheek. 'I look forward to seeing you both here again very soon.'

She was walking back to the car with Callum when her phone rang. 'Ooh, hopefully they'll give me a decision about you being cast,' she whispered to Callum. Her mood dropped when she saw it wasn't them calling, but her boss. 'No such luck. It's Riley.'

Not in the mood for any dramas from him today, Tasha took a calming breath and forced herself to answer his call. 'Riley.'

'Where the hell are you?'

Tasha saw Callum glare at the phone, unsurprised that he had heard Riley's angry tone. 'I'm at Hollyhock Farm with Callum.'

'Why aren't you here where you should be?'

Feeling her temper rising, Tasha closed her eyes briefly to steady herself before answering. 'He invited me to have a drink with his friends, which I thought was lovely,' she said slowly and without bothering to hide her irritation.

'Tasha, I've no idea what you're going on about. All hell has broken loose here and I need you back at the cottage. Immediately.'

She was about to continue speaking when the line went dead. 'Cheeky sod,' Tasha groaned. She looked up at Callum. 'That man can be incredibly rude sometimes.'

Callum scowled. 'I've no idea how you put up with him.' He got into the car and waited for her to do the same and strap herself in. 'He did sound irate though. I wonder what might have happened to cause it.' He raised an eyebrow. 'Or is this his usual way of speaking to you?'

Not wanting to admit that Riley's rude tone was something she often heard, Tasha sighed. 'It did sound as if something had happened – to upset him quite this much.' She smiled at him. 'I suppose we'd better get back so I can find out what it is and start sorting this latest drama out.'

She was relieved they weren't too far from the cottage and as Callum's car took them down the beautiful leafy lanes, Tasha wondered how much longer she could work with such an insufferable man as Riley. He really was impossibly rude at times and as much as she didn't like his attitude it was times like this – when another person had heard how Riley had spoken to her – that she really found mortifying.

When Callum didn't speak, Tasha wondered whether it was because he was angry with Riley, or – worse – that he was disappointed in her for taking such abuse. She considered trying to justify why Riley behaved this way but decided that there was no excuse for this nastiness and lack of consideration for her feelings.

Callum slowed at a yellow line, waiting for several cars to pass. He gave her a sympathetic look. 'You OK?'

She shrugged. 'I'm getting to the point where I feel ready to try and find another job,' she admitted. 'But there aren't that many around. Only working for people not much better than Riley.'

Callum drove on again as soon as the road was clear. 'You'll do what's best when the time is right.'

She went to thank him but saw he was concentrating on the road. It was refreshing to have someone not try to force their opinion on her about her boss, like her parents did whenever she spoke to them. Tasha thought back to the times she had confided in her mum or dad about something Riley had done or said to her and it was only afterwards they began suggesting she find somewhere else to work that Tasha realised that although she soon got over each unfortunate event, her parents loved her and would probably never be able to do so. She wished they would trust her ability to make her own decisions. Surely that was what being an adult was all about. That, and making different choices when the initial ones hadn't worked out.

Callum drove down the long driveway, insisting that he was happy to drop her off before driving back up to the house. 'I'll come in with you and help you explain to Riley why you were at the farm. You were trying to help his filming schedule after all.'

'It's fine,' she insisted. Tasha's stomach lurched. She shouldn't feel this way about seeing her boss; it wasn't right but knew she could handle Riley, regardless of how annoyed he might be.

She got out of the car and turned to wave goodbye when she heard screaming and ranting. She stared at Callum, unable to speak for a moment, when a large smashing sound came from the house. Tasha gasped.

'That's it,' Callum said, immediately getting out of the car. 'I'm coming inside with you.'

Tasha liked being an independent woman and had learnt to deal with most things in her job, but she daren't imagine what was going on in the cottage and was happy for the backup. 'Thanks, I think I'd like that.'

'Shall I go first?' he asked.

She shook her head. 'No, it's fine. I'll be happy enough knowing you've got my back.'

Tasha hurried to the door and, on opening it, heard another loud smashing sound. 'I hope he's not breaking things from this house,' she said, surprised that Riley would do something like that, but presuming it must be what was happening.

'Hey!' she yelled, running towards the noise into the kitchen. Spotting Riley's girlfriend, Brooke, holding an expensive vase above her head ready to throw it onto the marble-tiled flooring, Tasha raised her hands, stunned to see the woman there after what Riley had assured her. How the hell had she got here this fast? Tasha shot a panicked look at Callum. Seeing Brooke raise the vase a little higher, Tasha shouted at her, 'Don't you dare break anything else.' She took the opportunity of the woman's shock at seeing her and Callum bursting into the room to snatch the vase from Brooke's hands.

She turned and handed it to Callum who immediately put it safely out of harm's way onto the furthest worktop.

Tasha gasped at the shocking sight of all the broken porcelain and glass shattered on the floor.

'How did you get here so quickly?'

'I caught the red-eye of course. As soon as I saw the headlines in the early hours, I booked a flight here.'

'But why? You and Riley broke up.'

'Hah, is that what he told you?'

Tasha seethed. The damned liar. Why had she been willing to believe him so readily? She could have warned Erin if she had known Riley and Brooke were still seeing each other after all. She saw a glint of anger in Callum's eyes and hated to think he might feel let down by Tasha not stepping in and trying to protect Erin.

Brooke went to pick up a plate.

'What the hell are you thinking?' she demanded, shaking her head. 'Put that bloody thing down, now!'

Where the hell was Riley? Hearing footsteps, Tasha looked over to the door and saw him hurry into the kitchen from the utility room.

'You took your time,' he snapped.

'Me?' She gritted her teeth for a moment in an effort to stop herself from saying exactly what was on her mind. 'I came here as soon as you called, if you must know,' she said sarcastically. 'Anyway, never mind me, why didn't you do something to stop her trashing this room? Look at all this breakage.' Tasha glared at him. 'How are we going to explain how this happened to the poor owners?'

'I can speak to them, if it's easier?' Callum suggested, his face ashen.

She was grateful for the offer. 'No, thanks. This is for us to sort out. I'll do it. We will obviously pay for all broken pieces to be replaced and just hope there's nothing here that's irreplicable.' Tasha gave Brooke a pointed glare.

Tasha knew better than most how frustrating Riley was to deal with, but most people had enough respect for others' belongings not to want to damage their possessions.

'Maybe I should be the one to apologise to them,' Brooke said, her voice quiet and quivering.

'I think that's the very least you can do,' Riley snapped.

'I do wish the pair of you would communicate better,' Tasha said. 'Then at least you'd both be on the same page about whether you have broken up, are on a break, or simply not speaking to each other.'

'You didn't know?' Callum asked.

She turned to him, having no intention of Riley's selfishness causing a rift between her and Callum. 'If they don't know what's going on between them, I don't see how I can possibly keep up. Anyway, if I did know they were still together, don't you think I'd tell Erin?'

'You'd betray me?' Riley asked. 'You work for me, remember.'

Tasha spun round to face him. 'Exactly, I work for you. My contract does not stipulate that I also lie for you, Riley. So don't you dare start giving me a hard time for having morals.'

Remembering why Brooke had lost her temper with Riley, Tasha calmed slightly. 'I will contact the property manager first,' she said. 'I'll tell them everything will be replaced or paid for and it's up to you and Riley to decide who foots the bill, but one of you will need to do it.'

Tasha turned to Callum. 'You get on; we'll be fine here. Thanks for coming in though. I appreciate it.'

'No problem. I'll catch up with you soon.'

She hoped any anger Callum might have felt towards her was now placated. For now though, she needed to concentrate on damage limitation because it was perfectly obvious by Brooke's make-up-streaked face that broken porcelain was the least of Tasha's concerns.

23

CALLUM

Callum was relieved Tasha hadn't needed him to stay any longer. At least now he could go and find his sister and warn her to stay out of Brooke's way until Tasha had found a way to calm the poor woman down a bit.

As he drove up to the house, he pictured Riley's face and felt some satisfaction that the man had seemed startled by Brooke's reaction. Serves him right, Callum thought, parking the car and going into the main house. Riley needed to learn there were consequences if you trampled over another person's feelings. As far as Callum was concerned it was about time the man had to deal with repercussions.

Not wanting to alert the rest of the family to the dramas unfolding down at the cottage, Callum made his way from room to room downstairs looking for his sister. He came across his father and soon-to-be stepmother Betsy sitting in the orangery and sharing a bottle of wine as they discussed the success of the party.

'Hello there, son,' James Preston said, raising his glass of red wine to Callum. 'Care to join us? This is a rather good Bordeaux your grandad insisted we enjoy.'

'No, thanks. I'll probably have to go out again later. Have either of you seen Erin?' A thought occurred to him. 'Did she have to open the salon today?'

'Yes,' Betsy said before taking a sip from her glass. 'She said something about two important clients being booked in to see her today. If you're looking for her you'll probably find her there.'

'Thanks.' He wondered where his grandad had got to. 'Grandad still out with his friends?'

'Yes, he's been treated to another meal somewhere by a few of them.' James laughed. 'I think he has enough bookings in his diary for the week to keep him busier than he has been in a long time.'

'He'll love that,' Callum said, cheering up. He thought of the newspapers and the photos that had been included of some of the party guests. 'Has anyone seen any of the official photos taken by the photographer we booked, do you know?'

James laughed again. 'Oh yes.'

Callum wasn't sure if that was a good thing or not. 'What did they think?'

His father chuckled. 'It depends.'

Anxious, Callum asked, 'Oh hell. On what?'

Betsy batted James's arm lightly with her hand. 'You are such a tease. Stop winding the poor guy up.' She rolled her eyes. 'The party photos were generally very good and people are choosing the ones they'd like to order. As far as the ones taken by that paparazzi bloke, the consensus seems to be that those who found themselves in the photos were delighted, including your grandfather. A few of the other guests seem to be a little put out that they didn't have something to show off about.'

Callum couldn't work out why anyone would be upset to be excluded. 'I'm not sure I understand.'

'Well,' his father said, 'I think it had something to do with the wording in the articles. Whoever sold the story led the journalists to believe this was your grandfather's home and that the family were some sort of aristocracy over here. I think they liked the idea of people believing they were related to someone that grand.'

Callum laughed. 'Grandad isn't at all grand though.'

'I agree.' He took another sip from his glass. 'But you know what it's like when a big family get together and the one-upmanship starts. People lose their usual reason.'

He didn't have any experience of that happening, but not wishing to waste time before going to see Erin, Callum nodded. 'I see.' He raised his hand in a wave. 'Please tell Grandad if you see him that I'll catch up with him later.'

'Will do, son.'

Callum drove straight to St Helier and parked as close to Erin's salon as possible, not wanting to waste any more time before checking on his sister.

Having been stopped several times by people he knew on the short walk to Erin's hair salon, Callum was feeling more and more relieved Erin had needed to be away from the house and distanced from any confrontation with Brooke.

He entered the plush salon, thinking as he always did each time he came here how much his younger sister had accomplished. When he thought back to how she had yearned to be a veterinary nurse when she was younger, it had been a surprise to them all when one day she had completely changed her mind. He watched Erin standing behind a client styling the woman's hair while she chatted to her, looking over the woman's shoulder into her reflection.

Not wanting to interrupt while Erin was working, Callum went over to the reception and sat down.

'Hi, Callum,' Toni the receptionist said. Callum stood and moved away, not wishing to get in her way, but she raised her hand. 'No, you're fine there. I've yet to wash one client's hair.' She looked over at Erin before returning her gaze to him. 'Your sister won't be long now and will have a few minutes to chat while I look after the other client.'

'Thanks, Toni. How's things with you?'

'Fine.' She moved slightly closer to him and lowered her voice. 'Erin was telling me all about the party... and the photos.' She spoke the last part of her sentence so quietly Callum struggled to hear her. 'Told me about Riley Sharp, too.' This bit was mouthed but it was clear who she was referring to. 'Lucky Erin, if you ask me.'

Callum scrunched up his face. 'Really? You don't think he's a bit pretentious? Full of himself?' He stopped himself adding anything worse.

Toni looked startled. 'Why would I think that? Anyone that gorgeous can't be too bad.'

Callum wasn't sure he agreed with her logic but resisted saying anything. 'If you met him you'd probably not be so immune to his personality.'

She laughed. 'I should be so lucky.'

'About what?' Erin asked, walking over to the desk and waving for Callum to move. 'Please look after Mrs Sloane for me, Toni.' She smiled at her client. 'I hope you have a wonderful anniversary and I'll see you next month.'

'Thank you, as always, Erin.'

Erin gave her another smile, then took Callum by the arm and led him to her small kitchen at the back of the salon. 'What's happened?'

'Hello to you, too,' he said, unsurprised that Erin had got straight to the point of his visit.

'Never mind that. Why are you here? You never come and visit me at the salon.'

'That's a lie.'

She glared at him like she did when she was just about to punch him. Not that Callum expected his sister to do anything like that now they were grown-ups.

'I wanted to warn you that Riley's girlfriend has arrived and is trashing the cottage.'

'Brooke Farrow is here? In Jersey?'

'She is.'

Erin pulled a face. 'Ahh. She's upset then.'

He frowned, wondering why his sister seemed surprised. 'I'd say that's an understatement. Anyway, wouldn't you be if your boyfriend had been photographed kissing another woman, and the photos were then published everywhere online?'

Erin stared at him with her mouth open for a couple of seconds before her face crumpled. He could tell she was trying hard to keep from crying. She peered around him to check they weren't being listened to before quietly adding, 'I promise you I had no idea he had a girlfriend, otherwise I never would have kissed him.' She covered her eyes with one hand briefly before giving him a beseeching look. 'I've never knowingly kissed someone else's partner.'

Aware Erin was struggling, Callum pulled her into a hug. 'I know,' he whispered. 'But it's happened now and clearly there's going to be fallout from this.' It was a struggle to hide his irritation with Riley for getting his sister into such a nasty situation.

'I suppose I'll just have to grin and bear it, won't I?'

Callum nodded. He decided not to add that from what he had seen of the damage to the cottage crockery, Brooke had a way to go yet before Riley or Tasha managed to appease her. Aware that he needed to tip Erin off in some way so she was prepared for any confrontation, he added, 'You should be ready in case Brooke wants to meet you.'

Erin stepped back and looked up at him. 'I never imagined I'd meet someone as glamorous as Brooke Farrow,' she said miserably. Erin lowered her gaze and was obviously embarrassed by her involvement. 'Is she very cross?'

He couldn't lie. 'She is, I'm afraid.'

Erin groaned. 'I can't blame her for that; I would be too.'

'It didn't mention your name in any of the articles I saw,' he said, hoping to reassure Erin. 'But I presume journalists will now be vying to try and be the first person to track you down.'

Her mouth dropped open and her face paled. For a moment Callum thought she might faint and wished he hadn't been so blunt. He took her hand. 'Sorry, that came out wrong.'

Erin gave him a doubtful look. 'I can't see how that information could be shared any other way really.'

He supposed she was right. 'The point I'm trying to make is that I think you should keep away from the cottage, at least until Riley...' He frowned. 'Or Brooke come to the house to find you.'

She stared at him without speaking. 'Maybe I should stay upstairs in my flat.' Before Callum could respond she shook her head. 'No. We've got the house for a week and I want to be with my family.' She straightened her shoulders. 'If Brooke wants to have it out with me, I'll do the right thing and face her. It's the least I owe her, don't you think?'

Callum shrugged. 'Maybe, but don't forget you didn't knowingly do anything wrong.'

'That's true. I thought they had broken up months ago.' She sighed. 'They say you shouldn't believe everything you read in the papers.' Her face lit up. 'Maybe she won't believe this?'

Callum winced. 'I'm afraid she does believe it.'

'Are you sure?'

'Unfortunately, I am.'

Toni came over to join them. 'Sorry,' she said quietly, 'but your next client is ready for her cut and blow-dry.' She put an arm around Erin's shoulders. 'Are you all right?'

Erin shrugged. 'Not really, but I'll tell you about it later when we've closed up for the evening.' She exhaled sharply. 'I'd better get on,' she said, giving him a grateful smile. 'Thanks for coming to check in on me and letting me know what's going on. Shall I see you back at the house after work?'

Callum was relieved Erin had work to keep her mind from dwelling on the ugly situation. 'Yes, that would be great.' Remembering he was due back at the studio within the hour, Callum tapped his watch. 'I'd better get a move on too. See you back at the house.'

As he walked quickly to the radio station, Callum wondered what would happen next with this dreadful situation. Damn Riley for being so insensitive with both women's feelings. He had no excuse, as far as Callum was concerned.

24

TASHA

Riley marched off in a temper and it took a while before Tasha eventually managed to coax Brooke to sit outside on the pretty terrace. She made her a cup of tea and took it outside to her. 'You sit here while I go and find Riley.'

Brooke's eyes narrowed. 'How typical of him to sidle off and hide somewhere after having been the cause of all this drama.'

Brooke was right, but although Tasha agreed with her, she felt she should attempt to keep her personal opinion about her dreadful boss to herself. She knew from experience how often Riley and Brooke fell out, only to get back together again weeks or even days later. She had no intention of being their scapegoat if that happened this time. She couldn't imagine ever forgiving someone who betrayed her like Riley had done to Brooke, especially when her humiliation was so public.

'Is the tea all right?' Tasha asked, pouring another cup for Brooke and placing it on the small table in front of her.

Brooke looked at it and nodded. 'Thank you. It's perfect.'

'Right, then I'll leave you. He can't have gone too far,' she added hopefully.

Tasha knew it would be easy enough for Riley to hire a private plane to take him back to England, or even France. It was such a short distance, only being about fifteen miles, as far as she could remember. Or was that by boat? She tried to think where the closest airport might be in France but had no idea.

Leaving Brooke scrolling through her phone, Tasha raced back into the cottage and immediately began searching each room for Riley. Where the hell was he? she wondered, leaving his bedroom and rushing to the room next door. As she reached the door, Tasha thought she heard a voice say something. It was hard to make out as the person was murmuring, but she sensed it was Riley so retraced her steps and found him in the smallest bedroom, sitting by the window chatting to someone on his mobile.

He looked up as she closed the door behind her. 'Sorry, Dale, something's cropped up. I'm going to have to go, but I'll call you again later.' He ended the call.

When he didn't speak, she said, 'What are you playing at, Riley?'

Looking offended, he went to argue, but Tasha raised a hand and shook her head. 'No, don't bother trying to fob me off with some story. I'm far too worn out for that.' She stepped closer and lowered her voice in case Brooke had followed her inside and was listening from the hallway.

'I wasn't going to.'

Not bothering to argue, she continued, 'I've been babysitting your girlfriend, who is sitting outside drinking tea and as far as I can tell winding herself up further by looking at all the news items and photos of you and Erin on her phone.' She rubbed her aching neck to try and ease it. 'I suggest you go down there now and apologise.'

He stood and scowled at her. 'I have done. Several times.'

Tasha clenched her fists. 'Then do it again, because if you want to try and stop this from escalating, you need to act fast.' When he didn't immediately agree, she tried a different tactic. 'Or don't you care that you've dragged poor, unsuspecting Erin into yours and Brooke's latest falling-out?'

At the mention of Erin's name, Riley's shoulders dropped slightly and his angry expression vanished. 'I really didn't mean for any of this to happen.'

'I'm sure you didn't,' Tasha said, trying to be nicer to him. After all, she mused, Riley was the one who needed to change his attitude and try his best to resolve this for both his and the women's sake. 'But it has happened and now you need to find a way to calm everyone down and make things as right as you possibly can.'

He walked over to the door but instead of leaving the room, turned. 'What should I say to Brooke?'

Frustrated that this grown man knew how to upset people but had no idea how to put things right, Tasha tried to think. 'As I said, you need to apologise. You told me you thought the pair of you had split up after your last row, isn't that right?'

'It is. I did.' He rubbed his chin and she saw that he still hadn't shaved, which was very unlike Riley who always preferred to appear immaculate.

Tasha gave him a pointed stare. 'Go and tell her the truth. I'm sure she'll appreciate that far more than if you try and spin some rubbish tale painting you as the innocent person.' She smiled. 'Because, Riley, whether you think it or not, people much prefer the truth even if it is unpalatable.'

'Really?'

She felt her irritation increasing again and pushed it away. 'Yes, I promise you it's true.'

He turned from her and put his hand on the doorknob but didn't leave.

'Riley,' she whispered. 'Stop wasting time. The longer Brooke has to wait for you to appear, the more annoyed she'll become.'

He turned the handle and left. Relieved to have found a way to persuade him to go and do the right thing, for once, Tasha slumped onto the bed. Working for Riley was far too stressful for her liking. She really needed to make some discreet enquiries about vacancies. Surely there was something available for her that would be less problematic.

She peered out of the window and looked down at where she had left Brooke. She was relieved to see Riley sitting on the chair next to her, his hands waving in his usual animated way as he tried to explain his way out of trouble.

Good, she thought, happy to have a chance to escape from the house without him knowing.

Needing to get away from Riley's latest drama, she grabbed her phone and sunglasses, and left through the back door. She walked quickly up to the main house, disappointed not to see Callum's car parked in front where he usually left it. Unsure what to do next and not wanting to play gooseberry with Brooke and Riley, she decided to take a walk up to the road and explore some of the nearby lanes.

She had been walking for about twenty minutes, enjoying the cool shade from the trees lining either side of the lane, when a car slowed behind her and stopped.

'Hello there.'

Her heart leapt to hear Callum's voice. Unable to keep from smiling, she turned to face him. 'I thought I'd take a bit of a walk.'

He narrowed his eyes, amusement making them twinkle. 'You've run away really, haven't you?'

Tasha laughed. 'I have. Brooke is still at the cottage and I finally managed to persuade Riley to try to explain himself to her.' She thought of Erin. 'Did you see your sister?'

He nodded. Then, giving her a thoughtful look, leant over and opened the passenger door. 'Why don't you hop in and come for a drive with me?'

Delighted, she did as he asked. 'Where are you taking me?' She pulled her seat belt across her and pressed it into the catch.

He grinned and tapped the side of his nose. 'Ah, now that would be telling.'

Unable to stop herself, Tasha laughed. 'For some reason if any other man said that to me I'd be nervous and demand to be let out of the car.'

Callum's head turned instantly in her direction. 'What?' He looked at the road again but Tasha could tell she had worried him. 'I hadn't realised that was an odd thing to say.'

'I think it depends on who says it.' She reached out and touched his arm lightly. 'Sorry, I didn't mean to worry you.'

'No, it's fine.'

Relieved she had managed to get their evening back on track before ruining it, she asked, 'I can tell you're considering something.'

They stopped at a yellow line and he looked at her, eyes twinkling in amusement. 'I'm trying not to feel too happy to discover you've put me into a category away from all other men.'

Tasha was pleased he thought that way.

He began driving again when the road was clear. 'What does that mean exactly anyway?'

Tasha laughed and tried to think how best to explain her feelings. 'It's meant as a compliment.' When he didn't react, she added, 'That is to say, I feel instinctively comfortable with you.'

'I see.'

She wasn't sure whether he was happy with her answer, or not. 'And it's not because I don't find you attractive,' she added, not wishing him to think that was why she felt the way she did.

Callum glanced at her. 'I'm glad to hear it and to know you're happy to spend time with me.'

Unsure whether she had yet to find the right way to explain how she felt, Tasha decided to leave things as they were and simply shut up and enjoy their evening.

Believing she recognised the road they had turned onto, she asked, 'Can I ask what sort of place you're taking me to?'

He threw his head back and laughed. 'No, because I haven't decided yet.'

'Isn't this the way to Hollyhock Farm though?'

'It would be if I kept going straight, but we're going left further along.'

Tasha relaxed back into the seat, enjoying herself. 'I don't think I've ever been taken on a mystery tour before.'

'Is that what this is?' Before she had a chance to answer, the car slowed more quickly than she expected and Callum indicated just before turning right and taking them in another direction. 'Let's go this way.'

'Beauport.' As Tasha read the sign she wondered why it meant something to her. She must have read the name on a map, or heard someone mention it. Then it dawned on her why she had saved the name to memory. 'Isn't this where there's a lovely beach at the bottom of a lot of steps?' she asked, wondering if she had the energy to climb back up them when they left.

Callum gave a nod. 'It certainly is. It's a lovely walk around there on the headland and there's a beach.' He glanced at her and laughed. 'You've heard about the steps, I suspect.'

'I think I read a review about the beach somewhere when we first arrived on the island.'

'We can go elsewhere if you'd rather.'

She shook her head, not wishing to ruin his excitement to show her the place. 'I'd love to go there.'

25

TASHA

Callum turned into the road leading to the parking area on the headland. Once parked, they walked along a path until they reached the top of the steps leading down to the beach. Despite what she had said, she was anxious about going down the steps. She had always been nervous of heights and it wasn't only that but the thought of having to come back up to the top of the cliffs again.

Callum seemed to sense her concerns because he reached out to her. 'Here, take my hand. These steps can be a bit precarious and I know they're not to everyone's liking when it comes to ways to get down to a beach.'

She grimaced. 'I have to admit they worry me a bit. I can be rather clumsy.' She put her hand in his.

She was relieved that Callum took their descent very slowly, allowing her to relax slightly. She realised she was also enjoying being able to hold his hand and was touched that he chatted to her about the view, stopping every so often for them to take in the blueness of the sea that seemed to merge with the sky.

'It is yet another stunning place on this pretty island of yours.'

'Look at the colours of the sea,' she said, noticing and pointing with her free hand. She looked up at him, happy to see him smiling. She loved being in his company and it gave her a warm fuzzy feeling to know he had chosen to spend more time with her. Continuing, she added, 'The colours are amazing and range from the deepest navy to the most amazing turquoise I've only ever really seen in photos my parents took of a trip they made to the Caribbean years ago.'

'Not bad, is it?'

She sighed. 'It's stunningly beautiful and very inviting.'

'I love that you like it here,' he said, giving her a thoughtful look she couldn't decipher.

She loved feeling so comfortable in Callum's company. She didn't think she had felt this connected to a man for a long time.

'You all right?' he asked.

She snapped out of her reverie and nodded. 'I was just thinking of something I mustn't forget, that's all,' she fibbed, too embarrassed to voice her thoughts. Wanting to spend as much time with him as possible, she said, 'Maybe we could go for a drink or ice cream after the beach. My treat.'

'After walking up all those steps you mean,' he said as they finally reached the sand. 'I think we'll probably need it.'

Happy with the thought, she took off her trainers and waited for him to do the same.

She sighed happily. 'I'm so glad I left them to sort things out in the cottage and came across you on my walk to nowhere.'

Callum smiled. 'So am I.'

The sea wasn't far out at all and Tasha loved that it only took a couple of minutes for them to be able to cool their feet in the rippling waves.

'It's wonderfully warm,' she said, dreamily holding her trainers in her right hand. 'This is bliss.' She lifted her face to the sun and, closing her eyes, held her arms out wide. 'You did well bringing us here, Callum.'

She sensed he was watching her and opened her eyes to find him staring at her, a gentle smile on his face.

'What?'

He shrugged. 'I was just thinking that the way the sun is shining on you made you look as if you had a halo around you. I was trying to imprint the vision in my memory.'

She was taken aback for a moment and couldn't speak, simply gazing at him. They stood in silence, their eyes locked. She wondered if he was about to kiss her and hoped he might. She was just about to slip her arms around his neck and kiss him, when a child shrieked, distracting her. Tasha opened her eyes and looked for the child, relieved to see she was squealing happily. She let her arms drop back to her sides. She turned her back to the sun and it took a moment for her eyes to recover from the brightness. When they did she saw Callum bend to pick something up.

'What's that?'

He rubbed his thumb over it and handed it to her.

'It's a piece of pottery.' He held it out and Tasha took it from his palm.

She studied the white glazed pottery with tiny blue painted flowers. 'It must have come from a beautiful piece.' She wished she could see the whole plate, or whatever it had originally been part of. Tasha liked the thought of keeping a reminder from such a special day. 'Do you think I can keep it?'

'I don't see why not.'

Happy, she dropped the piece into her pocket.

As they passed several rock pools, Tasha felt the urge to step into one. It was warmed by the sun and she took a moment to wiggle her toes and relish the new sensations she was enjoying.

She went to speak when a ball slammed into the rock pool, splashing her up to her face. Shocked, Tasha shrieked.

'Sorry, miss.' A little boy ran up to her as she took Callum's outreached hand and stepped out onto the sand. The child stood a short distance away, and Tasha sensed he wasn't sure whether to approach the ball or not.

'It's fine,' she said. 'You can come and fetch it.'

'Are you OK?' Callum asked.

She laughed, seeing the funny side. 'I must have looked silly standing there covered in sea spray!'

He grinned. 'I think he got a fright when he saw how big the splash was that his ball made.'

'Good,' she said, amused. 'Maybe he'll be a little less enthusiastic with his kicks in future.'

'Shall we see the cave?'

She nodded and let him lead her further into it, enjoying the feeling of her hand in his. Tasha went to remark that they were still holding hands, then it occurred to her that if she did Callum would probably let go or worry that she wasn't comfortable walking with their hands together, which wasn't the case. So she kept quiet and decided it was another thing to keep for her memories when she was back at home in England and missing this place. And him.

'This is magical.'

He sighed. 'I'm glad you think so.'

She looked at Callum as he seemed to study first her eyes, then her mouth. His gaze didn't move for a few seconds and she hoped he was going to kiss her. Then he seemed to think better of it and, looking into her eyes again, smiled. 'Shall we go on?'

She presumed he meant with their exploring and nodded.

As she walked slightly behind him, their hands still in each other's, Tasha wished she'd had the courage to kiss him. Then again, she mused, to do so would only be starting something neither one of them could take forward. After all, whatever each of them thought of the other, she would soon be leaving the island and not coming back for months.

If at all.

Even if Riley did return to film a second series, the way she felt about him right now she probably wouldn't still be his assistant, if she managed to find another job working for someone less demanding.

'Everything all right?'

She gave Callum a reassuring smile. 'I was thinking about leaving Riley,' she admitted, wanting Callum to know why she was thoughtful at such a perfect time.

He stopped walking. 'You're really going to do it?'

She shrugged. 'I'm not a hundred per cent sure, but I'm considering it more and more now. His dramas take up too much of my emotion and I'm sure I can find work elsewhere that isn't quite so draining.'

He looked serious. 'Or maybe working for someone who doesn't expect you to be on call twenty-four-seven.'

She smiled. 'Being on call goes hand in hand with this job really. Especially at times like these when he's on location and we're staying in the same place. It's the problems he manages to create that affect me most, really.' She thought how Callum might be feeling about the newspaper photos and Brooke's arrival on the island. 'I hope Erin is doing OK.'

'I think she is and, I admit, she was a little upset.' He groaned. 'Horrified, really, that she had been kissing someone who was still in a relationship with someone she thought was his ex.' He frowned. 'I have a nagging feeling she likes Riley rather more than she imagined she might.' He raised an eyebrow.

Tasha felt sorry for the woman who clearly had little experience of being connected to a well-known actor. 'I worry what might happen when his fans take to social media about her. Even if he and Brooke were separated while he got together with Erin, but Brooke has her own fan base and if she intimates that she's been betrayed, or let down by him, then heaven only knows how they'll go for Erin.'

'What do you mean?' Callum asked, aghast. 'Is Erin's safety a concern?'

Tasha grimaced. Why had she spoken without thinking things through first? Now she had gone and worried Callum and ruined their wonderful outing. She wished she had kept her concerns to herself. 'I'm sure she'll be fine,' she said, hoping to reassure him. 'She has me to speak to and I'll do my best to regulate Riley's social media accounts. If Erin has any concerns at all, she really must contact me about them.'

'But what about the fans?'

His hand slipped from hers and he rubbed his chin, and Tasha felt the loss of his touch instantly.

'I really shouldn't have said anything. Look, I'll sit with Riley and Brooke, or Dale will speak to the pair of them, and Brooke's manager. Together they'll come up with a narrative that saves everyone's pride.'

'But who will speak for my sister?'

'I promise you I'll ensure no one forgets Erin in all of this.'

'She has a business she's passionate about.' He shook his head. 'She's worked hard building up her clientele and would be devastated if a couple of kisses one evening at a party ruined everything she's worked so hard to build up.'

Seeing he was getting more upset by the minute, Tasha took

his hands in hers. 'Callum, I promise you I will keep Erin in the forefront of my mind.' She wasn't sure whether to add her next thought but seeing the worried look still obvious on his face decided she should. 'I suspect Riley likes Erin quite a lot, if you know what I mean.'

Callum looked doubtful. 'He does?'

She nodded. 'He won't want her to suffer because of his mistake.'

'How can you be so sure?'

She thought of the Riley she often saw when he was on his best behaviour and also the man who could at times be very thoughtful. Like the time she had gone down with flu a couple of years before when they were in Cannes and she had to stay in her room at the hotel and leave another assistant to accompany Riley. She had worried he would be furious at the inconvenience, but instead he had sent out for medications, called for a doctor to keep checking on her and made sure the hotel kept Tasha supplied with tempting snacks and plenty of healthy smoothies.

'Because I know Riley quite well and below all his vanity and bluster lies an occasionally thoughtful and caring man. And he does like Erin, so he will do all he can to make sure she isn't hurt by this drama Dale has caused.'

Callum went to respond but her phone rang.

'Sorry,' she said, taking her phone from her pocket and seeing who was calling. 'I need to take this.'

After she ended the call she said, 'Sorry, that was Dale.' She wished she didn't have to take her phone with her everywhere. 'He's sent over some paperwork I need to go through with Riley. I'm afraid I have to go back to the cottage.'

'That's a shame.'

She sighed. 'I agree. I've enjoyed myself very much.'

His face brightened. 'That makes me very happy.'

They put their trainers back on, then Callum stared pointedly at the steps. 'I suppose we'd better navigate these things.' He reached out his hand to her and once she had taken it they began the slow climb up from the beach to the car.

As they walked, Tasha wondered what would greet her when she arrived back at the cottage.

26

CALLUM

Having dropped Tasha back at the cottage, Callum drove back along the driveway and parked outside the main house, unable to stop thinking about what might have happened if the child hadn't kicked their ball into the rock pool. He was almost certain Tasha had been about to kiss him and wished he had taken the opportunity to kiss her when he had the chance. It was too late now, though, he thought, realising that whatever might have greeted Tasha at the cottage at least everything seemed peaceful here.

As he walked to the front door he heard cheerful voices and smiled. For everything that had happened since the party, it was a relief that it hadn't affected his grandfather's enjoyment of this precious time spent with so many of his family and close friends and that they were all still having a lovely time.

'There you are, my boy,' Keith called out as Callum walked into the orangery. 'Where the devil have you been?'

'I took Tasha to Beauport beach.'

He ignored his father's barely suppressed delight and Betsy's nudge into his father's side. Callum knew his father worried that he wasn't in a relationship despite Callum reassuring him that he didn't need to have a partner to be happy. He had his work and enough going on in his life already.

'Come and join us.' His grandfather peered past him. 'Isn't she with you now?'

Callum shook his head. 'Unfortunately not. She had to go and work.' He thought how much he enjoyed spending time with her and how much having her in his life would enhance each day. But of course that wasn't possible.

'Before I sit, do any of you want another drink or something to eat?'

'We're all fine, I think,' his grandfather said. 'We only sat down ourselves about half an hour ago. You get yourself something though.'

Callum went to the kitchen, took a bottle of beer from the fridge and opened it. As he swallowed a mouthful of the cool liquid he thought of his sister and hoped Tasha had been right when she assured him that Erin would be fine. Erin might be strong, independent and savvy, but she was his little sister and he hated the idea of keyboard warriors making her life difficult for something that was no fault of her own.

'What you thinking?' Erin asked, making him jump. She laughed. 'What's got into you? You're never usually jumpy.'

Not wanting to worry her, he shook his head. 'I was deep in thought. You never come into the house that quietly,' he teased. 'I can usually hear your noisy footsteps coming from miles away.'

She stuck out her tongue. 'Rude. And not true.' Erin walked over to the fridge and pulled it open. 'I do love a full fridge, don't you?'

'I don't know.' He laughed. 'I don't often see mine with much in it apart from leftover food from the night before.'

'Sounds similar to mine.'

'Talking of which, I thought you were staying at your flat tonight because you were upset about what happened with Riley and needed a bit of time to yourself? What's changed your mind?' As he asked the question he wondered if she was hoping to bump into Riley if she returned to the house.

'No reason other than I thought as I had most of my family in the one place I should probably make the most of seeing them all and spending time with them.'

She took a few grapes from a tub and closed the fridge door, then taking the cover from the cheese platter on the side cut a small piece of Roquefort and popped it into her mouth, following it with the grape. 'Hmm, delicious. I might make up a plate of that and take it to the orangery.'

'Good idea. They're all out there now.'

Callum walked out of the kitchen and, noticing the front door was open, waited to see who it might be.

'Of course they won't mind,' he heard his mother say. 'Just go in. I'm sure she'll want to speak to you anyway.'

Wondering who might be about to enter the house, he was surprised to see it was Riley. Seeing Callum standing there, he stopped dead in his tracks.

'Ah, Callum. I was, er, wondering whether—'

'What are you doing here?' Erin asked from the kitchen doorway. She looked at Callum. 'Did you invite him?'

Callum raised both hands. 'Don't blame me. I had nothing to do with this.'

Their mother marched past Riley and shook her head as she looked first at Callum, then at Erin. 'Honestly, I didn't think I had brought you two up to be rude to visitors.'

Erin flushed. 'I hardly think—'

Their mother raised a finger and wagged it back and forth in front of Erin. 'Now is not the time to be silly, darling. You need to take this young man somewhere quiet where you can both talk and clear the air.' She indicated the front door. 'Why not go out into the garden. It's lovely out there.'

Callum thought of the hidden photographer who took the photos of them. 'I hardly think that's a good idea.' He sighed. 'But I agree with Mum that the pair of you should talk privately.'

'Fine.' Erin glared at Riley, but Callum couldn't miss how her reddening cheeks gave away how she still had feelings for the actor. 'We'll go to the smaller living room at the back of the house.'

Callum wasn't sure where that was, but nodded his agreement with the idea. 'Let me know if you need anything.'

She handed him her plate of food. 'You may as well have this. I don't fancy it any more.'

He took it from her and watched Riley follow his sister down the corridor.

'I do hope those two patch things up,' his mother said.

Callum couldn't understand her attitude. 'You can have this food, if you want. I'm not hungry.'

His stepfather Barry entered the house and seeing Callum holding the food out to his mother who didn't seem interested in it either, took it from Callum's hand. 'Well, if no one wants this delicious-looking food, I'll take it.'

'Go ahead.' Callum turned to leave space for them to make their way to the orangery. 'You'll find the others out there.'

Barry immediately walked through to join the others but his mother didn't move.

'What is it, Mum?'

'You're not joining us?' she asked.

Callum wondered what Tasha might be doing if Riley was here chatting to his sister. Aware his grandfather wanted to make the most of seeing family members he rarely spent time with and considering that he saw his grandfather several times a week, he decided to make the most of the chance to spend time with Tasha before it ran out. He was tempted to call and see whether she would be happy for him to pop down to see her. He decided there was no harm in asking her while his grandfather was engrossed in chatting to his guests. If she wanted to make the most of her peace, she could say no.

'I'm not sure. I'll just make a quick call but will let you know if I'm going out for a while.'

'Fine, but don't be long.'

He wondered why his mother wanted him to hurry when they both knew she would spend her time catching up with the rest of the family.

Callum took out his phone and decided to message Tasha instead.

> Have just seen Riley at the house and wondered if you were free for an hour or so? C

He was about to put his phone back into his pocket when it pinged. Either she was happy to hear from him and wanted to see him or knew without thinking about it that she wasn't in the mood to spend time with him. He hoped it was the former.

> Was hoping you'd contact me. Come down as soon as you like. T

Callum reread the message as he walked to the front door, his mood lifting at the thought that Tasha probably wanted to make the most of seeing him, just as he did, before she left the island.

He set off at a jog, then slowed to a walk. Maybe running there was a bit too eager, he thought, amused at his overthinking the situation. As he tried not to hurry past the colourful and scent-filled borders to the cottage, he couldn't help thinking how meeting and getting to know Tasha had made him feel far less jaded about life and more like he used to feel before breaking up with his fiancée Zena two years before.

He recalled his grandfather's advice at the time when coming across Callum sitting miserably in his grandfather's garden. 'I know this feels like the end of the world for you right now, Callum, but I promise there will be a time when you don't hurt this badly.' He had hesitated and Callum had asked him to say what else was on his mind. 'There will even be a time, although you won't believe me just yet, when you'll meet someone new who will make you glad that Zena did call things off.'

Callum had gone to argue, but his grandfather would have none of it. 'No, Callum. You mark my words. One of these days you'll look back and recall what I'm telling you now and know I was right.'

'And what makes you so sure that'll happen?' Callum had responded in disbelief.

'Because, my lad, you're a good, kind chap who cares about others, and one day someone will recognise there's more to you than what people see on the surface.'

Could this be the someone his grandfather had been alluding to? He pictured Tasha and thought about how kind, hard-working and fun she was, and hoped so.

27

TASHA

Tasha listened to Brooke continuing her rant as she paced the living room, intermittently staring out of the window like a modern-day Cathy yearning for Heathcliff in a badly acted play, then glaring at Tasha, hands on her hips as she yelled at her.

'He's a complete and utter bastard,' Brooke screamed. 'And what I want to know is what you intend doing about it?'

Tasha needed Brooke to go before Callum arrived. The poor man had enough to contend with in his own life without having to bear the brunt of Brooke's dramatics. She also didn't want him to witness this hysteria and worry that it might be aimed at Erin.

'As much as I'd love to sort everything out for you, Brooke,' she said in her calmest voice, 'even if it was my job to boss him around, which it isn't, we both know Riley doesn't listen to anyone.' She gave Brooke a sympathetic look. 'I mean, if he doesn't listen to you, why should he take any notice of what I've got to say?'

Tasha wasn't sure how Brooke would react to this comment, but felt hopeful when the woman closed her eyes and dropped her hands to her sides as if all the fight had gone out of her.

Tasha didn't much like the woman, but no one deserved to be treated disrespectfully.

'You're right, Tasha,' she said wearily. 'It's my own fault for taking him back after the last time he did something like this to me. Why I ever expected our relationship to be any different now after all our rows, I don't know. It was silly of me.'

Tasha shook her head, feeling sorry for the woman who, despite being a diva herself, clearly had feelings for Riley. 'I'm sorry it's turned out this way, Brooke, I really am.'

'Hellooo?'

She heard Callum's voice coming from the front door and noticed Brooke immediately perk up.

'Who's that?'

Wishing she hadn't responded so quickly to Callum's message and given herself more time to persuade Brooke to leave, Tasha walked over to the doorway. 'That's a friend of mine. I'm afraid we have business to discuss, so—'

Brooke shrugged. 'It's fine,' she said, waving a hand in front of Tasha's face to cut her off mid-sentence before crossing the room to the door. 'I've got things I should be doing too.'

Tasha glowered at Brooke when she turned and raised an eyebrow in her direction as Callum walked in. 'And why haven't we met before now?' Brooke said, her voice gentle and suggestive at the same time.

'I'm not, um, sure.'

Tasha heard the confusion in his voice and went to join the pair of them. 'You're here for our meeting, I see.' A moment's confusion flashed across his face, vanishing almost instantly.

'Have I, er, come too early?' he asked, looking at his watch as if to check the time.

Tasha shook her head. 'No, not at all. Brooke and I were

chatting and forgot the time. Didn't we, Brooke?' she added when Brooke didn't answer.

'No need to worry,' he said, cocking his head in the direction of the front door. 'I can wait outside if you need more time?'

'Well...' Brooke began, but not wishing to give her any excuse to stay a moment longer and be here when Riley came back from wherever he had marched off to during their row, Tasha stepped forward.

'There's no need for that – Brooke was just leaving.' Thinking she should not be quite so rude, Tasha turned to Brooke. 'Unless you have more you wish to discuss?'

As Brooke considered her question, Tasha willed the woman to think better of staying and agree to leave.

Brooke eventually smiled. 'Not at all. Nothing that can't wait, for the time being anyhow.' She walked up to Callum and reached out her hand. 'I'm Brooke Farrow, by the way. Riley's soon-to-be ex-girlfriend.'

Callum smiled politely and shook her perfectly manicured hand. 'Nice to meet you, Brooke. I'm Callum Preston, a friend of Tasha's.'

Tasha was grateful to him for adding that and wondered what Brooke's reply might be.

Brooke smiled at him, then at Tasha briefly before responding. 'Oh, by the way, when Riley does finally build up the courage to return, tell him from me to expect to hear from my lawyer.'

Tasha gasped. 'Why?' she asked, horrified.

'Because I'll be suing him, obviously.'

'For what?'

Brooke flounced out of the door without answering, slamming it loudly behind her and leaving Tasha stunned into a silent shock.

'You didn't expect her to say that, did you?' Callum asked, walking over to her.

She shook her head. 'No. And it's all we need, if I'm honest with you.'

'Shall we go to the kitchen?' Callum asked, causing her to look at him. 'I think you could do with a drink of something.'

She realised he was right. 'Yes, I think that's a great idea.'

She led the way into the kitchen, realising she was thirsty after all the talking she had been doing over the past hour, trying to first pacify Riley and then reason with Brooke. The pair of them were well suited, Tasha decided. Both spoilt and impossible most of the time. Although, she had to admit, both could also be lovely people when the mood took them to act that way.

But suing him? That was a bit much even for Brooke.

'What would you like to drink?' she asked Callum as she clicked on the kettle. 'We have cool drinks. In fact, I think we've got everything here.'

'I'm fine, thanks. I'm still recovering from my grandfather's birthday celebrations.' He went to fetch the milk from the fridge while Tasha took out a cup and saucer for herself and set them down onto the granite worktop. 'I wouldn't want to be the property manager having to set this place up for someone like Riley. I bet his expectations are higher than most people's.'

She spooned tea leaves into the fine porcelain teapot and poured boiling water onto them. 'They certainly are. Shame he doesn't behave as well as he supposes other people should.'

Her tea made, Tasha led them onto the terrace and sat next to Callum. 'I'm glad you've come.'

'I'm happy to be here. Hey, you don't think Brooke could still be out there somewhere?'

Tasha shook her head. 'She had a car waiting. If you didn't see it, maybe it was parked a little further down the driveway.'

'Good.' He looked at her for a moment. 'Do you think she really will sue Riley?'

Tasha shrugged. 'I've no idea. Those two are always suing someone, so it's possible, I suppose.'

'But what would she sue him for?'

Tasha gave a tired laugh. 'Who knows. And to be honest, I'm past caring. Riley has the backup and the funds to defend himself in a court of law, so he'll be fine whatever it is.' She decided to change the subject. Then thinking of a way to see Callum again, recalled receiving an email from the director's secretary just before Brooke's arrival. 'It seems they liked the recording I sent in of you delivering those lines. You're on a shortlist of two actors to take over that small part I put your name forward for.'

'Really?'

She smiled. 'Don't look so unhappy about it. Who knows, it might be fun.' She wasn't sure that was possible trying to act for the first time opposite Riley but didn't say so.

'Anyway, why don't you come and watch the filming?'

He frowned. 'I didn't know that was an option.'

'Would you like to?' she asked, thinking it would be a good idea if he wanted to be chosen.

'I suppose I would, yes. I mean, I haven't ever seen a TV series filmed before, so it'll be a new experience.'

Tasha didn't bother hiding her delight that he had agreed. 'Great. I'll have your name added to the list of guests. I'll give you more information about times when I have them.'

'Thank you, that's very kind of you.'

After the evening she'd had with Brooke it cheered her up to know she would have another opportunity to spend time with him. 'It's no problem at all. Anyway it makes sense you being there as you clearly know the place well.'

Tasha's phone pinged. 'Sorry, I should see what this is about.' She took her phone from her pocket and looked at the screen. It was a message from Riley's manager, Dale.

> Heard about B coming to the cottage. Have arranged another rental, which should take you through to end of filming. Will send through address soon. Moving lunchtime tomorrow. Dale

Her mood dropped.

'Bad news?' Callum frowned, looking concerned.

She turned her phone for him to read the message.

'Ah, so you'll be off in the morning then.'

She felt a little better to see Callum's obvious disappointment. 'Seems like it.'

He stared at her for a moment. 'I was enjoying you staying so close to the house.'

'Me too.' She smiled. 'But it can't be helped, I guess.'

He shrugged. 'We only have a couple more days at the manor, so us being neighbours was due to come to an end soon anyway.'

Tasha sighed. 'I've never lived so far away from neighbours in my life as I have at this place.'

'That's true. I live in a flat so mine are on either side and above and below me. Not the same at all.'

28

CALLUM

The place didn't feel the same after Tasha and Riley had moved from the cottage, although she had emailed to let him know he had been given the part in the series. By the end of his stay at the manor Callum was glad to return to his own flat. He suspected the rest of his family were ready to get back to some sense of normalcy too. He stood in his spotless living room thinking the place was so pristine it was difficult to believe his mother and stepfather had been here at all, let alone stayed for almost a week.

Callum was missing seeing as much of Tasha but spotting a fresh cabbage loaf on the worktop, cheered slightly. He always loved the delicious soft, white bread with its extra crispy crust and wondered what else his mother had brought for his return. Intrigued, he opened the fridge door and seeing the shelves packed with fresh French cheeses, neatly packaged sliced ham, several cooked meals neatly piled on top of each other ready for him to heat up, he smiled.

How typical of his mother to want to ensure he had all he needed. Callum was glad for once that she still didn't seem to think he was grown up enough to care adequately for himself, despite living away from home for the past ten years. He wondered why he expected anything less.

He was eager to prepare for next week's radio shows and sat down at his laptop to start work. He wasn't sure how long he had been busy when his front door opened and Erin raced in.

'Why aren't you answering your phone?'

'I hadn't realised I'd received any calls.' Remembering turning the sound off a few hours earlier, he picked up his phone and checked he hadn't missed any calls from his grandfather or Tasha. Seeing only three missed calls and each of them from his sister, he saved his work and sat back in his chair.

'Go on then, I can tell you've got some news.' He hoped it wasn't anything to do with the Riley drama. Trying to gauge her mood, Callum doubted it could be. Erin seemed far too cheerful for it to be anything to do with that situation. 'Well?'

'I'm going on location.'

Unsure what she meant, he shrugged and shook his head. 'Sorry, what?'

'Someone from the hair department just called me and told me their usual hairdresser had been taken ill. I gather you recommended me.'

Callum thought back to him asking Lettie. 'That's amazing, sis.'

'It is and all thanks to you. They looked up my website and photos and reviews from my fabulous clients and I've been called on set because they urgently need someone to step in.' She beamed at him. She flung out her arms and did a twirl, almost knocking one of the glasses on a nearby shelf.

'Hey, careful of those. Mum won't be impressed if you break them. They were a flat-warming gift from her and Barry.'

She looked at the shelf. 'They're fine. I didn't touch them.

Anyway, what do you think? Exciting, isn't it?' Her face fell. 'What if I'm not good enough?'

'We both know you are,' he said, relieved he had thought to ask Lettie to keep her in mind and that an opportunity had arisen. 'This is brilliant for you, Erin. Congratulations. They'll be lucky to have you there.' A troubling thought occurred to him.

Her eyes narrowed. 'I sense a but coming.'

He forced himself to continue. 'What if you're seen on location with, or near, Riley? Don't you think that'll be playing into the paparazzi's hands?'

'But this is different. I'd be there on a professional level. Surely no one will question that?'

He wasn't sure whether she didn't see the problem, or just didn't want to. 'And who will look after the salon while you're away?'

'My manager will, Callum.' Erin glowered at him when he didn't answer. 'Don't ruin this moment for me. You can see how happy I am and we both know how brilliant this could be for my business.'

'If you're happy to take that chance, then go for it.' He smiled. 'You know I'll support you whatever you decide to do.'

Her expression softened. 'I know you will. You're always there for me.' She pulled a face. 'Even when I'm being impossible.'

He laughed. 'Especially then.'

Erin picked up Callum's work notepad and began reading his messy writing.

Not ready to share the identity of the following week's interviewees, he snatched the pad from her hand and put it down on the table. 'I don't know why I'm worried,' he said, recalling his own invitation to watch the filming. 'I'll be there a lot of the time too.'

She stared at him. 'You will?' Then after a moment's thought, gave Callum a knowing smile. 'This wouldn't have anything to do with Tasha, I suppose.'

'It might do.' Seeing his sister's eyebrows rise in a questioning look, he sighed. 'She suggested I watch the filming to help me prepare for my small role in the show.'

'Ah, that's the excuse she chose then.'

'What are you insinuating?' he asked, hoping his sister might have noticed something in Tasha's behaviour that mirrored his feelings for her.

'Nothing.'

Why was his sister so infuriating when he needed her to just say something? 'No, go on. Tell me.'

She turned to leave, stopping at the doorway. 'It's just that I saw the pair of you getting cosy a few times.'

He thought back to when he had spent time with Tasha at the manor property but couldn't recall ever acting in a way that might make anyone suspect he liked her. 'Rubbish. You're just winding me up now.'

She laughed. 'Maybe I am.' Then leaning forward and tapping the side of her nose, she said, 'Or, could it be that I'm not?'

'Bugger off, Erin,' he grumbled, not wanting to be teased any longer. 'Some of us still have work to catch up on.'

'Bye, big brother.'

'Whatever.' He wanted to let her know he was happy for her before she left. 'And well done.'

'Thank you,' she shouted as she closed the flat door behind her.

Callum opened his notebook and found the page he was looking for, with suggested questions for one of his guests, and began typing them up. He stopped working as something dawned on him. Hadn't he wondered about his mother not realising he was an adult now, despite being almost thirty? What a hypocrite he must be to worry so much over his sister, just as his mother did for him. Erin was an adult too. She had her own business and was more than capable of putting most people in their place.

He turned the page of his notes, ready to begin typing again. Was he right to consider Riley simply as a regular person, or did the man who mostly surrounded himself with yes-people have more arrogance and a stronger feeling of entitlement than others? He gave the idea further thought and decided he would keep his distance so as not to annoy Erin by being overprotective, but he'd be ready in case she did need him.

After all, wasn't that what family members were for?

29

TASHA

Tasha listened to Dale and Riley's Zoom chat for a few minutes before waving at Riley and indicating the door. He barely registered that she was about to leave but gave her a curt nod. Making the most of having time to herself, Tasha decided to pop into town. She hadn't been to the shopping area in St Helier yet and wanted to buy a couple of things to take home to her parents. Even though they usually had some sort of snarky remark about her working for Riley, she still liked to find them a souvenir each time she travelled anywhere with him.

She decided to take the bus, having noticed a bus stop a short way down the road from the apartment where they were now staying. It would be nice to travel like a normal person for a change rather than in a smart car with a driver and Riley being stared at and photos being taken constantly.

As she waited with several other people for the bus to arrive, Tasha thought about filming starting the following day. She was looking forward to it, not because it would be another day on a film set but because she would see Callum again. It hadn't been twenty-four hours since she saw him last but even though Riley had kept her busy running around sorting out clothes and ordering in food for him, she still missed the man who had unexpectedly woken something in her she'd thought dormant after so long being happily single.

What was it about Callum that brought her emotions alive again? He was friendly and very good-looking. She thought of his piercing blue eyes, fair hair and chiselled jaw and wasn't surprised someone had thought him attractive enough to want him in a glossy commercial.

The bus stopped and Tasha waited her turn to get on.

'I don't know what it is,' an elderly lady standing next to her said. 'But whatever you're thinking about has put a right big smile on your face.'

Tasha thought of Riley and how if she didn't already know her boss was not attracted to her, she certainly did now. Callum was the sort of man Riley saw as competition, and the mere fact that he had no issues with Callum proved she was right to think that way. The feeling was mutual.

'Boyfriend, is it?'

Tasha realised she would like Callum to be just that. 'Not yet.' She lowered her voice. 'Maybe never.'

'Well, lovey, there's no harm in hoping now, is there?'

She supposed not.

The woman's attention was taken from her by a friend who hurried over to her, and they were soon deep in conversation. She had seemed very nice, but Tasha was happy to be left to her own thoughts once again.

The bus ride to town was far nicer than most bus trips she had taken. As the bus took them on a higher road overlooking another lower one, she looked past it to the beautiful bay with what appeared to be a fort on a small island and to the right of those modern flats. What a pretty island, Tasha mused, deciding to get off at the next stop and see where the roads took her.

She hadn't been walking for very long when she came across a building that she thought she recognised.

She was vaguely aware of a Golf pulling into the parking area and just as she passed heard someone calling out her name.

'Tasha? It is you.' She turned to see Callum standing, his laptop under his arm. He pressed his key fob to lock his car and walked over to the other side of the low wall separating the car park from the pavement. 'What are you doing in this neck of the woods?'

'I thought I'd come to St Helier to buy a few bits for Mum and Dad.'

He nodded. 'The shopping area is quite a way in that direction.'

'It is?' She thought about her bus trip. 'I didn't consider that when I got off the bus before the station.'

'If you wait a moment, I can walk with you. Unless you'd rather be alone, of course.'

She shook her head, still taken aback to have seen him so unexpectedly. 'No, I'd like that.'

They were soon walking together and she wondered if he might suspect she had been meaning to come to the station to see him. 'I suppose you bump into people you know here all the time.'

'It depends. Sometimes it happens, but there are people living on this small island who I haven't seen for years, even decades.'

Surprised, she gave him a doubtful look. 'I can't imagine that happening on such a small island.'

'You'd be surprised. Anyway, it might be small but there are over one hundred thousand people living here now. The numbers have increased massively over the past forty years or so.'

'That does surprise me.' She smiled at him.

'What?' he asked, laughing.

'You must be well known here though. A bit of a local celebrity, being on the radio and all that?'

He shrugged. 'Only to the people who listen to the show. Know me, that is. I'm no celebrity. Your chap Riley is one of those. I wouldn't be suited to that life at all.'

'No? Why not?' She didn't imagine he would be but was interested to know why the notion didn't appeal to him.

'I like my privacy too much. No one is bothered about someone like me. Riley, on the other hand, must have a hell of a time with fans coming to his home, or bothering him when he's out with friends, or girlfriends, or whatever.'

She couldn't tell whether Callum was genuinely interested, or if he was concerned for Erin. 'He lives in a secure apartment that's impossible to get into unless you either live there or are invited.'

'How can you be so sure?'

She frowned. 'Put it this way, the lift goes directly to Riley's apartment. It goes to other floors, too, but he has a code to take it straight up to his hallway.'

She saw Callum raise his eyebrows in surprise and smiled. 'He usually has someone nearby looking out for him too. Just in case some chap decides to challenge Riley to a fight.'

'People do that?'

'Not often, but he's been the tough guy in a few films and occasionally you'll get someone who's had a bit too much to drink and wants to show off to friends.' She shook her head. 'If they knew Riley well they would know his muscles look great on camera, but he's never used them to fight anyone.'

'I see.' They stopped, waiting for a set of traffic lights to change so they could cross the road. 'It's fascinating to think how different someone can be from their public persona, don't you think?'

She thought back to all the times she had been surprised when she first did this work and got to meet many of the people she had thought impressive on the screen. 'I don't think much would shock me now.'

Callum laughed. 'I suppose not.' He stopped near what looked like a big frog on a granite plinth.

'What a strange statue!' she said without thinking. 'Sorry, I didn't mean to sound rude.'

'That's a crapaud. A local toad.'

'I see,' she said, not really seeing at all. She realised they had reached a long street with shops on either side. 'I suppose this is where we part ways then?'

'It is, but if you want a lift back to where you're staying, I can either come and pick you up when you're finished, or you can walk back to the studio. I should be finished in—' he checked his watch '—just over two hours. In fact, I'd better get a move on if I don't want to be late.'

'I'll be fine, thanks.' She smiled at him, surprised but delighted when he bent forward and went to kiss her cheek.

Mistaking what he was about to do, Tasha turned to face him so his lips connected with the corner of her mouth. She realised what she had done and grimaced. 'Sorry, that was a bit awkward.'

'Not at all.' He gazed at her momentarily before running off in the direction they had just come, leaving her stunned and very happy.

30

CALLUM

As Callum jogged back to the radio station, he couldn't help thinking how happy he was that Tasha had misread what he had intended doing. Did that mean she wouldn't mind him kissing her? Or was it simply that she had turned on instinct but not meant anything by it? He wasn't sure.

The show went well but Callum was glad to be home at the end of his shift. He went for a run along the water's edge from La Pulente to L'Étacq, enjoying the warm breeze as it swept past his face. When he finished, he took off his trainers, socks and T-shirt and took a swim in the cold seawater. Tomorrow, filming of his scenes would begin at the farm, and he couldn't wait to see how everything worked.

* * *

The following morning, Callum rose early, wanting to get to the farm at a decent time so as not to miss out on anything. He collected his sister on the way there and listened to her nervously chatting one minute then being excited the next about what her day would hold.

'They said they'd look out for me,' she said, holding her bag on her knee which, Callum assumed, must contain her scissors, brushes and whatever else she used for clients' hair. 'I hope I know how to do what they expect me to. I'd hate to embarrass myself by doing things wrong.'

He glanced at her and shook his head. 'Erin, you've run your own salon for five years now and I bet a lot of your regular clients only come to you because you know how to make the best of their hair. You'll be fine, I promise you.'

She groaned. 'I do hope you're right, Callum.'

'I am. Trust me, for once.'

She laughed. 'Fine, I will.'

He hoped his sister's time working on set did go as well as he insisted it would. Erin worked hard and was very talented, or so he kept hearing from other people. He was proud of his sister and suspected that this work for the television series could lead to more interesting opportunities.

It would be fascinating to see Riley in action, he supposed, as the car took them closer to Hollyhock Farm. Riley might be a well-known actor but Callum couldn't recall ever seeing him in anything. Then again, he didn't really watch much television and hadn't been to the cinema for a few years. The only time he had recently watched anything was if he was going to interview an actor for his show. He mostly preferred reading novels or listening to music and wondered if he had missed out on much by not bothering with many films, but doubted it.

He was sure today was going to be interesting and looked forward to seeing what all the fuss was about. He parked behind the large barn where Lettie always sent people's vehicles when there was a large party. He heard someone instructing people to try the scene with several differences.

'I guess we go this way,' he said over his shoulder to Erin as he pressed his fob and locked the car.

They walked silently along the pathway between the two barns. Callum was anxious that he wouldn't get in the way of anyone trying to work. They reached the end of the path and stood side by side, taking in the scene in front of them. He noticed a trailer with 'Hair and Make-up' on the door.

'I imagine that's where you need to be.'

Erin grimaced. 'It is.' She exhaled sharply. 'Right, here goes nothing. Don't leave without coming to find me in case I need a lift home.'

'I won't. Have a good day. And Erin?'

She turned to him. 'Yes?'

'You'll be brilliant. Try to relax and enjoy every moment.'

She smiled and he was glad to have said the right thing.

'I will. You too.'

He watched her enter the trailer then stood watching a scene being filmed on the other side of the yard. He looked around hoping to spot Tasha but couldn't see her anywhere, so decided to stand out of the way and keep observing.

After watching Riley in a scene, Callum decided that whatever he thought of Riley as a man he couldn't fault his acting skills. He might seem like a spoilt brat on occasion, but Callum had seen Riley go from being angry in a previous scene to seeming close to tears having apprehended a woman for accidentally killing a friend in this one. His emotional range was impressive, and Callum decided that despite his initial misgivings about having another detective television series being filmed on the island that maybe he would actually sit and watch *Sam Thorne Investigates*.

After almost an hour, someone tapped him on the shoulder. He turned, delighted to see Tasha smiling at him.

'Having fun?' she asked quietly.

'It's certainly different to anything I've watched before.' He wasn't sure whether to add something that had occurred to him or not.

'What is it?' She laughed. 'I can tell there's something on your mind.'

'Just that they seem to take a long time doing the same thing over and over again.'

She rolled her eyes. 'They don't usually do that when filming something like this. There might be a few takes, but with so much to get through most actors know their characters quite well, especially this far into filming.'

'So what's different this time?'

She lowered her voice further. 'Riley is struggling a bit, despite us repeatedly going over his lines yesterday.'

'Maybe something is worrying him.' He looked over at the actor wagging his finger in front of some poor young chap's face. 'He doesn't appear to be very happy right now.'

She stared at Riley for a moment. 'Hmm, you're right. I'd better get over there and see what's wrong. We don't have time for one of his tantrums.' She went to walk off, then stopped. 'I meant to say I've seen Erin. She seems happy, thankfully. It was good of her to step in at the last minute.'

Callum nodded. 'I think she was delighted to be able to help.'

'Still, it was kind of her and I, for one, am very grateful.' He saw Tasha look in Riley's direction. 'I wonder if knowing Erin's on set might encourage Riley to behave a little better. I know he wants to impress her.'

'If he does then she won't think much of him berating that bloke over there.'

'Good point. I'll go over there now and let it slip to Riley that I've seen Erin and hope that cheers him up a bit.'

'Good luck.'

31

TASHA

Tasha could tell by the expression on Riley's face and his waving hands as he leant close to the production assistant that he was giving him a difficult time. Furious, she walked over to him, determined to take his attention from the poor man who was the focus of Riley's latest rant.

'Hi, sorry to interrupt,' she said, smiling at the man who appeared to be clenching his teeth. She didn't blame him for being annoyed; Riley's behaviour was unacceptable.

He looked at her and his jaw relaxed slightly. 'That's fine, Tasha,' he said. 'We were about done here anyway.' He looked at Riley. 'Weren't we?'

'Well, actually...'

Tasha sensed it wouldn't take much for the man to lose his temper with Riley. She wouldn't blame him either but knew they could not afford any further delays if filming was to be completed by the end of the week.

'What did you do that for?' Riley waved after the assistant as the man marched off.

Tasha kept her voice low, reminding herself she was

speaking to her boss, however much she might wish to lose her temper with him at that moment. 'I thought you might want to know something sooner rather than later, that's all.'

Riley finally focused on Tasha. 'What is it?'

Now she had his attention she hoped Riley would forget all about whatever the poor assistant might have done to irritate him.

'It's about Erin Preston.'

'Erin? Nothing else has happened, has it?'

She presumed he might be concerned that Dale had been up to his old tricks again. Or maybe Brooke.

'She's fine. I only thought you might want to know she's here.'

His interest piqued, he leant forward. 'What, now?'

Tasha nodded. 'Yes. She was asked to step in and cover for the hairdresser.'

Riley immediately began to walk in the direction of the trailers, so Tasha rushed after him.

'Hey, you can't go and see her now.'

He stopped and turned to her, scowling. 'Why ever not?'

'Because she'll be working.' Realising that wouldn't deter him, she added, 'And you're needed on set.'

'They can wait for a few more minutes.'

Tasha kept up with him, wondering what other reason she could use to get him back in place for the next scene.

They reached the steps to the trailer and Riley turned to her. 'Why are you still following me?'

'I don't want you to forget the time and delay the next scene.'

He sighed loudly. 'Tasha, you're a brilliant assistant. The best, in fact. But I don't need you micromanaging me. Now, go and find something else to do. I promise I'll only be a few minutes.' He gave her his brightest, most photographed smile. 'I only want to say a quick hello to her.'

Aware that doing what Riley asked was what she was paid to do, Tasha stepped back. 'All right. I'll wait for you over there with the others.'

Tasha went to return to where the other actors in the scene were waiting to start filming again and spotted Callum speaking to one of the producers. She wasn't close enough to hear what they were discussing, but Callum seemed to be interested in whatever it was. Unsure whether to go over to speak to him, she decided to wait until they had finished their discussion.

'Hey, Tasha.' Callum waved at her as the chap walked away. Both were smiling and she wondered why.

'You look happy.'

He tilted his head from side to side as if unsure. 'It's probably surprise and a bit of shock rather than happy.'

Unsure what he meant, Tasha waited for him to continue. When he didn't she decided to find out for herself. 'Is there a reason, or would you rather not say?'

Callum spotted someone behind her and smiled. 'Hi there.'

She turned to see who it was and saw Lettie walking with Brodie whom she had met on the first day of shooting. He was carrying the baby. 'I hope they're not too disturbed by everyone here today.'

'I'm sure they'd say if they weren't happy.' He smiled. 'Lettie will always put her animals' welfare before anything else; don't worry about that.'

'Good. I'd hate her to be concerned and keep it to herself.'

Lettie walked over to Callum and kissed him on both cheeks. 'This is very exciting, isn't it?'

Tasha calmed slightly as Callum gave her a I-told-you-so smile. 'I'm glad you're happy.'

Brodie grinned. 'We're fascinated by the whole thing. Lettie and I were out here a couple of hours ago when everyone started arriving.'

Callum pulled a face at the baby, making her giggle.

'You two should come to the farmhouse for lunch, if you'd like.'

'I'd love that, thank you,' Tasha said, happy to be able to take time away from everyone else for a bit.

'That's kind of you.' Callum smiled. 'Erin is here too, so is it OK if I bring her with me?'

Brodie rolled his eyes. 'Of course.'

'Oh, wow. So they did call Erin in to help with the hair?' Lettie said, looking delighted. 'I'm so pleased. When Callum asked me to put her name forward just in case they needed someone urgently I didn't actually expect it to happen.'

'It was kind of you to do that for me. She's always wondered what it would be like to work on a set and now she'll get the opportunity to find out.'

Tasha saw something cross Callum's face and wasn't sure whether it was amusement or something else. 'What is it?'

'He's got a secret,' Lettie whispered.

Brodie slipped an arm around Lettie's shoulders. 'Leave the poor man alone.'

Callum laughed. 'It's not a secret; I just haven't mentioned it to you yet.'

Intrigued, Tasha waited for him to continue. When he didn't do so immediately she couldn't stop from asking him about it. 'Well, are you going to tell us then?'

He raised his hands. 'You already know, Tasha, because it was you who put me forward for it.'

'What?' Lettie asked impatiently.

'I'm going to be in a couple of scenes later today.'

Lettie's mouth dropped open briefly. She nudged Brodie. 'Did you know about this?'

'Not until now.'

Callum pulled a face. 'You don't have to sound so shocked.'

Lettie gave a knowing nod. 'It's because of his modelling, isn't it, Tasha? That's why you thought of him.'

'It helped that he's done shoots before and I could find a couple of adverts online to show to the producer.' She stared at Callum not minding being teased by his friends. Her stomach flipped as she studied him, so handsome in a sun-kissed sporty kind of way, unlike Riley's more cheeky, boyish looks. It dawned on Tasha how unlike Riley Callum was who, despite his modelling in the past, didn't act as if he was anything special. He was just a good, kind person who was fun to be around and just happened to be utterly gorgeous.

Lettie spotted someone she wanted to speak to. 'Come along, Brodie, let's go and see how they're getting along over there.' She looked at Tasha and Callum. 'Come to the house whenever you're hungry.'

Tasha saw Callum's anxious frown. 'Maybe after Callum has finished his scenes?'

'Yes, that would be good,' he agreed.

She thanked them and waited for Lettie and Brodie to leave before turning back to Callum. 'I think they were trying to be subtle then.'

'They were.' He stared at her for a moment.

'Go on then, tell me more.'

He sighed. 'This is going to be very different to my modelling,' he said, frowning. 'Anyway I only really did those to help pay for my uni fees.'

'You haven't done anything since then?'

'A couple of shoots, but nothing much.'

She could tell he was almost embarrassed to talk about it. She spotted Riley coming out of the hair and make-up trailer. 'So much for him only being a couple of minutes chatting to Erin.'

'Ah, so that's where he was. I did wonder.'

Tasha could see Callum wasn't too happy to discover Riley had been in contact with his sister again. 'He only wanted to say a quick hello.'

Callum looked at her and raised an eyebrow. 'That was rather a long hello, though, don't you think?'

She shrugged, aware he was right. 'Unfortunately, there's not much I can do about what Riley chooses to do.'

'I know,' Callum said, taking her hand in his. 'Sorry. That guy bothers me. I know he's your boss, but I wish he'd find someone else to focus his attention on other than my sister.'

Tasha knew she would feel the same way if it were her sister on the receiving end of Riley's interest. 'Thankfully, he'll be working for most of the rest of the day. I doubt he'll have much time at all to speak to her again.'

'He'll be spending some of that time in a scene with me, as far as I can gather.'

'I can't wait to watch you being filmed.'

He frowned. 'Don't expect too much of me, will you?'

She laughed. 'You'll be fine. I just know it.'

32

CALLUM

Callum followed the woman who had come to take him to the make-up person and hoped he would find Erin there to see a familiar face and also check how she was doing. He was relieved he only had to pretend to speak to one of the women in the cast and then be in another scene where Riley was to act becoming angry with him.

Callum was led into the trailer and saw his sister hard at work, curling one of the actress's hair and chatting to her, and judging by the glint in his sister's eyes Callum could tell she was very happy to be working there.

She spotted him and smiled. 'That's my brother.'

The actress sat up a little straighter as Callum passed behind her chair. He sat down on the one next to her.

'Are you one of the actors?' the woman he vaguely recognised asked.

Callum shook his head. 'I'm in the show, but only have a tiny part.'

Erin gasped. 'That's so exciting though.'

He thought so too but didn't like to show too much enthusiasm, especially not in front of one of the professional actors. 'It's only two small scenes and I barely say anything in those.'

'Still a fun experience though.' The actress turned her head to address him. 'I wonder if you'll be in any of my scenes?'

'I've no idea.' He spotted Erin pressing her lips together, trying to hide her amusement and couldn't think what she found funny about the exchange.

The door opened but before he had a chance to look and see who had just entered the room, he felt the actress's fingers curl around his own.

'I'm Beth, by the way.' He was taken aback by the sudden depth in her voice.

'Tasha!'

Hearing Erin call out Tasha's name, Callum immediately turned to look at the doorway. He went to smile but just caught her eyes snapping back from where they had been focused on Beth and his hands clasped together. Not wishing Tasha to get the wrong idea, he gently withdrew his hand from Beth's, surprised when she tightened her grasp.

'How are things going?' he asked Tasha, wishing he could think of something more insightful to say but needing to show her he was pleased to see her.

'As well as can be expected.'

Callum started to rise to walk over to Tasha. Erin pressed her hand on his shoulder. 'No, you don't. I need to change your hair slightly before you go anywhere. It's too messy how you usually wear it.'

'But I'll come back,' he argued.

Erin's hand remained where it was. Aware he had little choice but to do as his sister told him, he turned his gaze back to Tasha. 'Where shall I find you?'

She shrugged one shoulder. 'I'll be out there somewhere.'

Her expression softened and he wondered if it was because she could tell he was worried about her reaction. 'I'll look out for you.' She smiled at Beth. 'Morning, Beth.'

'Tasha.'

By the sound of their polite but cool reaction to each other, Callum surmised that the women didn't think much of each other. Deciding it probably wasn't wise to ask Tasha about Beth, he pushed the thought away.

'I just came by to say hi to Erin.' Tasha kissed his sister on her cheek. 'It's good to have you working here. How are you enjoying it?'

'I'm really enjoying it so far.' She cocked her head in Callum's direction. 'And as long as this one doesn't let the side down in any way, I'm sure I'll continue to do so.'

He was used to his sister making him the butt of her jokes. 'I'll do my best not to mess things up.'

'I'm sure you'll be brilliant,' Beth said, stroking his forearm and getting a pitying look from Tasha.

'I'm sure he will be,' Tasha said eventually.

Tasha left and Callum was relieved when Beth was called for shortly afterwards.

As soon as the door closed behind her, Erin stood behind him and laughed at him in the mirror. 'Do you often get that sort of reaction from women?'

He sighed. 'No, thankfully.' He puffed out his cheeks. 'For the first time ever, I'm beginning to feel a bit sorry for Riley. I imagine he gets that sort of thing a lot.'

At the mention of the actor's name, Erin's amusement vanished.

'Is everything all right between you and him? I thought he came to speak to you earlier but assumed you didn't mind.'

She shrugged and began tidying his hair. 'He's fine.' She

frowned. 'I think he's trying to impress me, but I'm just not used to his way of life. Not impressed by it either.' Her lips drew back in a smile and she leant slightly forward, keeping her voice low. 'I do like him though. Is that mad, do you think?'

Not wishing to hurt his sister, but wanting to answer her question honestly, Callum thought about his answer before replying. 'Tasha hasn't said much about him but she did say that although he could be a bit infuriating, he was also a decent chap. Neither of us know him very well, so it's difficult to say how he does behave in relationships, but I think it's clear that he does like you and, whether I like him or not, he did seem very upset about the whole Dale and Brooke thing.'

'He did. I also think he likes me.' She carried on brushing and styling his hair. 'I just don't know how serious he is about me.'

'I see.' He wasn't sure that he did fully. 'Are you concerned that it might be a short-term fling he's after?'

She nodded. 'I'm not really into that sort of thing, but how will I know where it will lead if I do start seeing him if I don't even give him a chance?'

She had a point. He pushed his hair back from his face. 'I look odd with it down like that.'

Erin laughed. 'You did a bit.' She put her comb onto the worktop. 'So, what do you think I should do?'

He tried to work out whether she actually wanted an answer from him, or if she was simply hoping Callum would come up with the answer she was hoping for. He had no intention of getting caught up in that trap again, having learnt his lesson years before when he had stupidly admitted what he really thought about Erin's first serious boyfriend. She hadn't spoken to him for weeks after that debacle.

'I think you're sensible enough to decide what to do for the best without my help.'

She pushed his shoulder. 'That's no help at all.'

'Listen to your instincts, Erin. That's what I do.'

She laughed. 'And how has that worked for you so far?'

He narrowed his eyes at her in the mirror. 'Just finish what you're doing and let me get out of here, will you?'

Satisfied with his hair, a make-up artist then dabbed a bit of powder onto his face. 'To take away the shine,' she said when he grimaced. 'There,' she said, patting him on both shoulders. 'That's all you need.'

'That's a relief.' He got up out of the chair before she could change her mind and decide to start fussing over his face or hair again.

He walked over to the door and reached out to open it, when someone pulled it open from the outside. Callum stepped back to give the person room to enter and saw Riley.

'You're still here,' Riley said bluntly. 'I can come back.'

'It's fine,' Erin said, coming over to stand next to Callum. 'My brother was just leaving.'

Callum left them together, smiling to himself when he heard Riley ask Erin if she wanted to join him for lunch.

33

TASHA

Tasha ended her call to Dale assuring him Riley was behaving for the most part when she spotted Callum descending the stairs from the trailer. She wondered whether he had noticed her annoyance seeing him holding hands with Beth. She hadn't thought Callum was the sort of man to mess a woman around, but what did she know? If she was truly honest with herself, Tasha knew her insight into men's characters and behaviours were very limited. Serves her right, she supposed, for putting so much emphasis on her career rather than her personal life.

It was so long since she'd had a significant other that she barely remembered what it felt like to have to consider another person in your daily plans. Or, she realised, to spend evenings and holidays with someone else. She smiled to herself as it dawned on her that it was probably close to six years since she had taken any time for a holiday.

'How's it going?'

She had been so busy daydreaming that she hadn't noticed Callum walk up to her. 'Fine, I think. Did I see Riley going to the trailer a short while ago?'

Callum nodded. 'As I was leaving I heard him ask Erin to join him for lunch.'

'They should be ready for your first scene soon, but we can then go and meet up with Lettie and Brodie for something to eat.'

He grinned at her. 'I'm looking forward to that.'

Tasha studied his face. 'You look different with your hair swept to the side like that.'

He didn't seem happy about it. 'I'd never choose to wear it this way.'

'I think it suits you in a kind of...' She struggled to think of the right way to describe what she meant.

'Preppy sort of way?'

Tasha threw her head back and laughed.

The sound was so infectious Callum found himself joining in and laughing too. 'Hey,' he said, pretending to be offended. 'It wasn't that amusing.'

She wiped her eyes with the backs of her fingers. 'It was though.' She took her hanky from her pocket and blew her nose. 'Sorry. That really tickled me.'

'Why?' he asked, still amused but confused.

'All you need is a cable-knit cream sweater over your shoulders and a smart pair of chinos.'

He waved her away. 'Rude. That's what you are.'

She shook her head, still laughing. 'Sorry.'

'It's fine,' he assured her. 'I'm teasing.'

'Anyway,' she said, finally gaining control of her laughter. 'I didn't say you weren't hot, looking like you do.'

His smile vanished and he stared at her, a stunned expression on his face.

Tasha's stomach clenched when she realised she had voiced her thoughts. She cringed. 'Er, I didn't intend saying that out loud.'

His face softened. 'Don't be sorry. I'm not offended.' He turned his palms upwards and shrugged. 'I might not choose to dress this way but I'm happy to hear you approve.'

'Callum Preston?' One of the runners hurried over to join them. He gave Tasha an apologetic look. 'Sorry to interrupt, but they need Mr Preston now for his scene.'

'I'm on my way.'

He gave Tasha a knowing look, clearly aware she was relieved someone had turned up just at that moment to save her any more embarrassment.

She watched him walk away, mortified by what she had said. He was hot though, she mused, reminding herself immediately afterwards that whatever he was, she never would have meant to announce it to him in the way that she had done.

'Urgh.'

'Something the matter?' Riley asked as he appeared from the trailer looking very pleased with himself.

She was relieved to have work to focus on again so that she didn't keep playing what she had just done over and over in her head. 'It's fine. You OK though?'

'I am.' He heard his name being called and turned to respond. 'I see your friend is ready to do his first scene.'

'He is,' Tasha said. 'It's not something he's used to, so please be gentle with him.'

Riley raised an eyebrow. 'I'll do my best not to trip him up or anything.'

Aware Riley was joking but also that he could just as easily do exactly what he had said, Tasha walked with him to join the others. 'Whatever you do, just remember, if you want to impress Erin Preston, then upsetting her brother or making a fool of him is the very last thing you should do.'

Riley's step faltered. 'Yes, that's a good point. Fine. I'll be kind to the guy.'

'I'll wait for you over here.' Tasha found a sheltered place next to the barn wall out of the sunshine. It was hotter today than she had expected. In more ways than one.

34

CALLUM

The director indicated where Callum should stand for his brief scene and explained what he needed to do. As he waited for Riley to check a couple of his lines, he wished he had come up with a reason not to take part in the filming. It was one thing standing still and holding a pose while you were photographed by a professional in a studio, but another entirely when you were filmed supposedly being someone else. Not that he had much to say, only a few words.

Riley walked up to him with a slight frown on his face, which appeared to vanish as soon as he spotted Callum looking at him. He then shot Callum a brilliant smile that seemed to light up his face. Riley's demeanour also changed and as he joined Callum, he gave him a friendly pat on the back.

'Good to see you again. I hope you enjoy filming here today. We'll do our best to make it a memorable experience.'

'Er, thank you. That's very kind of you,' Callum said. He saw the team nearby raising eyebrows and seeming happy with the exchange and supposed that if he didn't know the pair of them he would assume they were very good friends.

'Are we ready to roll?'

Callum reminded himself of his lines and prepared for their scene to begin.

Riley's eyes narrowed as he leant in closer to Callum. 'What the hell are you doing here? Have you been following me?'

Callum did his best to look affronted. 'Why would I do that?'

'You're here, aren't you?' Riley came across as malicious, and Callum had to focus on his next line rather than showing how impressed he was at the man's sudden change in action for his part.

Callum pushed Riley's hands away from him and scowled, as he had been shown. 'Can't a guy go for a drink without it having to mean something?'

Riley moved back slightly, his demeanour menacing. 'Just keep away from me, do you hear?'

'I'll be happy to.'

He caught movement at the side of his vision and when Riley next spoke, he briefly looked over and saw his sister smiling proudly at him.

Callum focused on waiting to respond to Riley's comment and watched as Riley continued to morph further from his real personality into the darker, menacing character he was playing.

The experience of working with Riley only went to reaffirm his suspicions that Riley wasn't the sort of guy he imagined would suit his sister as a partner. Did the man manipulate most scenarios to his advantage? Callum suspected that he might just do that. He was certainly used to getting his own way.

Callum thought of Erin and how strong and independent she was and felt a bit better. He doubted Riley would get his own way with her all that often. The thought made him smile.

'Cut!'

Surprised by the sound of the director's voice, Callum

realised he had been lost in thought and inadvertently forgotten to keep his expression serious.

'Callum, this is a serious scene. One that's supposed to make the audience feel anxious for your character being threatened by Riley's. You smiling won't help us achieve that.'

'Sorry, I don't know why I did that.' Callum didn't like to admit he had lost concentration and tried not to show his discomfort at messing up the scene.

'Please try to concentrate this time.'

Callum nodded. 'Of course.' He spotted Riley give a discreet eye-roll to the director as if to say, *This is what happens when you bring in someone who doesn't know what they're doing.*

Riley seemed to sense Callum watching him and shot him a glance, raising his eyebrows and smiling. 'Could happen to anyone, mate.'

'That's good to know.' Callum knew Riley was only trying to appear friendly because Callum had caught his exchange with the director, but was looking forward to finishing his part in the episode, so let Riley think he hadn't seen anything.

'Right, let's do this one more time.'

It wasn't a question; that much Callum did know. He took a deep breath and prepared to try again.

35

TASHA

Tasha's irritation with Riley rose sharply when she saw him being sarcastic about Callum's mistake. Why couldn't he just allow someone else to do well for once? Typical Riley always having to be the hero! She knew he would have enjoyed Callum feeling embarrassed in front of everyone about making a blunder. She watched the scene play out, mouthing Callum's words as he said them, glad she was standing out of his sight line so he didn't notice her doing it.

At the end of the scene, she realised her shoulders were so high with tension they almost met her ears, and she had to consciously lower them and relax.

'Poor Callum.'

Surprised to hear Erin's voice coming from just behind her left shoulder, Tasha turned to her. 'Sorry, I didn't see you there.' She stepped to the side to give Erin space to stand next to her.

Erin moved slightly forward. 'I didn't like to speak in case I interrupted the filming but I thought Callum did very well, didn't you?'

'I did,' she agreed, looking in his direction.

Erin returned to the hair and make-up trailer.

Callum noticed Tasha when they were done and walked over to her, looking forlorn.

'Did you see what I did?'

She could tell he felt badly about what had happened and rested a hand on his forearm. 'You did very well.'

He gave a sarcastic laugh. 'I messed up, but it was my own fault for not focusing on what I was doing.'

Tasha had the sudden urge to find out what had amused him. 'Why did you smile?'

He smiled again before answering, intriguing her further. 'I was thinking Riley has a lot to learn if he thinks he can boss Erin around and get away with it.'

Amused to picture Callum's beautiful sister with someone so used to charming people in order to get his own way and it not working for once, Tasha laughed. 'It will do him the world of good to spend time with someone like her then.'

'I agree.' Callum shrugged. 'I suppose he's not all that bad but he can be rather arrogant at times.'

'Now you are being charitable.' She looked over at her boss, who was preparing to shoot the next scene. 'I suppose we'll just have to wait and see.' She flicked a fly from his shoulder. 'I'm starving. Shall we go to the farmhouse and find Lettie and Brodie for a bit of lunch while there's still time?'

'I thought you'd never ask,' he said.

She smiled as Callum linked his arm through hers. 'I hope they've prepared for two hungry people to descend on them.'

'They will have done. There's one thing you can be sure of when you visit Hollyhock Farm and that is there is always an abundance of tasty food. Lindy, that's Lettie's mum, is a great cook and baker. She prides herself on always having fresh cakes in tins in the pantry and there's always pre-prepared food in the fridge that can be heated up.'

'She sounds amazing,' Tasha said honestly. Her stomach rumbled noisily.

Callum laughed. 'I think you're even hungrier than me right now.'

She pulled him to hurry him to the house, enjoying their time together again. 'Hurry up then, before someone else gets there and eats our share.'

Callum broke into a jog with her. 'Careful, you don't want my make-up to run.'

She burst out laughing. 'I don't think you have enough on for that to happen, or that you're hot enough.'

He slowed to a walk, pulling her to stop with him. 'Hey, are you trying to tell me you don't find me attractive?'

Seeing the mischievous twinkle in his gorgeous eyes, she shook her head. 'If you're hoping to force me into telling you I think you're hot again, you're going to be disappointed.'

He sighed heavily. 'Fine. Then I suppose we may as well get to that kitchen and eat. I need something to cheer me up.'

'That's rubbish.' She walked with him, enjoying the banter and wishing she had the courage to not only tell him how much she was attracted to him but also to grab hold of him and kiss him and show him how hot she really thought he was.

They were a few steps away from the kitchen door when it opened, making them both skid to a halt in surprise.

Lettie looked from one to the other of them, grinning. 'Sorry, I didn't mean to catch you off guard. I was watching from the window and saw the pair of you coming this way, so thought I'd welcome you.'

She stepped back and waved for them to enter the cool hallway. 'Your lunch is ready. Please go on through to the kitchen.'

'First on the left,' Callum whispered when Tasha hesitated to walk forward.

She stopped at the kitchen doorway and gasped at the sight of the huge pine table laden with various dishes: green salads, pasta salads and something that looked like a large bowl of Coronation chicken. There was a baguette, with a butter dish full of rich yellow Jersey butter.

'Wow, this looks amazing,' Tasha said.

'I'm glad you think so.' Lettie motioned for them to take a seat. 'Please, help yourselves and tuck in. Brodie will be here any minute and he will be ready to eat quite a bit.'

'Thank you for all this,' Callum said.

'I love doing it, as you well know.' She pushed two of the salads closer to them. 'Now, what do you both fancy to drink?'

Tasha went to respond but before she could someone called out to them from the hallway.

'Hello there. I'm looking for Tasha.'

She looked at Callum, trying hard to remain calm. Did Riley not consider this was her lunchtime too?

Lettie went to stand but sat again when Brodie passed the open kitchen door and went to speak to their guest.

'I hadn't expected to see Brodie back here so soon.'

Callum leant closer to Tasha. 'What does Riley want, I wonder?'

'For me to do something for him, no doubt.' She rolled her eyes.

They heard footsteps and Brodie said, 'They're through this way.' He mouthed an apology to Tasha as he entered the room ahead of Riley.

'There you are,' Riley said in his most charming voice. He gave an apologetic smile to each of them. 'I hate to interrupt your lunch, but I was hoping to ask Tasha for her help.'

Not wishing for Lettie, Brodie and Callum's lunches to be interrupted further, Tasha stood. 'I'll come with you now, Riley.' She turned to Lettie. 'I'm so sorry to leave without tasting any of this delicious-looking food.'

Lettie shrugged and shook her head. 'Don't worry about it.' She went to stand. 'If you can wait a moment I'll put something into a Tupperware for you.'

Before she could answer, Riley responded. 'No. Please don't do that.' He gave Lettie an appealing smile.

How typical of Riley to assume Lettie was referring to him, Tasha thought, amused.

Riley turned to her and pulled out her chair. 'Please don't worry, Tasha. I only came here to let you know I'll be finding something for Erin and I to eat from the canteen, so there's no need to worry about me.'

Tasha was taken aback by him being uncharacteristically thoughtful, then it dawned on her that he was clearly making a show of being considerate for Erin's benefit.

'Erin is with you?' Callum asked.

Erin appeared in the doorway and smiled, looking embarrassed at being there. 'Please, take no notice of me. I'm only here with Riley because he was hoping to find Tasha.'

Lettie stood and pointed at the food on the table. 'There's more than enough for everyone to eat. Why don't the pair of you take a seat and join us?' She beamed at them. 'I'd be fascinated to hear all about the filming, if you don't mind sharing, Riley.'

Tasha had to control herself from showing her amusement and wondered if Lettie had sensed how much Riley enjoyed being with people when he was the centre of attention. He loved talking about his favourite subject: himself. He took Erin's hand and led her to the other side of the table, pulling out a chair for her to sit on before taking a seat next to her.

'And it will be lovely to get to know you a bit more, Erin,' Lettie said. She turned to Tasha and Riley. 'Callum is my brother Zak's best friend, so Erin and I have met each other quite a few times over the years, but never really spent much time chatting.'

'That's right,' Erin agreed. She laughed. 'And when we do it's usually about our brothers and what they're doing. Zak is a sound engineer for bands and is away on tour, isn't he?'

Lettie nodded. 'He is. I believe he's in Germany at the moment.'

'That's right,' Callum said. 'He was looking forward to it.'

'Brodie, will you bring a couple more plates and cutlery for our new guests, please?' Lettie asked.

He gave her a knowing wink and did as she asked.

Tasha watched the scene play out in front of her as Riley immediately began talking about his career and the morning's work. If she did have to spend her lunchtime with Riley, she supposed that at least she was also doing it with Callum, and eating her new friends' delicious offerings.

She lowered her hands to her lap and felt Callum gently take hold of her hand nearest to him. He gave it a gentle squeeze and looked at her.

'You OK?' he whispered.

She nodded. 'I am.'

36

CALLUM

He let go of Tasha's hand so she could eat her food. How kind, yet how typical of Lettie to read the situation and immediately invite Riley and Erin to join them. She was a natural host and he supposed it was probably helped by growing up with a mother like Lindy who always had enough food to cater for any unexpected guests.

Callum smiled at his sister and swapped amused glances with her. She seemed happy and he wondered whether it was because her morning had gone so well, or because she was enjoying spending time with Riley. Riley's eyes kept returning to Erin and resting on her face for a few seconds before he seemed to remember he was in the middle of talking about himself.

Callum enjoyed seeing his sister happy but wished it could have been with someone other than this actor who was so very satisfied with himself. He wondered if older siblings always had a sense they should look out for their younger brothers or sister. Probably, he decided.

'Have you enjoyed filming this series, Riley?' Brodie asked before eating another forkful of pasta.

'I've enjoyed being on this beautiful island,' Riley answered, shooting a bright smile at Erin. He raised his eyebrows at Tasha, who Callum felt tense next to him.

As if Riley sensed Tasha's tension, he turned his attention to her. 'I couldn't do any of this without Tasha's help.' He smiled at her.

'It's my job.'

'And you do it very well, if I may say.'

'Thank you,' Tasha said, sounding grateful, but Callum didn't miss the undertone of irritation in her voice.

Lettie took a sip of water from her glass and set it back down on the table. 'Well, we've loved having the crew here and watching you all filming. It's a new experience for all of us, isn't it, Brodie?'

'It is,' he agreed. 'And thankfully the animals don't seem fazed by any of it.'

Riley seemed delighted. 'Thank you. I'm glad it's all going well and that you, or the animals, haven't been too bothered by us being here.'

Callum began eating his food until he realised Riley was talking to him. 'Sorry, I didn't catch what you said.'

'I was asking how you enjoyed your part this morning.'

Callum decided not to dwell on his mistake. 'I enjoyed it, as a matter of fact. I wasn't as nervous as I'd expected.'

Riley nodded. He seemed to be waiting to say whatever was on his mind. He grinned. 'Tell me, what were you thinking about when you smiled and we needed to go for another take?'

Callum wasn't surprised Riley wanted to draw attention to his mess-up. He had no intention of admitting his real thoughts to Riley though.

'I'm not really sure I was thinking of anything,' he said

vaguely. 'I suppose I had a momentary lapse of concentration – probably thinking how much I was enjoying myself.'

'Hmm.' Riley didn't seem convinced.

'Why?' Lettie asked. 'What did you think was on Callum's mind?'

Riley frowned and rested his elbows either side of his plate and then his chin on his hands. He gazed thoughtfully at Callum before returning his attention to Lettie. 'I thought it might be because he had seen my wonderful assistant standing on the sidelines watching my scene.'

He saw Tasha's hand nearest to him clench slightly and knew she was irritated. That might be her role but they both knew she was so much more than that, being available at all times of the day or night to reassure Riley, manage his mess-ups with ex-girl-friends, apologise to people on his behalf when he had offended someone and keep an eye on what he posted on social media when he had drunk too much.

'No, it wasn't that,' Callum argued.

Riley tilted his head slightly and narrowed his eyes, smiling. 'I saw you looking in her direction though.'

Callum purposely hesitated, wanting Riley to feel uncom-fortable for pushing the subject. 'My sister was also standing there.' He smiled at Erin. 'Weren't you?'

'That's right.' She blushed at the admission and immediately Riley's attention was diverted to her.

It was a relief, although Callum wondered how long his sister and Riley would stay interested in each other. How was she going to feel when filming finished and he left the island? Would Riley ask his sister to visit him? Whatever happened, he was sorry that when Riley left, Tasha would be going with him.

With lunch over, Callum thanked Lettie and Brodie for their hospitality and followed Riley and Erin with Tasha back to prepare for his last scene. Erin and Riley made their way to the hair and make-up trailer while Tasha took a call.

As Callum walked back to join the crew, he thought how it had been interesting to take part in the series in such a small way. He had not really wanted to do it, but now knew he would probably look back and be glad that he had.

'Ah, there you are.'

Callum saw the director walking over to him and felt a sense of unease. 'We were at lunch. I hope we haven't kept anyone waiting.'

The man shook his head. 'Not at all. I was coming over to ask you if you would agree to be in some stills for advertising the show.'

Callum didn't see why. 'I'm surprised you're asking me.'

'Why?'

'I've only got a tiny part.' He shrugged. 'I clearly don't know a thing about how all this works but, thinking of promotional photos from television shows I've watched, I've always assumed it's the main cast who would be used for this sort of thing.'

The director lowered his voice. 'I like the contrast between both your looks. You come across as the boy next door, whereas Riley has something darker about him. You're also from here and we need the locals to take the new series to their hearts and help spread the word on their social media platforms. I think both those things will work well and help entice as many viewers to watch as possible.'

Callum still didn't like to imagine Riley's reaction to this news.

'Well, what do you say? You can have time to think about it, of course. Not long though. Say, an hour?'

Callum laughed. 'Boy next door? I've never been called that before.'

An assistant standing near the director said, 'Boy next door who would make a perfect Tom Ford model.' She gave a flirtatious laugh before walking off.

'So, what do you think? Will you consider it? You'll be paid, of course.'

Callum wasn't fazed about being paid, but wasn't sure whether he could be bothered with Riley's reaction. He might not know the man all that well, but he knew enough about Riley's arrogance to suspect he would not be impressed about having someone with barely any lines standing in the same shot as him for promotional photos.

'Say yes,' Tasha said from somewhere behind his right shoulder.

He turned to her and laughed. 'Where did you spring from?'

'I was coming to chat to you and was intrigued to see the pair of you here.' She smiled at the director. 'Sorry to interrupt your conversation with Callum, Mike.'

He shook his head. 'Don't apologise, Tasha. If you manage to persuade him, then I'll be very happy.'

Deciding he needed to broach what was concerning him, Callum checked that Riley wasn't anywhere nearby before doing so. 'I'm not sure Riley will like the idea.'

The director didn't seem at all bothered. 'And?'

'He's your star. I'm not even an actor. You've already had to redo several scenes and I would hate for anything I do to cause further issues.'

Mike put a hand on Callum's shoulder. 'He might be the main character in the show, but that doesn't make him the one in charge. Not that Riley seems to remember that too often. We all know he's the reason some of the cast and crew needed to stay for filming. As far as I'm concerned he's lucky we had already recorded the vast majority of the series, otherwise we would have fired him and replaced him with another actor.' He frowned and leant slightly closer to them. 'And that latest drama with him being photographed with someone other than his girl-friend really isn't the sort of coverage we need to promote our show. I don't think it'll do him any harm to feel slightly threat-ened by having another good-looking man in the photos. If you don't have a problem being that person, that is?'

'It's true,' Tasha said quietly, glancing over her shoulder, probably to check Riley wasn't anyway nearby. 'And if there's to be another series, then there's a lot riding on this being launched to as many people as possible.'

Callum was shocked to hear them talking so openly.

He focused on the point the guy was making. 'But I thought a second series had already been commissioned?'

Mike groaned. 'Not yet, but we're all hoping it happens. Whether we like it or not, Riley has a big audience and most people believe he's the fun, charming chap he likes to portray.' He glanced at Tasha who was nodding and didn't seem at all bothered to hear her boss talked about in this way.

'So, will you agree to do the photos?' Mike asked, a hopeful tone in his voice.

Callum wasn't sure what to do for the best. It wasn't as if he had a career as an actor and needed the promotion. Would it matter that much if he didn't do it? Would he regret not doing it? Or be glad that he had turned the offer down?

'Go on, do it,' Tasha urged. 'It'll be fun.'

He wondered whether the fun from her perspective would be in seeing Riley's reaction. Was she wanting Callum to do this as payback for Riley messing everyone around for the past few months? For behaving so badly that delays were caused, costing the production money and time? Hearing his sister's voice and Riley's laughter as he'd left her at the doorway to the trailer,

Callum thought of Erin and how Riley's adverse reaction might affect her.

'I'm not sure it's the right thing to do.'

'What isn't?' Riley asked, joining them.

Without thinking, Callum said, 'For me to agree to join you for the series promotion shots.'

He realised what he had done when Mike's eyes widened and Tasha cringed.

37

TASHA

Tasha took the moments following Callum's comment to brace herself for Riley's onslaught. He looked stunned and didn't react. Then, shooting her an accusatory look, as if she could do anything to stop this, he glared at Mike.

'This was your idea, I presume?' Mike went to answer, but Riley raised a finger in front of the man's face and shook his head angrily. 'No. You do not get to do this to me.'

'Riley, wait—' Mike began but Riley was having none of it.

'No. I won't have this.' Without looking in Callum's direction, Riley jerked his thumb towards him. 'He is a stand-in. For another bit-part actor.' He forced a laugh. 'Why would fans of the show want to see him? Tell me that.'

Tasha saw Mike's face redden and the muscles in his jaw working furiously. He was angrier than she had ever seen him.

'Firstly, Riley,' Mike said through clenched teeth, 'regardless of how you seem to see yourself, this is about enticing as big an audience to the series as possible.' He shot a glance at Callum who, Tasha could tell, was becoming increasingly uncomfortable with his part in the unfolding drama. 'Callum Preston, whether you like it or not, has the looks, and—' he nodded, seeming satisfied with himself for choosing him '—the presence on screen to appeal to much of our audience.'

Riley's expression darkened. 'Are you trying to insinuate that you are using him as some sort of competition?' He laughed. 'For me?'

Tasha was surprised to see that was exactly what Mike had been doing. The realisation shocked her too. 'But Mike, Callum isn't an actor. He's a DJ.' She looked at Callum, hoping he would back her up by agreeing.

'She's right,' Callum said after a brief pause.

Mike scanned the area around them. 'I think we should take this into my trailer and discuss it further in private.' Without waiting for any of them to agree, he told the crew to prepare for the next scene while he took a short break.

Tasha knew that their voices had been loud enough for everyone nearby to hear what had been said and was concerned about how this might pan out.

Riley didn't move, but stood where he was and scowled.

'Come along,' Tasha said in a gentle voice. 'We should go and hear what Mike has to say.'

Riley's eyes flashed at her, as if he was surprised to see her standing there. 'What do you mean "we"? This has nothing whatsoever to do with you.'

It was typical of Riley to take his fury out on his staff and this wasn't the first or even the twentieth time he had turned on her in this way. She might be used to him acting this way but it didn't hurt any less.

'I only thought—'

Riley spun to face her. 'Well, save yourself the bother. You're my assistant and don't forget it. You do as I ask you. What Mike wants is nothing to do with you working for me.'

Embarrassed, Tasha concentrated on not showing that she was upset about him speaking to her in such a rude, condescending way.

'That's enough,' Callum snapped, his voice low as he stepped in front of Riley. 'You do not get to disrespect Tasha in that way.'

Riley stabbed Callum in the chest with his pointed finger. 'And you don't interfere with me and my assistant.' He sneered before adding, 'You might be sleeping with my assistant, but I'm her boss and I'll speak to her as I like.'

Tasha had had enough. She gave Callum a grateful smile, thankful he wasn't rising to Riley's bait and giving in to the urge – which she could see clearly in Callum's eyes – to hit him.

'Thanks for standing up for me, Callum,' she said, taking a steadying breath in an attempt to stop her voice quivering. 'But I can speak for myself.'

'Of course.'

She waited for Callum to walk away and follow Mile to his trailer. Smarting to have been put in this situation by Riley, Tasha clenched her teeth, willing herself to remain calm. She hated to think she was about to prove her parents right when they had argued that she was being foolish expecting to find a satisfying, long-term job working as a PA to an actor, but she had insisted that following her dream was what she wanted and assured them working for Riley would be her dream job.

There was nothing for it now though. She had struggled to justify her reasons for continuing to work for Riley as his behaviour deteriorated. She had her limits though and losing her self-respect was not something she could accept, regardless of how smug her parents' reaction to her doing exactly as they had predicted might be.

She turned to Riley. 'I've had enough of your nastiness. Your complete lack of respect for me is appalling. Actually it's embarrassing, especially after all my hard work and dedication to looking after you for the past three years.'

His mouth dropped open. 'Now look here, Tasha, I only meant to—'

She shook her head dismissively. 'You know what, Riley? I simply don't care.'

'About what?'

'About you, about what you think, but most of all, about your stinking job. Today has been the final straw. I've had enough of you treating me badly. You can take this as my resignation. I'll put it in writing as soon as I get back to the apartment.'

'Now hang on a second, Tasha.' He glared at her indignantly. 'You can't do this.'

Tasha was shocked to see that Riley really believed what he was saying. 'That's where you're wrong. I can do exactly as I wish. And right now, that is to end my employment working for the rudest man I've ever met.' He went to argue, but she shook her head. 'Don't bother. Now, I think you should hurry and get to Mike's office before he's had enough of you too and fires you from the series.'

Spotting several members of the crew trying not to seem as if they were listening to every word, Tasha just wanted to get away from the farm. The humiliation of being spoken to like that in front of everyone was mortifying and she couldn't wait to escape.

The magnitude of what was happening seemed to slowly dawn on Riley. He looked from her to Mike's trailer, then back at Tasha again. 'Wait for me to speak to him, then we'll discuss you leaving again. I have more to say on the matter.'

38

CALLUM

Callum made his way to Mike's trailer, glancing over his shoulder to check Tasha seemed to be OK. It was probably a good thing she had asked him to go, because as much as he wanted to remember his place and let Tasha deal with her own boss, it had taken all his determination to resist thumping Riley. How dare the little snot speak to Tasha in that way? And to embarrass her in front of all those people too. It was unacceptable and he wished he could teach the nasty piece of work a lesson.

He walked up the few steps and knocked on the door.

'Come in.' Mike sounded snappy and Callum wondered if he had been expecting Riley. He opened the door and leant inside.

'Sorry, I'm not sure whether you did mean for me to follow you here, or if you were just wanting to speak to Riley alone?'

Mike waved for him to get inside. 'Close the door behind you, will you?'

Callum did as he was asked and took a seat that Mike indicated.

'I'm sorry about that scene out there, Callum. How he gets

away with the public believing he is such a sweetheart, I've no idea.'

Callum wanted to try and placate the director, aware the extra couple of weeks' filming was adding pressure onto everyone involved. 'I'm sure Riley will realise what he's done and make amends.' As Callum spoke, he knew that was not nearly enough and that Riley needed to learn not to behave in such a disgusting way in the first place.

'Right, before Riley arrives, I want to ask you what you think about the promotional photos, videos? Will you be in agreement about taking part? Do you have an agent I can discuss this with?'

Callum was taken aback that Mike still wanted to proceed with his idea. 'I would love to do it,' he said, deciding on the spot that there was no harm in doing it. He thought there was no problem in seeing if something came from him being in that spotlight and what it might do for his career. It would also be a metaphorical clap for Riley to pay him back for his behaviour towards Tasha and others.

Mike immediately cheered up.

'I don't have an agent, but if you have someone you can introduce me to, I'd happily speak to them.'

'Great.'

There was a knock on the door before Riley opened it and walked inside. He glared at Callum before ignoring him and taking a seat next to him. 'You wanted to speak to me, Mike?'

Callum enjoyed Riley's irritation when Mike ignored him but continued to address him. 'Thanks, Callum. Leave everything to me. I'll sort a few things out and give you a call tomorrow, if that's OK?'

'Perfect.'

Without saying anything further, Callum left the trailer. He stopped at the bottom of the steps, trying to come to terms with what had just happened. He wondered where Tasha could have gone, so he returned to the set, but after a few minutes without seeing her, he walked up to one of the runners.

'You don't know where Riley's assistant Tasha went by any chance, do you?'

The girl pointed towards the alleyway between the two barns. 'Through there, the last time I saw her. She called for a cab and that's where the cars are parked.'

He thanked her before running to the car park to see if she was still there. As Callum exited the alleyway, he scanned the field where various cars and lorries were parked but couldn't immediately see her. Damn. He had wanted to make sure she was OK and check there was nothing he could to do help her.

'You looking for me?'

Hearing her voice, he spun round, relieved. 'You're still here. I thought I'd missed you.'

She frowned. 'I was waiting for you to come here, actually.'

He was unsure why for a moment, then it dawned on him. 'You want a lift?'

She smiled, looking relieved. 'I'd love one, if that's OK with you.'

He put his arm around her shoulders. 'Now that's something I can do very easily,' he said, leading her back to his car. Unsure how to broach the subject of what had happened with Riley, Callum just walked back to the car with her.

Once inside, he carefully drove out of the field and down the driveway. Tasha hadn't spoken since they had got into the car and he was concerned about her. 'How are you feeling?'

She sighed heavily. 'Angry, embarrassed. Aware that I really have no choice but to leave my job now.'

He looked over at her and seeming to sense his eyes on her, Tasha turned to look at him.

'I'm so sorry he caused that scene. His behaviour was deplorable.'

She looked away and out of the window. 'I agree. He was horrified when I told him I was resigning, but surely even Riley can see how he's left me little choice. I have my own self-respect to think of.'

Callum let her speak, not wanting to say the wrong thing. He concentrated on the lanes.

'The only positive is that he did that in front of people who have more than likely been on the receiving end of his nastiness themselves. I won't be the only one, that's for certain, but I have worked for him for three years and enough is enough.'

Unable to help himself, Callum asked, 'Has he been that rude to you before then?'

'Not quite. Oh, don't get me wrong, he's been insufferable many times, but not to that extent. And not to put me in my place so pointedly, or in company.'

'Stupid man,' Callum replied, not meaning to voice his thoughts. 'Sorry.'

'No need. You're right. By being this rude to me he must know I won't put up with it and will need to leave him.' She groaned. 'Anyway I don't care whether he knows it or not. I've had enough and I'm leaving him. Tonight.'

Callum was shocked. 'You mean you're not working out your notice? Or don't you have to?' he added.

'I'm past caring what I should or shouldn't do. If Riley can speak to me in that tone, then I can react how I damn well please. I'm appreciate you giving me a lift to the apartment.' He felt her hand rest on his arm. 'And if it's all right with you, I'd be grateful if you could wait while I quickly pack my things, so you can take me to a hotel, or guest house, somewhere to spend the night.'

'You can stay at mine,' Callum said without thinking.

'Sorry?'

He looked at her and saw she was shocked. Then, realising that Tasha might take his offer the wrong way, added hastily, 'I have two bedrooms and you're more than welcome to move into the spare room for as long as you like.'

'Really?' she sounded surprised and, he noted, a little tearful.

'Of course.'

'That's so kind of you. Thank you.'

'No need for thanks, Tasha. I'm only too glad to be able to help you after what you've been through today.'

39

TASHA

'This is very kind of you, Callum,' Tasha said again as Callum parked his car outside the apartment she was sharing with Riley. 'All of this would be so much harder without your support.'

'I'm glad I'm able to be of help.' He looked at the front door. 'Would you rather I came up with you while you pack, or should I stay down here and wait in the car?'

As far as Tasha was concerned she had already taken far too much advantage of Callum's generosity. 'I'll be fine.' She got out of the car and bent down, resting her palms on the door to speak through the open window to him. 'I'll be as quick as I can.'

He smiled. 'There's no rush. I can catch up on emails here. Bellow from the balcony if you need me to help carry your bags down for you.'

'Thanks, but I'm sure I'll be fine.'

She hurried into the lobby and took the lift up to the penthouse, relieved to know that Riley would be busy at the farm filming his next scene. Hopefully they would keep Riley long enough for her to pack, write him a note and get well away from the apartment and avoid any unnecessary confrontation with him.

Feeling slightly calmer at the prospect of not having to face Riley again until she was calmer and ready to do so, Tasha grabbed her case and smaller bag and set to packing her things. She decided not to bother wasting time by folding everything neatly. Callum had put himself out enough for her today.

Tasha hated the thought of imposing on him but needed somewhere to stay to get her head straight. Although she had felt like leaving Riley many times over the past three years, and had threatened to do so on several occasions, she hadn't ever made any solid plans about what she would do next.

What happened if she didn't find work, or somewhere to live? Could she in all honesty contact her parents and ask to return home to stay with them for a few weeks until she worked out what do to next while putting up with their I-told-you-sos? She was miserable at the thought of doing that when her parents would only repeat their initial concerns when she had given up her career in banking to work for an actor.

No, she wasn't in that much of a predicament to ask them for somewhere to stay. Not yet, anyway.

Having checked the drawers and cupboards in her bedroom and en-suite bathroom, Tasha took a walk around the living room and open-plan kitchen to double-check that she hadn't forgotten anything. Once she left this place she had no intention of returning. When she did speak to Riley again, it would be on her terms and when and where it suited her.

Hearing the lift outside in the hallway, Tasha tensed. Surely Riley couldn't be back here already?

Wanting to get out of the apartment as soon as possible, she ran into her bedroom, slipped on her jacket and picked up her case and her bag, slipping her phone into the back pocket in her trousers. She would send him an email later explaining about his diary dates for the next week and forward his flight information for his return to London the following week. Riley would be furious to be left this way, but it was too bad. He should have thought about that before insulting her as he had done.

She thought of Dale and wondered whether she should copy him into her email to Riley, deciding it was a good idea. Dale knew what he was doing when it came to logistics in Riley's busy life. He would know what was needed if she gave him all the necessary details in advance.

Satisfied that she wasn't being too unkind by leaving, Tasha reached out to take the door handle but before she had a chance to grab it the door flew back, making her jump back to avoid being hit.

'You're still here then?' Riley said sniffily. He made a point of looking at her case and bag. 'Although only just.' He stepped inside the room and closed the door behind him. 'I think the least you owe me is an explanation about where the hell you think you're going, Tasha. Don't you?'

She glared at him, her stomach a jumbled mess of anxiety as she tried to keep her cool and not give in to his anger. 'Where I'm going is none of your business, Riley.'

He gave a mocking snort. 'I think you'll find that it is while you're under my employ, which, unless I'm very much mistaken, you still are.'

'No, I'm not.'

He frowned, seeming confused. 'Look, Tasha, why don't you put those bags down and let's talk sensibly. I'm sorry I behaved as I did. You're sorry you resigned—'

'But that's where you're wrong, Riley. I'm not sorry, and whether you are or not, I really don't care. I've been getting more and more miserable with each passing day working for you.'

'Why?'

Was he serious? 'Because you're rude and obnoxious. What's more, nothing you can pay me is worth putting up with your nonsense,' she added, aware his next response would be to offer to throw money at her. 'Not everything is about money, Riley. At least not with me.'

His expression softened and once again she saw the charming side of Riley appearing. 'Tasha,' he said calmly as he reached out to take her case and bag from her grasp. 'Let's calm down and talk about this. There's no need to act hastily, now, is there?'

'If I was acting hastily, Riley, I would have left your employ months ago.' She stepped back, still holding tightly on to the handles of her baggage. 'Please open the door.'

'You're seriously leaving? Now?'

'The door.'

He glared at her and for once she saw a hint of fear in his eyes. 'But Tasha, what will I do without you?'

'Dale will help you with all you need,' she said, certain he would, albeit reluctantly. 'I'll email you both a bit later with all the information you need.'

He stared at her in disbelief. When she didn't speak, Riley opened the door. 'Do you even know where you're going?'

She had no intention of telling him that Callum had offered her a room in his flat and was relieved Riley hadn't noticed Callum waiting for her in his car.

'I'll be fine.' She walked out of the apartment without looking back. 'As I said, I'll email you with everything you need.'

40

CALLUM

Callum watched Riley get out of a taxi and march inside the lobby, the glass doors closing behind him. He looked unhappy. Callum hoped Tasha was all right and debated whether he should go upstairs to check. He knew she'd asked him to wait in the car for her but wondered if maybe it would be OK if he went up anyway and waited outside the apartment in the hall for her, just in case he heard any disturbance going on inside.

Then, he remembered Tasha saying she would call down for him from the balcony if she needed him. Callum reasoned that she would want him to do as she had said.

A few minutes after seeing Riley go up in the lift, Callum noticed the lift doors open once again. He waited, relieved to see Tasha leaving the lift and carrying her suitcase and a couple of bags. Callum quickly got out of the car and went to help.

'Are you all right?' he asked, taking the luggage from her grasp and putting them into the boot of the car. 'I saw Riley go inside and wasn't sure whether you'd want me to come up.'

She smiled. 'I'm fine. I'd like to go now though before he has a chance to register that I really have gone and comes down here to try and persuade me once again to stay.'

Tasha got into the car, and Callum quickly closed the boot and joined her.

'I'll have you at mine in a few minutes,' he said, hoping to reassure her.

They drove to his flat in silence. He could tell she was lost in thought and wanted to give her time to come to terms with what had happened, so didn't speak.

'I'll be OK after a good night's sleep, if you're worried about me,' she said eventually.

'I'm glad.' Unsure whether to broach the subject of Riley, Callum decided he needed to ask what had happened to know whether to worry about Riley tracking Tasha down and confronting her sometime over the next few days. After all, she could tell him to mind his own business if she wasn't in the mood to share anything with him.

He glanced at her as they stopped at traffic lights. 'How was he when he saw that you were leaving?'

She shrugged. 'As you'd expect, I guess. He was shocked, although I can only presume that was because he was so certain I would never have the gumption to leave. Then he asked me to stay, but I told him I had no intention of doing so and would contact him later with all he needed to know for the next few weeks.'

Callum rested a hand on hers, hoping to comfort her. The lights changed and he immediately removed it to drive on. 'I think what you need is a few days to rest and recover from all the stress you've been under recently, working for him.'

'You know what? I think you could be right. I can't really think straight at the moment and I think a lot of that is hurt that someone I've worked so hard to look after could show me up like he did today.'

Hating to hear her sounding humiliated, Callum shook his head. 'The only person Riley showed up today was himself.'

He sensed she was looking at him and quickly gave her a sideways glance, followed by a gentle smile.

'I wish it felt that way.'

It hurt to hear her sounding so downtrodden. 'Hopefully after you've had some time and space away from him to reflect, you'll realise I'm right.' A thought occurred to him. 'And when he's had time away from you, I'm sure it'll begin to dawn on him what a complete prat he looks to everyone and what an unnecessarily nasty thing he did to you today. No one will be surprised you've left him. Not even his manager, I imagine.'

He thought of Erin and wondered how Riley would explain his behaviour towards Tasha to his sister. Callum doubted Riley would get away with his sister not learning about the incident, especially as she'd be working on several actors throughout the day. Someone was bound to gossip about it. He knew Erin well enough to suspect she would not be impressed and would have a few things to say to Riley about his treatment of Tasha.

'What are you thinking?' Tasha asked quietly.

Callum told her his thoughts about his sister and how he imagined she would react. 'If Riley thinks he'll only have you to defend his actions to, then he's sorely mistaken.' The thought pleased Callum. 'As painful as this will be for you right now, I have a feeling Riley is about to learn a big life lesson not to treat women badly,' he added, feeling angrier. 'Especially not people who have worked tirelessly to ensure his life runs as smoothly as you make sure it does.'

'Made,' she said. 'As in, past tense. From now on, Riley can do what he likes as far as I'm concerned. I'm done with being his servant.' She shrugged a shoulder. 'Or I will be when I've collated all the information I promised to send him and Dale.'

He was glad to hear it. 'Yes, well, it serves him right as far as I see it.'

'I agree.' Her voice sounded slightly stronger and more forceful and Callum was glad of it.

Turning into the entrance of his flat, Callum parked in his designated space. 'Here we are.' He took the luggage from the boot, locked the car and led Tasha up the two flights of stairs. 'This is us.'

41

TASHA

Tasha wasn't sure what to expect as Callum opened the front door to his flat. Her mood immediately lifted as she stepped into the pristine, minimalist, sunlit living room.

'Welcome to my home,' Callum said, his arms outstretched.

He led her past the good-sized galley kitchen down a short corridor to two large bedrooms with a Jack and Jill bathroom in between the rooms.

'Oh, it's lovely, Callum.' She stood in the middle of the living room and enviably gazed at the huge bookshelves lining one of the walls. 'Do you mind me asking if you designed this or were you lucky enough to take this on from someone else?'

'It was in a bit of a state when I bought this place. I enjoyed turning it into something that suited me, although I admit it did take a bit longer than I had at first imagined it would.' He laughed, his brow furrowing as if he had just thought of something. 'I'm not sure why you sound so surprised though.' He tilted his head to one side. 'Don't I look as if I'd live in a nice place?'

She saw the glint in his eyes and knew he was teasing. 'It's not that,' she said, wanting to explain. 'I suppose I hadn't known what to expect but this is very impressive.' She laughed. 'That doesn't really answer your question very well though, does it?'

'It'll do.' He indicated the kettle.

'Tea for me, please.'

Callum pressed the kettle on to boil. 'I'm just glad you like it enough to be happy staying here.'

'I'm very grateful to you for opening your home to me.' Recalling her promise to Riley to send him information, she took her phone from her trouser pocket and checked the screen.

Fourteen missed calls and various messages ranging from insisting she return, to promises that if she did Riley would change his ways. Tasha knew him better than that and doubted he would be any different if she did agree to return to work for him.

She held up her phone.

'Riley?' Callum asked, taking two mugs from a cupboard and setting them down on the worktop.

'How did you guess?' She sighed.

'Why don't you tell me what happened?'

He listened while she spoke and Tasha could tell Callum was angry with Riley but trying hard not to show it.

'You do know you're welcome to stay here for as long as you'd like?'

She swallowed back tears. 'Thank you, I appreciate that. I shouldn't be here too long though. Maybe a week, or two, if that's not pushing it? I'm not sure what my next steps will be and I would love to see more of this place now I'll have the free time to do that.'

'I think that's a great idea. You've been working long hours for him and you're probably in dire need of a break. It'll do you good to take it easy and relax. Focus on yourself for once.'

She felt tears threatening to appear once more, and cleared her throat, aware that if she didn't spend some time alone without Callum being so thoughtful she would have no choice but to give in to them and cry.

'I'd better go to my room and unpack,' she said, her voice wobbly. 'Then I'd better respond to him, otherwise he will keep trying to get hold of me. I shouldn't be too long.'

'Take whatever time you need. I'll bring your tea into you when it's ready.'

'That's kind. Thank you.'

Tasha unpacked her things quickly then sat on the edge of her bed. The bed felt comfortable beneath her and she looked forward to sleeping in it later on. It was only now that she was away from Riley and somewhere peaceful that she began to realise how exhausted she actually felt. Another message pinged into her phone, so Tasha picked up her laptop and opened it, needing to get her contact with him over and done with.

It took a little while to go through his diary and emails for her to collate the information Riley would need for the next few days and weeks. She copied Dale in to the emails, adding a note at the end of the message that Dale could email her if he needed any further explanation about any of it.

Tasha pressed send and immediately relaxed. Moments later her phone screen lit up.

Tasha saw Riley was trying to call her again and closed her eyes, feeling exhausted. She let the call go to voicemail, but then realised she was going to need to call him back and listen to him trying to persuade her to withdraw her resignation if she was going to get any peace.

Riley answered immediately, causing her to believe he had been waiting for the call. She was not surprised.

'Tasha, I can't believe you're doing this to me.'

How typical of him to only think of himself, she mused, unsurprised.

'Tasha?'

'I'm still here, Riley.' She tried to calm her flustered thoughts. 'You've probably seen the email I sent to you and Dale.'

'I haven't read it yet,' he said sullenly.

She hadn't expected him to have done. 'I'm sure Dale will though.'

'You're really sticking to this resignation then?'

'I am.'

'I don't understand why you're doing this. I know I was rude, but you know how stressed I am at the moment.' She waited for him to continue, knowing him well enough to sense the change about to come in his tone. 'It's that Callum Preston's influence on you, isn't it? Don't think I didn't notice him waiting for you outside the apartments in his car.'

And there it was.

Tasha felt her temper rising. She had expected him to need someone to blame because Riley rarely ever thought he could be the one to have caused any damage, but it irked her to think he could believe she was soft enough to let anyone influence her to leave a job.

'I would hope you know me better than to think I would make choices just because someone else expected me to.' She hoped he got the message that she was not only referring to Callum but to Riley's expectation that she would change her mind simply because it suited him.

'I suppose I do.' There was a moment's silence and she knew he was building up to play the hard-done-by person. 'How can you do this to me, Tasha?'

'Do what?' she asked, irritated with him for being so predictably selfish.

'Abandon me just when I need your support most of all.'

'Riley, we both know you have enough people around you to make sure all your needs are well catered for.'

'So you're refusing to change your mind?' he asked huffily.

'I am.' It was an enormous relief to reiterate her initial decision directly to Riley. 'I'm going now. Dale can contact me if there's an emergency but I've decided I need some time to rest and gather myself after working for you these past few years. I'd like to say it's been an incredible experience.' Feeling mean, she added, 'Which some of the time it was, but you expect a lot from someone, Riley. Even if you aren't aware that you do. Long hours, not brilliant pay and what might have seemed exciting initially,' she said, thinking of all the film sets she had been thrilled to visit and the actors she had met over her time with Riley. 'But I'm over all that now.'

'What do you want then?' He sounded exasperated.

She decided that if he didn't know her well enough, having shared a lot of accommodation and spending so much time in each other's company, then she had no inkling how to begin trying to explain her feelings to him.

'What I want right now, Riley, is to have some time to rest and think. And that's what I'm going to do.'

'Wait! Don't go before telling me where you're staying.'

She had no intention of doing that and giving Riley the chance to arrive at Callum's place unannounced to cause another scene.

'There's no need for that, Riley.' The thought of him knowing where she was staying filled her with dread. 'You have my number if you need it, but please only use it in an emergency. I'm sure Dale will do all he can to help you if you have any issues finding my replacement.' She was about to end the call when he spoke.

'What about your outstanding salary?'

Typical of Riley's mind to veer to money. He seemed to believe everyone could be led by offering them money, or at least mentioning it.

'You have my bank details. I'm sure Dale will work out what I'm owed and can settle any outstanding wages into my account.' She had had enough of the call. 'I'm going now, Riley, and I'd be grateful if you gave me some space. Think of it as me being on holiday for a week or so.'

'Will you be using your flight to return to London then?'

She had no idea but wasn't about to let him know how up in the air her plans really were. 'Bye, Riley, and good luck filming the rest of the series.'

She ended the call and lay back onto the bed. What was she going to do next? She really hadn't thought that far.

There was a knock at the door. 'Mind if I bring this tea into you?'

She sat up. 'I'll come out and join you.'

Tasha studied her reflection in the mirror and ran her fingers through her hair. She looked dreadful. She wasn't kidding when she told Riley she needed time out. And based on the dark circles under her eyes and how tired she felt, she shouldn't waste any more time getting it.

42

CALLUM

For the first time ever, Callum hated leaving his flat for work each day. He would have much rather spend time with Tasha, chilling, going out for lunches, or simply for a walk. She needed this time to herself, but as each day had passed, he had seen her relax more and the colour come back to her cheeks.

She had only been staying at the flat for a little over a week but already his home felt more complete with her staying there.

They still slept in their own rooms but the more time they spent in each other's company the more they seemed to gravitate towards each other. He ached to hold her, to kiss her, but she had seemed so traumatised by leaving her job and unsure what to do next that he felt Tasha needed the space to figure out what she wanted to do before he became too involved with her. He cared too much for her to put his own feelings before her needs but hoped that sometime soon she would be ready to take the next step in their growing closeness.

Callum smiled to himself as he got out of his car and looked up at her sitting on the balcony reading a book. How had this place ever felt like home before without Tasha there to complete it?

She noticed him and smiled down at him, waving. 'Is it that time already?'

* * *

Callum thought how happy and carefree she seemed today and remembered the several messages in his pocket asking him to return calls to Riley.

The receptionist had been confused that Riley kept calling.

'Don't you want to phone him back?' she asked when she handed him the fifth piece of paper with Riley's latest request for Callum to call him.

'Not really.' Callum didn't elaborate. He suspected the receptionist was happy to speak to Riley whenever he called anyway, so the only person to be put out by Callum's lack of interest in phoning Riley was Riley himself.

He returned to the flat wondering whether to suggest he and Tasha go out for a quiet meal at one of the beachside restaurants, or maybe take a gentle evening stroll on the beach. He arrived home and found Tasha sitting on the balcony, her eyes closed and an open book lying face down on the small bistro table next to an almost empty cup of coffee.

He didn't want to disturb her, having witnessed for himself how long she had slept the nights she had been staying in his flat. She clearly needed this time apart from Riley to figure out whether to go back to working for him, or move on to something else. He enjoyed seeing her make the most of the sun, having time to be still and just do exactly what she felt like doing.

Not wishing to disturb Tasha, Riley went and showered. It

had been another warm day. He wanted to be ready to go out in case Tasha decided that's what she was happy to do.

The cool water was refreshing and Riley took his time washing his hair and standing underneath the waterfall shower, feeling invigorated. He got out of the shower, dried himself and went to his room to dress.

Wearing a fresh linen shirt and shorts, he left his room and stepped into the hallway, only just missing slamming into Tasha. 'You're awake.' He wasn't sure why he had made such an obvious statement, but even though they had spent the past few days together he still couldn't get past feeling slightly awkward in her presence.

He really needed to get a grip. He wasn't fourteen any longer.

She seemed amused. 'I hadn't realised I'd dozed off until I woke hearing the shower. I wondered what the sound was for a moment, then realised you must be home.'

He stared at her, enjoying seeing her this comfortable in his home and thought how wonderful it would be to enjoy this sort of exchange every day.

Tasha frowned. 'What is it?'

He shook his head, not wishing to add any further disruptions to her life. What Tasha needed now was his support, not his admission that his feelings for her were deepening every day. 'It's nothing.'

'Are you sure?' she asked, clearly not believing him.

Callum realised he needed to give a reasonable answer. 'I was wondering whether you'd like to go for a stroll on the beach. There's a lovely one I haven't taken you to see yet and it we could have dinner either before or after, if that suits you.'

Her face broke into a smile. 'I'd love that. Thank you.'

43

TASHA

After a light meal at a pretty beachside restaurant, Tasha accompanied Callum down granite steps onto the beach. It was still very warm and after they'd taken off their shoes, she relished having the warm, soft, pale sand under her feet. The sun was slowly setting and the sky now a mass of pink, lilac and golden hues.

She slipped her hand into Callum's and he looked at her, smiling.

'Enjoying yourself?' he asked.

'Very much.' She didn't add that she dreaded her stay with him ending. Callum was everything Riley wasn't, kind, thoughtful and a perfect host. He seemed to sense when she needed time to contemplate her thoughts, unlike Riley. If only her ex-boss had some of Callum's pleasant traits, then her job would have been incredible.

She wasn't sure whether it was the thought of leaving Callum in two days' time that upset her so much, or the knowledge that what she had expected to be her ideal role had turned out to be nothing more than a massive disappointment.

Wanting to change her mindset, she thought back to how relaxing it had been at Callum's flat. She had enjoyed getting to know him a little better and even had time to read a book for once.

Her thoughts returned to Callum. She suspected Callum had something on his mind and decided she needed to encourage him to open up a bit.

'What's the matter, Callum? I can tell there's something bothering you.'

She waited for him to respond. 'Let's walk, shall we?'

Callum gave her hand a gentle squeeze. 'I was wondering what you're going to do next,' he said eventually.

She looked up at him, unsure whether he was really sharing his thoughts but didn't want to sound as if she doubted him so kept her thoughts to herself.

'I'm not entirely sure,' she admitted, realising she really did need to make a decision and not continue to rely on Callum's hospitality. The poor guy was used to living alone and having his own space, and as much as she had loved staying at his flat she would hate to feel as if she'd outstayed her welcome.

They walked in silence.

A few minutes later, Callum stopped walking and went to say something just as she did too.

'You go first,' she said.

He shook his head and smiled. 'It's fine. You go.'

Happy to have finally come to a decision, but sad that it meant these blissful few days would come to an end, she said, 'For the first time in three years I think I know what I'm going to do.'

He smiled proudly at her. 'That's brilliant. You can do whatever you want and I believe your future is there for the taking.'

She wasn't sure exactly what he meant but feeling empowered by Callum's belief in her, she sighed. 'I suppose it is. I think the trouble is that I've spent so long running around making life easier for Riley that I've forgotten how it feels to put myself first.'

Callum pulled her into a hug. 'Good for you.'

Surprised by his sudden act of affection, Tasha hugged him back. 'Thanks for reminding me I'm my own woman, Callum.'

He leant back and looked into her eyes. His focus moved slowly down to her lips where it rested for a few seconds.

Tasha sensed he wanted to kiss her. Excitement swelled in her chest at the thought, only for Callum's gaze to lift until his eyes were locked with hers.

'You're an amazing woman, Tasha; I hope you know that.'

Delighted to hear his praise, Tasha concentrated hard on hiding her disappointment that he hadn't kissed her. 'I certainly needed the reminder, so thank you. I suppose we should go back so I can book my flight home.'

He seemed shocked. 'Flight?'

Tasha had been so caught up in his reaction she realised she hadn't actually voiced her decision. She gave him an apologetic smile, unsure whether his reaction was one of disappointment or simply surprise.

'Yes, sorry. I let my studio flat in Clapham go before coming to Jersey and had been looking for somewhere further out of London to live. Somewhere a little cheaper and with more greenery around it. Now that I don't know where I'll be working, I think it's safer for me to wait until I've found somewhere nearby to rent.' She frowned. 'I think I'm going to cast aside my reservations and stay with my parents for a while. We could do with patching things up and if it means they'll need to have the satisfaction of me admitting they were right to be concerned about me working for Riley, then that's what I'll have to deal with. I need to move forward though. I'm not good at just sitting around and doing nothing.'

She had expected him to laugh at her quip, but he didn't.

'I'll be sorry to see you go,' he said eventually.

She felt a pang of loss in her chest. 'You will?'

He nodded. He stared at her for a moment. 'Do you mind if I kiss you?'

His question was so unexpected that she almost laughed. *Mind?*, she wanted to ask. She couldn't think of anything she would rather do.

Instead she shook her head slowly. 'I wouldn't mind at all,' she said, unable to stop smiling. 'In fact, I think I'd like that very much.'

Callum's mouth slowly drew back into a smile and, taking her in his arms, he pulled her close to him and slipped one hand behind her head before lowering his head until his lips met hers.

44

CALLUM

As they kissed, Callum knew the last thing he wanted was for Tasha to leave the island. Let alone leave his flat.

Her arms tightened around him as her kiss became more passionate. Delighted, Callum gave in to the sensations and did the same. Kissing Tasha was amazing and if he was sad to know she would be leaving before, this only made the thought of her returning to the UK even harder to bear.

He wished he could tell Tasha not to leave but stay on at his flat; however, doing so would be selfish of him. What right did he have to interfere with her life? Hadn't she just got away from someone who had spent the past three years ordering her about? Callum decided that regardless of how he felt, Tasha needed to do what was right for her. He just hoped she would choose to return at some point.

They sat on the sand near the sea wall watching the sun slowly disappear into the horizon.

'This is incredible,' she said. 'There isn't anything marring the view of the sun going down. What an incredible place to see this.'

'I'm glad you think so.' He looked at her and, seeming to sense she was being watched, Tasha gazed up at him.

'Thank you, Callum.'

He wasn't sure what she was thanking him for. 'I'm not sure why I deserve your thanks,' he said eventually.

'Because of all the ways you've helped me while I've been on the island.'

She sighed.

Callum frowned. 'I still think it's a bit much that the director wants me to be involved in any way, especially when I only had a couple of scenes.'

'Yes, but remember you're well known and loved here on the island, and having you in some of the promotion will be a good way to get people who don't know who Riley is to tune in and watch. It's all about viewing numbers, Callum.' She laughed. 'Anyway, I'm sure you'll have fun and if nothing else it'll give you great content for your radio show. You might even meet new and interesting people you can invite on the show for interviews.'

She had a point, but it didn't make up for the fact that he would be spending more time with Riley, without Tasha being there.

'Don't look so glum,' she teased. 'It'll be fine.'

He shrugged. 'But you won't be there and if Riley was insufferable with you keeping him in check, I daren't think how he'll be without you.'

Tasha rested a hand on his knee. 'I didn't really make much difference to Riley's behaviour.' She rested her head on his shoulder. 'I must admit I'll miss you, Callum.'

He was glad she wasn't able to see how miserable the thought of her leaving the island made him. Choosing to try and encourage her rather than feel sorry for himself, he kissed the top of her head. 'You'll be fine. You've made the right decision.

Although, it's a shame that silly man doesn't try to put someone else's feelings first for once. I have an idea he'll only realise what he's lost in letting you go when it's too late.'

'That will be Riley all over,' Tasha said, sounding, Callum thought, sad at the notion.

45

TASHA

Tasha heard Callum thanking the delivery guy as she sat on Callum's comfy sofa, her laptop resting on her thighs. She checked her booking information and without giving herself a chance to change her mind, paid for her flight to London in two days' time.

She set her laptop aside and watched Callum set out their food on the table in front of her. 'This all looks delicious,' she said, taking a glass of wine from him a minute later and sipping the delicious Malbec.

'You not having anything?' she asked, taking another sip of her wine.

He smiled. 'My beer is in the kitchen, I'll get it now.'

'This food smells wonderful.'

He went to the kitchen, returning with a bottle of beer. 'Let's take these out to the balcony.'

She nodded and followed him.

'I'm going to miss this view,' she said miserably as she looked down at the bistro-style table and two chairs he had set up with a hurricane candle for them to enjoy most evenings when the sun set.

He pulled out a chair for her. 'I wanted to make your last evening here memorable.'

She didn't dare tell him how memorable it was, aware that if he had wanted her to stay Callum would most probably have taken the opportunity to say so after they had kissed on the beach. Instead he had told her that he thought she had made the right decision to leave Riley and return to the UK, seeming more concerned about Riley only realising when it was too late that his bad behaviour had caused her to leave.

They finished their meal and sat in silence gazing out over the fields near his flat.

'I've enjoyed having you here,' Callum said suddenly.

'I'm glad.' She reached out and took his hand. 'I've loved being here. I already feel rested and much calmer.'

'Good.'

She stared at him, thinking how difficult it was going to be to leave him.

'I'm going to miss you, Tasha.'

'You will?'

He frowned, then nodded. 'Of course.' He laughed.

'What is it?' she asked, unsure what he was getting at.

'I hoped you might say you'd miss me too.' His cheeks reddened at the admission and her heart melted to see him being vulnerable for once.

'I'll miss you very much,' she said, aware that now was the time to be open because soon it would be too late. 'I can't bear the thought of leaving here.' Tasha tried to swallow away the tears about to come. 'I know I've had a few glasses of wine, but I hate to think that the enjoyment I've had living here over the past few days will soon be over.'

He stood and gently pulled her around to his side of the table. Tasha couldn't think what to say as Callum took her into his arms and kissed her.

Unable to think of anything else, Tasha gave in to his kisses.

The urge to kiss him again increased. Tasha gazed into his deep blue eyes, her arms still around his neck, and felt compelled to take their relationship further. 'Shall we go to bed?'

His eyes widened slightly. 'Yes. I mean, if you're sure that's what you want?'

Tasha smiled. 'I can't think of anything I'd rather do right now.' She sensed hesitation. 'I know I've had a couple of glasses of wine, but I know what I'm doing.'

Aware she needed to take the lead to prove to him how much she wanted this, she let her hands slide from his neck, grazing over his muscular chest before taking his hand in hers.

'I believe this is the way to your bedroom?' she asked, smiling up at him over her shoulder as she led the way.

'Yes, it is.'

46

CALLUM

Two days later, when Callum opened his eyes, he lightly kissed the skin on her tanned shoulder, wondering how he was going to bear waking up without her in his arms. He had been dreading today and now it had arrived. By tonight Tasha would be back in England. She had already made some contacts with agencies for her next job but he couldn't tell whether she was excited about what to expect next or not.

He listened to her gentle breathing, the warmth of her breath against his arm sending sensations racing through him. He glanced at the clock, noticing they had a few hours before she needed to leave for the airport and decided that after finally falling asleep in the early hours after their lovemaking to let her sleep for a little longer.

Images of their nights together came rushing back to him. Being intimate with Tasha had seemed perfect from that first time, but last night had an added urgency to it as each of them tried to make the most of every moment they spent in each other's arms. His heartbeat raced. He wanted to make love to her now, but she needed to sleep a bit longer. Whatever he had expected when he admitted his feelings for her, this wasn't it.

Tasha stirred and the sheet slipped slightly to expose more of her back. Like every other part of her, this was also perfect. He felt the urge to lean forward and kiss the tanned skin but wanted to let her sleep for a bit longer.

He tried to imprint the sensation of his skin against hers to his memory, wishing it didn't have to end. He thought back to his plan not to lead her decision either way about whether she stayed on the island or left, but with each passing second his determination to keep his thoughts to himself weakened. He didn't want her to go. She sighed in her sleep and it occurred to him that he hadn't said as much to Tasha. Was he right not to admit his feelings to her? Could she make a different choice whether to stay or go if she did know he would rather she not leave?

She turned her head and looked up at him, then turned around to face him, draping an arm over his chest. 'Good morning,' she said, her voice croaky with sleep. 'I don't recall sleeping that well for...' she frowned thoughtfully '...forever.'

He bent his head to kiss her. 'I'm glad.'

She closed her eyes. 'I wish I didn't have to leave today.'

He wrestled with his thoughts, wanting to do the right thing by Tasha.

She opened her eyes and looked up at him. 'What's the matter?'

He gave her an apologetic smile, aware that any resilience he'd had to keep his thoughts to himself had now vanished. 'I want to admit something to you but don't know whether I'm being selfish to do it.'

She moved her head back slightly and rested a hand on his

cheek. 'Of course you should tell me, Callum. Whatever it is, we should be honest with each other.'

She was right. She had also said what he'd hoped to hear.

He took a deep breath. 'I don't want you to leave the island.' *Be honest*, he thought, forcing himself to admit his true feelings. 'I'm falling for you, Tasha. I had made up my mind not to stand in the way of your career, but after last night I think it's wrong not to be completely truthful with you and admit that I want you to stay here with me.' He looked away from her and stared out of the window. 'I'm sorry. I'm aware that's completely selfish but I thought you'd rather know how I feel.'

When she didn't immediately respond, he looked at her, trying to get a sense of how his admission made her feel. She hadn't pulled away from him, so that must be a good thing, he thought hopefully.

She kissed him on his neck. 'Thank you for telling me how you feel,' she said quietly. He could tell she was struggling to work through her own feelings and was beginning to wish he hadn't said anything, when she spoke. 'My feelings for you are increasing all the time,' she said, giving him a smile. 'And, lying here with you is something I want to be able to do every day I possibly can.' She met his lips in a kiss. 'I really don't want to leave you either, Callum.'

'Then don't.'

Her eyes widened. 'What do you mean?'

'If you want to stay for longer, then stay.'

She rested her weight on one elbow. 'What happened to you thinking I was doing the right thing by returning home?'

'I was trying to do the right thing.' He sighed. 'Which, if you want the best for your career, you probably are.' Not wishing her to think he was going back on what he had just said, he added, 'I don't know if it's possible for you to live here and still work in show business, but if you'd rather take your chances here, then I would be very happy for you to do that. I also completely understand if you feel you have to go.'

47

TASHA

She gazed into his eyes as she thought about what he had said.

'I think...' What did she think? The only thing Tasha did know for certain was that she didn't want to leave Callum. She also knew she had enjoyed her job immensely, apart from the past couple of years when Riley had become far too full of himself and as a result his manners deteriorated, and his rudeness increased. If only he'd find a way to revert to the boss she had known that first year and been so excited to work for.

'I want to stay here,' she admitted. 'I hate the thought of leaving you. Of leaving this. Waking up in your arms is blissful.' She thought of the previous night and the one before it and felt the heat rise in her cheeks. 'But I need to find a job.'

'You love what you do,' he said, sounding sad but understanding. 'Do you think it might help to talk to Riley about this?'

'If only it was that easy.'

'What do you mean?'

She shrugged. 'I've broached the subject many times but he doesn't take me seriously.'

Callum frowned. 'He might, now that you've actually left.

He's had more than a week without your help, don't forget. I'm sure he'll have missed you and might be able to find a compromise that will work for you both.'

'Are you trying to persuade me to stay or go back to Riley?' she asked, only half amused.

'I want you to do what's best for you, that's all.'

She thought of her parents and how different their reaction had been to Callum's. He was such a good man. Kind, loving, fun. If only she had the financial means to take time off work and spend the next few months there, or find a different job on the island. Not that it would solve much if she then had to leave him after getting used to living this way. No, it would be far harder to bear.

Frustrated, she kicked back the bed sheets. 'I don't know.' Then it came to her. She had always worked, been sensible, at least as far as she was concerned; and never completely gone with her heart, especially in a relationship. She loved Callum and had enough experience in her failed relationship with Toby to know that he was worth giving some things up for.

'I've made up my mind about something.'

He looked anxious. 'You have?'

She nodded. 'I'm going to postpone my flight for a couple of days and enjoy being here.'

'With me?' he asked before laughing. 'Sorry, silly question. That makes me really happy.'

She liked that he didn't assume what her reaction would be. 'Yes, of course with you. If the offer is still open, that is?' She wished she could commit to staying on permanently but she needed to be practical.

He pulled her into his arms and kissed her passionately, leaving her almost breathless. Letting go, he said. 'Does that answer your question?'

Tasha laughed. 'It does.' She got out of bed.

'Where are you going?' he asked, disappointment on his face.

'To change my flight, unless you want me to wait and do it later?'

He shook his head. 'No, you do that while I shower and think of ways to reassure you you've made the right decision.'

Tasha couldn't wait to find out what he would plan.

An hour later as Callum drove along the east coast of the island, Tasha stared up in awe as the car passed Mont Orgueil Castle.

'It's such a beautiful day,' she said, glad she had thought to wear a cotton T-shirt and shorts. 'Where are we going? Surely there isn't much further we can go before we come to the end of the island?' she teased.

'Ahh, but there's still so much you haven't seen out this way.'

'Such as?'

'Tiny bays, woods we can walk through, St Catherine's pier and the café at the beginning where you can eat, then buy a delicious creamy ice cream afterwards, or take a seafari to the Ecrehous.'

'We're going to one of those places then?'

He shook his head and laughed. 'Nope.'

'Then where?'

He didn't reply straight away, but indicated right, slowing the car before turning down what seemed like a short lane. Even before they parked, Tasha saw they were right by the sea.

'Is this one of those bays?' She looked to her left, noticing a round granite tower painted with thick red and white stripes.

'This is Archirondel,' he said, getting out of the car.

He took her hand and walked to the edge of the pebbly beach with bright flowers in planters and palm trees next to a seating area for a small, but busy café to their left.

'It's magical down here.'

'I'm glad you like it.' He led her to a free table and pulled back one of the heavy wooden chairs, waiting for Tasha to sit before sitting opposite her. Callum pointed out to the sea. 'Look, a couple kayaking. We could do that if you like?'

She recalled trying that sport once before while on holiday with her ex. 'I don't think so.'

'Something tells me you might have tried it before.'

'I did. Not only wasn't I very good, but I also got seasick, and the instructor had to take me back to the shore past all the other kayakers. I was mortified.'

Callum reached out and took her hand, giving it a light squeeze. 'That's not why I brought you here anyway.'

'That's a relief.' She saw the waiter carrying three plates of food that looked delicious. 'I was hoping we were here to eat breakfast.'

'And that's what we will do.'

The waiter spotted them and took their orders.

'This is one of the prettiest spots I think I've ever been to,' Tasha said, after finishing the last mouthful of her full English breakfast. She took a sip of tea before gazing at him.

'And there are so many more I plan to show you now we have time to see some of them.'

She smiled. 'I love that idea.'

'It's getting hot,' Callum said. 'And I might have the perfect way for us to walk off our large breakfast and stay cool at the same time. Do you fancy visiting St Catherine's Woods?'

'I'd love that.'

After paying for their meal and not wishing to take up the small amount of parking when they would be moving on from Archirondel, Callum drove a short distance away to a small parking area before walking with Tasha past tall Jersey pines on one side and the beach on the other as they made their way to the pretty woods with its stream running through it.

'This is beautiful,' Tasha said as they stood in the dappled shade holding hands, as she took in the space around them.

'I'm glad you think so.'

'Do you come here often?'

He shook his head. 'I've just realised I haven't been back here. My parents used to bring Erin and I here for walks after Sunday lunch sometimes. We'd run around climbing on fallen tree trunks and paddling in the stream while they strolled and chatted.'

'Your childhood sounds idyllic.'

He nodded. 'Looking back, I now realise how lucky I was. I love living here. I know a lot of my friends moved away, preferring big cities, and I did try that for a time but couldn't wait to come back.'

'And I'm lucky enough to get to stay here for a bit longer.'

He looked down at her. Tasha felt that immediate flip in her stomach. He was so hot and she couldn't believe how lucky she was to be seeing a man this decent and gorgeous.

He slipped his arm around her shoulders and kissed her. 'For as long as you want.'

Tasha beamed up at him. 'I don't think I've ever been happier,' she admitted.

'I don't think I have been either.'

48

CALLUM

The next morning Callum's phone vibrated, interrupting them kissing. Callum stifled a groan. He tried to ignore it but the caller was determined to wait until someone answered. Thankfully the ringing stopped as the call went to voicemail.

'Maybe you should answer it?' Tasha said, resting a hand on his stomach and making Callum think that was the last thing he wanted to do at that moment.

'It's not seven yet,' she said, giving him a sympathetic smile. 'For someone to call this early could mean there's an emergency.'

'Ever the professional,' he said, kissing her on the tip of her nose. 'I suppose I should see who it is.'

He moved away from her reluctantly and reached out to pick up his phone. Then, seeing it was his mother who had a tendency to call at inopportune moments, thought he would call her back in a bit. Before he had the chance to ask Tasha to continue with what she had been saying, a message pinged onto his screen.

Call me. Urgent. It's about your sister. See
attached pics. Mum

Callum sighed. What had Erin done now that couldn't wait
until later in the morning? 'I'm sorry. It seems that my sister has
done something that's concerned my mother. I need to look at
some photos Mum has sent me.'

'Go ahead.'

Tasha turned on her side, facing away from him, the skin of
her thigh grazing his lightly as she moved, resting her bottom
against his hip.

Callum's breath caught in his throat and for a moment he
wondered if he could leave the photos just for a little while.

No, he should do the right thing. He closed his eyes, frustrated with his mother's interruption, then opened the photos,
frowning when he saw photos of Erin at a party with Riley. He
began to feel irritated with his mother for getting irate about
perfectly innocent photos, when he swiped to the next one and
saw what had upset her.

'What the hell?'

Tasha immediately turned to face him. 'What's happened?'
she asked, sitting up and peering at his phone screen. She
gasped.

He stared at his sister. Riley stood beaming at her, his arm
around her waist as Erin held out her hand to the woman he recognised as the make-up artist who had prepared him for his few short
scenes. Erin beamed at the woman who gazed in awe at the large
diamond solitaire engagement ring on his sister's finger. It wasn't so
much seeing that, but the wedding band next to it that shocked
Callum. It took him a moment to comprehend what this meant.

'They're married?'

'It certainly looks that way,' Tasha said, sounding as stunned as he felt.

He tore his eyes from the photo and stared in disbelief at Tasha. 'When could they have done it?' A dark thought wafted into his mind. Callum tried to push it away but after discovering that Tasha had not immediately alerted him or Erin about Brooke after the drama of the photos of his sister and Riley kissing being in all the papers, he knew he needed to address what was on his mind.

Before he could say anything, Tasha's expression darkened. 'No, I did not have any prior warning about this, if that's what you're about to ask me.'

He was relieved she had been the one to say it, removing the need for him to do so.

Callum looked from her to the photos again. 'I know,' he said, feeling guilty for even considering that she might have known without trying to do something about it. Although what Tasha could realistically do, he wasn't sure. 'I'm going to have to call Mum. She'll be beside herself about this.'

Tasha held out her hand, so he passed the phone to her. She peered at the photo and shook her head. 'This must have been taken at the wrap party. I forgot that was happening last night.' She scowled up at him. 'Someone from the party probably took this and sold it to one of the newspapers. They didn't waste any time, did they?' She picked up her own phone from the nightstand next to her. 'Send me this, will you?'

He forwarded the photo to her, wondering what she was about to do with it.

'I'm going to contact a couple of the crew and see what they can tell me,' Tasha explained.

'Thanks.'

Callum slipped out of bed, pulled on his underwear and went into the kitchen to call her.

'Mum?' he said, keeping his voice low.

'Oh, so you are there then?'

'I know you're upset, Mum, but until we speak to Erin there's not much I can add to what you've already seen.'

'This can't be real,' she said. 'Can it?'

'Oh, it's real all right,' he said, hoping his sister knew what she was doing. 'I've spoken to Tasha and she's calling a couple of people to try and find out more. I'll let you know if she comes up with anything.'

'She's there with you now?'

'Mum, I think that's irrelevant, don't you?'

He heard his mother mumble something to herself. 'I despair with you and your sister sometimes.'

Callum had no intention of discussing anything about Tasha with her. 'Mum, there's nothing we can do about this anyway. Erin is an adult and in her mid-twenties with her own business. We have to trust she's made a decision that's right for her.'

'Is that all you can say?'

He understood his mother's shock and wished there was some way he could reassure her.

'That silly, reckless girl.'

'Realistically,' he continued, 'I think the only thing we can do is be there for her in case this does all go wrong. If it does, we need to be there to support her.'

Hearing light footsteps coming into the kitchen, he looked over to the door and saw Tasha gently rubbing her eyes, wearing his dressing gown that was so long on her it reached the ground. She stopped in front of him and shook her head.

'Thank you,' he mouthed.

'Are you there, Callum?' he heard his mother ask.

'Sorry, Mum, I am.' He decided to end his mother's call on a positive. 'Anyway, who knows, Erin and Riley might surprise us all and enjoy a long and happy marriage.'

'And you really believe that, do you?' she asked, her voice dripping with sarcasm.

He had no idea but liked to think Riley could make his sister happy. 'It's possible.'

He bent down and gave Tasha a kiss on her forehead.

'I'm going to have to go, Mum. Why don't you speak to Barry about this. Maybe he'll have some suggestions. If I find out anything useful I'll give you a call later.'

'Thank you, darling,' she said, sounding calmer.

The call ended. Callum placed his mobile on the kitchen counter and focused on Tasha.

'I don't know about you but I need a cup of tea,' she said.

He did too. After their amazing day yesterday when anything seemed possible, Callum knew that today they would need to focus on his sister and damage control where his family were concerned.

First though, he wanted some quiet time with the woman he loved and decided he was going to cook them breakfast. He took Tasha by hand, opened the balcony door and led her outside. 'I think we need to eat something. I have a feeling today is going to be a very long day.'

49

TASHA

Tasha gazed in disbelief at the photos of Erin and Riley together. They did seem joyous and strangely enough as if they were a couple who had been together for years, rather than barely weeks. She noticed that in the second photo they were kissing standing inside a heart shape someone had made in the white sand.

Her face flushed as she recalled how incredible her previous night had been with Callum, and how she had lost herself in the romance and sensuality of being in bed with him. She wished it was her and Callum on that beach now, together. Although as much as the depths of her feelings for him seeped into every second of the day, she wasn't ready to jump into marriage.

She studied Riley's face in the photo, hoping his feelings for Erin were real and not just another whim he had given in to.

'I need to call him,' she said, handing Callum's phone back to him.

He frowned, clearly confused. 'But you don't work for him any more, Tasha. Do you think that's wise?'

'I've no idea,' she said honestly. 'But I do know him as well as anyone and I'm concerned about your sister. I can't just sit back and do nothing without trying or at least finding out more about this for your mum.'

'That's kind of you. Thank you.'

She rested a soothing hand on his shoulder, thoughts flashing back to when she had kissed him there only a few hours earlier as he held her just after they had made love.

Tasha scanned the room, looking for her phone. Spotting it on the coffee table, she picked it up and called Riley.

'Tasha? This is unexpected,' he said, sounding smug. 'I didn't expect a phone call from you today. I presume you've seen the photos.' She didn't have a chance to respond before he added, 'Have you called to congratulate us both?', his voice filled with amusement. 'Because if you're phoning about anything else, it's too late.'

'Too late for what? I know you're already married, I saw the ring,' she said, barely able to contain her weariness with his tiresome antics.

'I meant you don't work for me any longer.' He sounded like this call was giving him a lot of satisfaction. 'I know how you like to boss me around, but my business is nothing to do with you any more.'

As if it did before? she thought but kept quiet.

He gave a sarcastic laugh. 'I suppose I should be grateful to you, Tasha.'

Confused, she asked, 'In what way?'

'I almost certainly wouldn't have taken this step if you still worked for me.'

Tasha clenched her teeth. How dare he drag her into this situation. 'How do you figure that out?'

'You would have no doubt cancelled the flights or simply refused to book them in the first place. You would have also insisted I take time to think before rushing into marrying someone I barely know.'

He was right; that's exactly what she would have done. She also knew he would have taken little notice of her. But Tasha had no intention of being his scapegoat.

'Are you trying to tell me you already believe you've made a mistake?'

He scoffed. 'Not at all. I love Erin, very much, and I know we're going to be very happy together.'

'Then what are you saying?'

'I won't be a moment, sweetheart.' He sighed. 'That was my wife wondering how long I'll be before joining her on our balcony.'

'I did work that out for myself, thank you.' She withheld a groan. 'You didn't answer my question.'

'I didn't, did I?' He went quiet and she presumed he was having a think. Impatient to finish the call, Tasha said, 'You must know this will have repercussions for Erin.'

'Rubbish. If anything, being married to me will protect her.'

'How?' He was delusional if he thought that, Tasha mused.

'She'll have the protection of my team.'

'What team, Riley? Dale is back in England and you need to find someone to replace me.'

He sighed angrily. 'Stop being so negative, Tasha.'

Sensing he wasn't going to entertain her for much longer and knowing Callum and Michelle would appreciate some answers, Tasha thought quickly. 'What about Erin's salon?'

'She has someone looking after it. Her manager, I think.'

Not wishing him to ruin his second chance with the film

company, she couldn't help adding, 'And what about the series, Riley?'

He didn't respond straight away. 'Riley, are you still there?'

'I am,' he said, his voice much gentler. 'Thanks, Tasha.'

'For what?'

'For still caring what happens to me even though you can't stand working for me any longer.'

'Riley, tell me.'

'Fine. We finished recording everything we needed, so I'm free for a few weeks to do as I wish with my lovely bride.'

Relief flooded through her. 'Right.'

He didn't speak for a moment. 'And as far as Erin goes, you can reassure Callum that I do love her. I know us getting married has come out of the blue, but we had a long weekend when I wasn't needed for filming on the last Monday of the shoot, so we flew to Vegas for some fun and ended up marrying there.'

'Ah, I see, so it was a flying visit then?'

'As you probably know, the wrap party was held here, so we're on the island and plan to have a honeymoon as soon as Erin has faced her family.'

Feeling slightly calmer, Tasha was relieved she had something to pass on to Callum. 'I'll let them know I've spoken to you and what you've said.'

'Thanks. I know Erin is nervous about their reaction, especially her mother's. She mentioned having quite a few missed calls over the past few hours, so this will make her feel a bit better.'

'I'm glad.' She thought about how frustrated Callum said his mother had been when she'd called him about the photos. 'Maybe suggest she give her mum a quick call anyway, just to reassure her.'

'Will do. And Tasha?'

'Yes?'

'You do know I didn't mean it when I said it was too late, and that you can come back and work for me any time, don't you?'

She sighed, wishing it was that easy. 'Thanks, Riley, but I think we both know that's probably not going to happen.'

50

CALLUM

The following morning, Callum opened his eyes and smiled. The pair of them had forgotten all about Riley and Erin's shock wedding as soon as they fell into bed.

He realised it would soon be time for Tasha to fly to England. His mood dipped. Needing to hold her, he went to put his arm around Tasha, but instead of his skin connecting with hers his hand met a cool pillow. He opened his eyes to see whether she was still in the bedroom somewhere but she wasn't there. He stilled, listening and hoping to hear her. When he didn't hear anything, Callum threw back the sheet and went to get out of bed just as Tasha appeared at the bedroom door holding a tray.

'Oh, you're up already.'

Seeing she also had a cafetière and cups on the tray, he didn't like to think of her holding the heavy tray for longer than necessary.

'I can get back in, if you like, or,' he said, thinking how much cooler it would be to sit on the balcony where there might be a slight sea breeze, 'we could enjoy this outside.'

'Good idea.' She turned on her heels and went towards the living room.

Callum slipped on underwear and, grabbing a T-shirt, quickly followed her. She stopped in front of the small sliding door and waited for him to open it, then stepped outside and lowered the tray to the table.

He put on his T-shirt and sat opposite her, wishing she didn't have to leave. 'Shall I pour?'

She nodded. 'Please.'

He handed her a cup of coffee and noticed the plate of fresh pastries from the French bakery down the road. 'You've been out.'

'I thought we deserved a treat.'

'What a lovely idea.' He waited for her to take an almond croissant then took a plain one and put it on his plate. 'The baker and his assistant are both French and as far as I'm concerned these are the best on the island.'

He tore one of the ends from the croissant and dabbed a small amount of the strawberry jam Tasha had placed next to a small butter dish his mother had insisted he might one day need.

'This is delicious.'

She beamed at him. 'It is.'

He ate another mouthful and watched as Tasha drank some of her coffee. She had a thoughtful expression on her face, and he presumed she was as reluctant to leave as he was to part with her.

Instantly losing his appetite, Callum picked up his coffee and drank a little before placing the cup back in its saucer.

'What's the matter?' Tasha asked, frowning.

He stared at her, determined not to show how upset he felt about her imminent departure. He despised emotional blackmail and had no intention of using it on her. If Tasha needed to move on and find her next chapter then he had no right to get in her way. He loved her and wanted her to be with him, but more than that he wanted to see her happy and if returning to England and finding work that she loved doing was how that would happen, then he would do everything he could to help her.

She reached out and took one of his hands in hers. 'Callum?'

'Yes?' He didn't want to discuss what would happen once she returned to England but knew he had little choice if he was to support her wishes.

'You know you said I could stay here, if I wanted to?'

Was she about to tell him she wasn't going? He pushed the hope aside, not daring to believe she was about to change her mind. 'Of course.'

'Well, does the offer still stand?'

He smiled. 'It does. Why?'

'I've been up for hours thinking.'

He hid his nervousness, desperate to know what she had decided. 'You have?'

She nodded. 'I've decided I'm not ready to leave yet.'

His heart raced. 'Good. I'm not ready for you to go either.'

She sighed. 'I'm so relieved.'

'Why?' he asked, confused.

'Well, it's one thing to offer for someone to stay in your home, but another entirely when they do decide to stay.' She shrugged. 'I'd hate to outstay my welcome.'

He laughed, unable to help himself. 'You could never do that, Tasha. I want you to stay as long as you want.' He lifted her hand to his lips and, turning it over, kissed her palm. 'The longer the better.'

Tasha stood and, coming around to his side of the table,

pushed it away from him to make more room. Callum wondered what she was doing, when she sat on his lap and put her arms around his neck.

'I promise I won't be an annoying flatmate,' she said, kissing him.

Callum wrapped his arms around her and lost himself in her kiss. If this was how his mornings were going to be from now on, or even if they weren't, he doubted he would ever find Tasha to be anything other than an ideal flatmate.

51

CALLUM

Later that morning, Callum's phone rang. He waited for the caller to get bored and ring off, but when they didn't he picked it up and saw it was Erin. Hearing Tasha singing in the shower, he smiled, loving how well they got along and how much more he was enjoying his life since she had come into it.

He answered the call. 'How does it feel to be a married woman, Erin?'

'Don't you give me a hard time too, Callum. I've had more than enough with Mum's theatrics.' She sighed huffily, making him smile to hear her familiar note of irritation. 'I would hope you'd be pleased to know I was happy at last.'

'At last? You're hardly a spinster sitting on a shelf in one of those Victorian novels. Anyway didn't you always insist marriage wasn't for you?'

'No, Callum. What I said was that I wasn't sure whether I'd ever find anyone worth marrying.'

'And now you have,' he said, still staggered to think of his sister dating Riley Sharp, let alone marrying the man. Before their conversation descended into an argument, he decided to return to their mother's reaction. 'Don't be too upset by Mum. You know she can be a bit dramatic sometimes and you are her daughter, so I suppose in this case she's entitled to be.'

'Eugh. I'm in my mid-twenties, Callum. I run a business and have lived alone since I left home at eighteen. I've no idea why she still feels the need to be so overprotective. She can't get used to the idea I've grown up; that's what it is.'

Wanting to calm his sister, he said, 'That's not true, Erin, and you know it. It was a shock to all of us, discovering you had married someone you barely know. Someone with such a public profile as Riley Sharp. Surely you can understand how this might take a moment for Mum to come to terms with.'

There was a pause before she responded. 'The only thing I can see now is how much I'm enjoying my summer being with him. I've fallen in love properly for the first time and he's adorable, whatever you might think. He treats me like a princess, and I love every moment I spend with him.'

Callum was glad his sister and Riley got along so well but felt compelled to explain their parents' concerns, hoping Erin would be understanding when she saw either of them. It wouldn't be a good start to her marriage if she fell out with her parents, especially if she needed them should things go sour between her and Riley.

'I'm happy for you, Erin. I really am but...' he hesitated, trying to get his words right so that he didn't antagonise her further '...you even said how he was engaged, or almost engaged, several times in the past, and we all know how tumultuous his relationship with his most recent girlfriend has been, with them breaking up and getting back together several times. Doesn't it worry you he's had such a chequered past?'

She didn't reply immediately and so he waited.

Erin groaned irritably. 'You mean Brooke?'

'I do.'

'I know you're concerned about me being safe and happy. For your information, Brooke is in Hawaii right now and having a ball there. So regardless of what everyone seems to think, I'm not stepping on anyone's toes and, for what it's worth, not that it's anyone else's business, my salon is being well looked after by my staff. Satisfied?'

He wasn't surprised Erin was angry with them all. He would be unimpressed if his family tried to dictate how he should lead his life. She deserved an apology.

'You're right,' he said, hoping to calm her. 'Sorry, Erin. I overstepped the mark and will let Mum and Barry and Dad and Betsy know that's what I think too. We just want you to be happy. That's all.'

'I know you do,' she said, her voice gentle again. 'And I love you all for caring so much. I'd just like you all to trust me to do what's best for me.'

'That's fair enough.' Callum relaxed slightly. 'I'll also let Mum know you're fine and doing perfectly well and that there's no need for her to worry about you.'

'Thank heavens for that.' She muted the call briefly. 'Look I'm going to have to go now.'

'Really? You don't have time to tell me more?' he asked, surprised.

'Not right now I don't. I can speak to Mum about all of this face to face. No need for you to worry. I just wanted you to know how I felt and have my back if Mum continued to make a fuss.'

How typical of Erin to have planned this before seeing them all, he thought, impressed. 'No worries. I'll see you soon. Oh, and Erin?'

'Yes?'

'Congratulations to you and Riley. I hope you'll both be very happy.'

'Thanks, big bro,' she said happily. Before Callum could say anything further, Erin ended the call.

Callum went to find Tasha and relayed what had happened.

'I've decided I've had enough of being the one to resolve family issues. We're not children any more and our parents would hate us to fuss about them. It's time they stopped doing the same thing to us.'

Tasha gave him a sympathetic smile. 'They're your parents. I think it comes with the territory. Or at least that's what my mum says.'

He gave her comment some thought. 'I suppose you're right. I'll give it a go though, just in case I can persuade them we're both capable of looking out for each other as well as ourselves.'

52

TASHA

Tasha showered and washed her hair, relieved to have finally made a decision and cancelled her flights. It was a little unnerving to take a chance and stay with Callum, but she was in love with him and wanted to make the most of the feeling that being in an exciting and romantic relationship gave her.

She was sitting on the balcony reading while her hair dried in the warm morning sun as Callum took his own shower when the doorbell rang. Tasha put her book on the table and stood to go and answer it. She got to the door just as Callum walked out of the bedroom, pulling a T-shirt down over his tanned, muscular chest, his hair still wet.

She stared at him and sighed, making Callum grin.

He pulled her into his arms and kissed her. 'I'm enjoying having you here.'

'So am I.'

The person knocked again. 'Hey, are you going to let us in or not?'

'Erin never did have much patience,' he grumbled, opening the door.

'Riley?' Tasha was taken aback to see him with Erin.

'I thought I'd bring him with me,' Erin explained. 'You have been ignoring his calls since the one when you asked about us getting married and he's been driving me nuts going on about you. I thought if he came here with me he could say what he needs to and you can do the same.'

Tasha suspected Erin wanted there to be as little antagonism as possible between her and Riley and supposed it would make things easier, especially now she and Callum were together. Not that Erin knew much about their situation yet.

Callum gave Tasha a questioning look. 'It's fine, Callum. I don't mind.'

Tasha led the way into the living room and sat down on one of the armchairs.

'We've been chatting,' Erin said, sitting on the arm of the sofa next to where Riley had taken a seat. She rested a hand on his shoulder. 'I explained to him why you probably left and how he should treat someone who works for him.' Tasha was surprised to hear Riley had listened to anyone. It dawned on her how much he must really love Erin if he was willing to do this so readily.

'Go on,' she said, folding her hands on her lap.

'Erin's right,' Riley said, focusing his attention on Tasha after a quick glance up at his wife. 'She explained to me how she treats her staff.' Tasha tensed, and he noticed, immediately adding, 'And especially those people she really respects, like I do you.'

Tasha felt mollified by his assertion but waited for him to finish what he was here to tell her.

'The thing is, Tasha,' Riley said, 'I've missed having you around.' He shrugged one shoulder. 'I've told you that already on the phone that time, but I want you to consider coming back to work for me.'

'Go on,' Tasha said, not giving away how she felt.

'Um, well, I'd obviously increase your wages and the number of holidays you are free to take each year. And to be honest with you, I'll agree to pretty much whatever you want.'

Assuming he had finished when he didn't continue, Tasha took a deep breath. 'I appreciate you coming here and offering me these things, but if I were to come back to work for you, Riley, there are a couple of other stipulations I need to make,' she said, aware that if she wanted to ensure things changed to suit her, now was her best chance to make that happen.

'Go on.'

'I know that in my line of work it's difficult to keep set working hours; however, Callum has offered for me to stay here in his flat and I will therefore want most evenings free to spend them with him. Obviously if we're away at an event, or filming, then that's different, but when I'm here... Which is another thing. I know you're based in England, but I like it here and would like to at least give it a go to see how I would settle here on the island.' She smiled at Callum. 'And see how my relationship with Callum pans out.'

He laughed. 'I'm hoping it'll be permanent,' he said, taking her hand in his.

She smiled up at him, loving the idea. 'Me, too.'

'You two are a thing?' Erin asked, interrupting their moment. 'I knew it would happen.' She tapped Riley's shoulder. 'Didn't I say that?'

He nodded. 'She did.'

'I'm so pleased.' Erin stepped forward and kissed Callum on the cheek, then did the same to Tasha.

Tasha loved that they were so happy for her and Callum, but

didn't want them to get carried away. Neither she nor Callum were going to run off and get married like they had done.

'It's early days for us yet,' Tasha said, taking hold of Callum's hand nearest to her. 'But we're enjoying it, aren't we, Callum?'

'We are,' he said, his face lit with happiness. She loved that she was the one to make him feel this way. Remembering what she was saying, Tasha tore her gaze from the man she was falling in love with and back to Riley and their negotiations.

Not wanting to miss the opportunity to finalise things between her and Riley, she held up her hand. 'With regards to us two, Riley, I'll expect you to also mind your manners. You humiliated me on set and that's not acceptable. If you do that to me again I will walk away from you and will not give you another chance.'

She knew she was pushing her luck with him, but it needed to be said. He didn't seem about to react in his usual defensive way when criticised, so she continued. 'And I don't only expect you to be more considerate to me but also to everyone else you work with in future. I don't think that's too much to ask, do you?'

He stared at her silently for a moment. Tasha braced herself for him to get angry, ready to tell him to keep his job.

'If it means having you back working for me, Tasha, then I'll happily do all those things.'

She was amazed and took a few seconds to gather herself enough to speak.

'Fine. Then I'll come back and work for you. Not until I've had a couple of weeks' holiday though.'

He shrugged. 'Whatever you want.'

'We've got news of our own,' Erin said, grinning.

'What now?' Callum asked, shooting Erin an anxious look.

She laughed. 'No need to panic. It's just that now we're

married, Riley will be able to live here, so that's what he's going to do.'

Tasha couldn't believe it. 'Really?'

Riley nodded. 'I've moved into Erin's flat above her salon for the time being while we look for our own property. Which is why you taking a couple of weeks off works well with our plans to get straight on and search for something.'

Tasha laughed. Typical Riley, always agreeable when it suited him.

53

CALLUM

After Erin and Riley left, Callum decided he and Tasha should get out of the flat.

'It's another beautiful day,' Callum said, looking out of the window at the cloudless blue sky. 'Why don't we go and see how they're getting on at Hollyhock Farm now the filming has ended?'

'I love that idea,' Tasha said, getting to her feet. 'It'll be fun to go back there. I'll need a couple of minutes to brush my hair, then I'll be with you.'

'Great. I'll send Lettie a text asking if she minds us going there and tell her we don't wish to disturb her if she's working.'

Lettie responded within a few seconds, telling him to take as long as they wanted walking around the land and to pop in when they had finished for some tea and cake.

He wasn't surprised she had invited them in for refreshments. Lettie had been brought up by Lindy, after all, and of all the times he'd visited the farm growing up Callum couldn't recall one time when Lindy didn't have something tasty to offer to guests.

Callum was looking forward to showing Tasha more of the property.

As soon as they arrived, he led her to the lower field where the alpacas stood staring at them like three nosy old ladies.

'They're adorable,' Tasha said, stroking the soft noses. 'And so tame.'

'Most of the animals here were rescued by Lettie's father over the years. The few cows he has left are also elderly but when he sold his dairy herd around eleven or twelve years ago to grow organic produce, he decided to keep them and just let them spend their old age where they had always lived.'

'That's so sweet,' Tasha said.

'They're a good family. I'm relieved the filming at the farm has brought in an added income. They've had a few problems over the past year or so.' He took her hand and led her away.

'Where to now?'

'The wildflower meadow.'

'I love it there.'

It only took a couple of minutes to walk there through one of the fields and down to a dip on the other side of the part of the farm where all the filming had taken place Tasha stopped and breathed in deeply.

He watched her gaze around them at the poppies, cornflowers, ox-eye daisies, buttercups and then turned to gaze up at him in stunned delight. 'I think this place will always remind me of you from now on,' she said.

Callum smiled, liking the idea. 'I've spent many lazy summer days down here with Zac, dozing and dreaming about our futures, keeping our feet cool in the stream.'

She gave his hand a squeeze. 'And did all those dreams come true?'

He thought about his job, his flat and now standing here

with his arm draped around the shoulders of the woman he loved. 'They have now.'

'I'm glad.' She lifted his hand and kissed the back of it. 'You deserve to have everything you want, Callum. Most of all you deserve to be happy.' She lowered his hand. 'Can we lie by the stream and dip our feet in the water now too?'

'I'd be disappointed if you didn't want to do exactly that.'

He took off his trainers and waited for her to do the same, then led her along the meandering path that Lettie had mowed through the wild grass, leaving the wildflowers growing prettily on either side.

'This feels so good under my feet,' he said.

'I was thinking the same thing.'

As they neared the stream, he heard the water bubbling over the rounded stones in the stream. 'Here is a good place.'

She sat without answering, a wide smile on her face. Tasha lowered her feet into the water and gave a satisfied sigh. 'Bliss.'

'It's a bit cold.'

'It's heavenly.'

Lying back on the grass, his head resting on his hands, Callum didn't think he had ever imagined being this happy. He closed his eyes against the brightness of the sunshine.

Within seconds a shadow fell over his face. He opened his eyes to look up and smiled seeing Tasha's face above his as she lowered her lips to kiss him.

Taking her in his arms, Callum rolled her onto her back and kissed her as they both lost themselves in the romance of the moment and their intense attraction to each other.

'You really are perfect,' he murmured a few minutes later. 'I can't imagine being without you now.'

She slipped her arms around his back and held him tightly.

'That is the nicest thing you've ever said to me. I feel the same way about you.'

'You do?' It was all he needed to hear. 'I want you to know that whatever happens with your job in the future, I'll do whatever you need to make sure we stay together.'

'You love it here though,' she said softly. 'Your life is here, Callum.'

He shook his head. 'No. I hadn't been aware of it until now, but being with you has shown me what was missing from my life all along.'

'I love to hear you say that. I really do,' she said, pushing a strand of hair from his forehead. 'But I never want to make you unhappy.'

He loved her for caring, but he knew now what was important to him. 'I do love it here, but my life going forward is with you, Tasha. I love you, so much, and I'm happy to live wherever your work takes you.'

'You're the first man in my life to put me first. Do you know that?'

He didn't but it was good to hear how much that meant to her. 'I think we're going to be even happier than we imagine.'

She sighed. 'I'm already far happier and more content than I ever thought possible, so this is enough for me.'

He pulled her against him and kissed her again, grateful to be lucky enough to have someone as perfect as her in his life.

'I was just thinking how lovely it would be to come back here at night and lie here looking up at the starlight,' she said, snuggling against him a little while later. 'The sky is so clear here and I imagine it'll be amazing.'

'I'm sure it will be. I like that idea,' he said. 'We'll definitely have to do it.'

She kissed him. 'I never expected that coming to Jersey with Riley would end up changing so many things.'

He smiled, enjoying seeing her contented.

She wrapped her arms around his back and hugged him tightly. 'I can't believe that I met and fell in love with the most amazing man, or that I'm now based on this lovely island and, what's more, Riley seems to have reverted back to the person I was so excited about working for three years ago.' She looked up at Callum and frowned. 'I know his behaviour has a lot to do with trying to impress Erin, but I'm happy to go along with things and see how it goes.'

Callum kissed the top of her head and hugged her. 'If anyone can keep Riley in order it'll be my sister.'

Tasha laughed. 'I agree.' She gazed at him. 'I feel as if I'm living in a dream and I don't ever want to wake up.'

Callum stared into her green eyes and knew he had never been happier or ever wanted more than to share his life with her.

'Thankfully this is no dream,' he said, bending to kiss her. 'And I think the two of us are going to have the most amazing future together.'

She kissed him lightly on the lips. 'I think you could be right.'

* * *

MORE FROM GEORGINA TROY

The first book in another romantic, escapist series from Georgina Troy, *New Beginnings by the Sunflower Cliffs*, is available to order now here:

https://mybook.to/SunflowerCliffsBackAd

ABOUT THE AUTHOR

Georgina Troy writes bestselling uplifting romantic escapes and sets her novels on the island of Jersey where she was born and has lived for most of her life. She lives close to the beach with her husband and three rescue dogs. When she's not writing she can be found walking with the dogs or chatting to her friends over coffee at one of the many beachside cafés on the island.

Download your exclusive bonus content from Georgina Troy here:

Visit Georgina's website: www.deborahcarr.org/my-books/ georgina-troy-books/

Follow Georgina on social media here:

facebook.com/GeorginaTroyAuthor

x.com/GeorginaTroy

bookbub.com/authors/georgina-troy

ALSO BY GEORGINA TROY

The Sunshine Island Series

Finding Love on Sunshine Island

A Secret Escape to Sunshine Island

Chasing Dreams on Sunshine Island

The Golden Sands Bay Series

Summer Sundaes at Golden Sands Bay

Love Begins at Golden Sands Bay

Winter Whimsy at Golden Sands Bay

Sunny Days at Golden Sands Bay

Snow Angels at Golden Sands Bay

Sunflower Cliffs Series

New Beginnings by the Sunflower Cliffs

Secrets and Sunshine by the Sunflower Cliffs

Wedding Bells by the Sunflower Cliffs

Coming Home to the Sunflower Cliffs

Hollyhock Farm Series

Welcome to Hollyhock Farm

Second Chances at Hollyhock Farm

Love Blooms at Hollyhock Farm

Starlight Over Hollyhock Farm

BECOME A MEMBER OF

THE SHELF CARE CLUB

The home of Boldwood's
book club reads.

Find uplifting reads,
sunny escapes, cosy romances,
family dramas and more!

Sign up to the newsletter
https://bit.ly/theshelfcareclub

Boldwood

Boldwood Books is an award-winning fiction publishing company seeking out the best stories from around the world.

Find out more at www.boldwoodbooks.com

Join our reader community for brilliant books, competitions and offers!

Follow us
@BoldwoodBooks
@TheBoldBookClub

Sign up to our weekly deals newsletter

https://bit.ly/BoldwoodBNewsletter

Printed in Dunstable, United Kingdom